S0-ABB-161

Also by
DEBORAH RANEY

Over the Waters
A Vow to Cherish
Within This Circle

Insight

DEBORAH RANEY

Steeple
Hill®

Published by Steeple Hill Books™

STEEPLE HILL BOOKS

Steeple
Hill®

Recycling programs
for this product may
not exist in your area.

ISBN-13: 978-0-373-78644-2
ISBN-10:   0-373-78644-1

INSIGHT

www.SteepleHill.com

Printed in U.S.A.

For Terry Stucky.
Your insight is always appreciated.
Thanks for journeying with me,
rejoicing with me,
and helping me keep my feet on solid ground.

Don't be deceived, my dear brothers.
Every good and perfect gift is from above,
coming down from the Father of the heavenly lights,
who does not change like shifting shadows.
—*James* 1:16–17

Chapter One

Olivia Cline drew a handful of paintbrushes from a mason jar on the closet shelf and wrapped them in careful folds of newspaper before laying them in a waiting shoe box.

A hank of dishwater-blond hair fell into her eyes and she swept it to the side, tucking it behind one ear before loading a second shoe box with crimped tubes of oil paint.

"Hey, you." Derek poked his head through the doorway of the spare room, a cardboard box hefted on one shoulder. He cocked his head. "What are you doing?"

"Just packing up my art stuff. Don't let the movers take it, though. I'll bring it in the car when I come down."

Sighing, Derek rolled his eyes. He lowered the box to the floor and came to put his hands on her shoulders. "Olivia."

Her husband's voice was stern, but she'd trained herself to discern the twinkle in his eyes that accompanied it. The light glinted there now in the green flecks of his hazel eyes. He wasn't angry with her. She relaxed a bit.

The lines on Derek's brow smoothed and a crooked smile bloomed on his face. "For the first time in our lives we have the luxury of leaving the packing to professionals." He slid his hands down her arms, took the shoe box from her and set it back on a shelf in the closet. "Let the movers take care of it. You never use that stuff anyway. Why don't you get rid of it? One less thing to haul."

She tried to ignore the lump of resentment inching up her throat. Derek had come a long way in the last year, but there were moments… She swallowed hard. "Not yet. And I'd feel better if I at least pack the boxes. Did you see what they did with Grandma's dishes?"

"These guys know what they're doing. You can trust them."

Trust. The word dangled in the air between them. Aware that she was biting her tongue, Olivia shook away the storm of thoughts clouding her mind and looked past Derek, over the railing to the living room below. She might be learning to trust her husband again, but she definitely didn't trust the crew of clumsy galoots down there lobbing boxes like so many circus jugglers. Oil paints were expensive. And her sable brushes could be too easily crushed—if they weren't already in danger of rotting from age and lack of use.

Behind her, Derek cleared his throat. "I just thought this might be a good chance to get rid of that stuff. The new house isn't *that* much bigger than this place. Besides, you haven't done any painting in…what? Three years? Four?"

Six, to be exact. And that hurt. Derek never had understood how much she'd given up when she put her brushes away to take a "real" job. As he often reminded her, she was lucky she'd been able to use her artistic talents in her work. She owed her success as an interior decorator to her gifts as an artist, and in her eyes, the two years of art school under her belt were far more valuable than her bachelor's degree in business administration. They'd certainly been more fun to earn.

Oh, she liked her job. It would be hard to say goodbye to her clients and colleagues next week. But she secretly hoped she might get back to her art once they were settled in Missouri. Not that a little burg like Hanover Falls was any artists' mecca, but at least maybe she'd have more time for her art.

Derek was on a different track, though. He wanted a baby. *Babies.* She wanted a family, too. But now? So soon after…after all they'd been through? She wasn't sure. Maybe they needed a couple of years to adjust to the new town, practice everything they'd learned in a year of marriage counseling. They were still young. Barely in their thirties. They had plenty of time. Some of their friends hadn't started their families until they were almost forty.

But Derek had wanted children—at least four of them—for years. It was one of the things they fought about most, from the very beginning, when they were both still in school racking up astronomical student loans and living on macaroni and cheese in a shabby one-bedroom apartment. And not "shabby chic," either. Just plain shabby.

But now Derek had landed this great job, and everything they'd hoped for was falling into place. He would start work in Hanover Falls in a few days. So why did she literally tremble every time she thought about leaving Chicago and settling down to become the mother of Derek Cline's children?

Something clanged downstairs and Derek flinched. "I'd better go see what that was."

"Please do," she said. She followed him out of the room and looked over the railing. She didn't see any of the crew, but she spotted the painting still hanging on the wall in the foyer. With a little gasp, she brushed past Derek and raced down the stairs. This painting was one thing she was not willing to risk to this moving crew…make that *wrecking* crew, she thought as another crash split the air.

She hurried to the foyer and lifted the canvas from its perch on the narrow wall. The oak frame was nothing special and the canvas had buckled slightly. She promised herself she'd take the time to repair the painting before she hung it in the new house. Something about this piece had always anchored her, had always said "home" like nothing else she owned.

She inspected the landscape that had taken her a full month to complete. A wry smile tilted her mouth. One of Derek's pet peeves about her was that she was not easily impressed. But with this particular work of her own hands, she'd finally managed to impress herself.

All these years later, she still liked the way her brushes had captured hazy green afternoon shadows in the peaceful pastoral scene. Alongside her asymmetrical trees, three cows contemplated their reflections in a glassy pond. It was odd, when she thought about it, that this painting captivated her so. She was a city girl. Always had been. Usually, neon and stainless steel made her heart beat faster. But something in this bucolic scene spoke to her, touched a tender place inside her. A place she treasured without quite knowing why.

Though he'd never come right out and said so, she suspected Derek didn't even care for the piece. She still remembered his too-casual comment the day they'd first moved in to this apartment, when he'd noticed it leaning against the wall waiting to be hung in the foyer. "Are you sure that's where you want it?" he'd asked. "This will be the only part of the place some people see."

She hadn't challenged him then to come out and say what he meant, but his comment still stung a bit. And why was the painting still here now? Her gaze panned the bare walls of the large combination living room and dining room. Derek had orchestrated the packing of all their other paintings and artwork—all works of other artisans—first thing this morning. Why was this one still here? Did Derek think this move provided a convenient opportunity to leave her painting behind?

She stared at the artful splotches of sienna and white paint that resembled grazing cows. Her fingers caressed the rough strokes of paint. The piece had an impressionistic quality about it. To Olivia's embarrassment her friend Jayne had compared it to a Monet. But she'd been flattered, too.

"I don't care what he thinks," she whispered. But the defiance in her voice startled her. Obviously, she *did* care.

In the kitchen, Olivia found the roll of heavy brown paper the movers had been using to wrap items. She ripped off a long sheet and let it trail behind her as she moved to the foyer. She lifted the bulky frame and placed it on the folds of paper, swaddling it tenderly, as though it were a newborn. She taped the wrapping securely in place, then carried the unwieldy bundle out to her car. She propped it carefully on the floor of the backseat. When she packed the car to join Derek in Hanover Falls next week, she would use the last of the towels and bedding from the house as further padding for the fragile painting.

And she would hang it in a spot of honor in the house there. Maybe it would somehow make that house feel a little more like home for her.

A siren wailed on the streets beyond the cul-de-sac where the Clines' Chicago town house sat. Olivia filled a disposable coffee cup with water from the kitchen faucet and walked across the shiny oak floor to put it in the microwave. The heels of her pumps clattered on the wood, echoing throughout the small apartment. She would stop by Starbucks on her way to work for something more substantial. Instant coffee was almost worse than nothing, but it did help ward off the early-March chill of the empty rooms. She'd turned the furnace up five degrees, but still it felt as if the icy wind was blowing off Lake Michigan and straight through some invisible seam in the walls of this place.

She punched in another thirty seconds on the microwave and headed for the front door to retrieve the morning paper. Halfway down the hall, she remembered that Derek had cancelled their subscription as of yesterday. Deep scars in the carpet where their barrister bookcases had sat reminded her that her books, too, were already in Hanover Falls. She felt disoriented and lost in her own home. Everywhere she reached, she ended up grasping empty air. Nothing was where she expected it to be. She'd lived this way for almost a week now, and it was starting to make her crazy.

The microwave turntable groaned to a stop and the timer dinged. She turned over her wrist and glanced at her watch. Seven forty-five. Derek was probably stepping into his plush office at Parker & Associates this very minute. She pictured him "administrating"— or whatever it was Engineering Administrators did—in suit and tie.

A smile cut through her melancholy. Her husband would be in hog heaven about now. He'd always been in his element bossing people around. And he was good at it. He knew how to manage people in such a way they didn't realize they were being managed. It was his gift. He'd employed it with her in their decade of marriage more than she cared to admit. But that was all in the past now. The counseling had been good for them.

She took the steaming cup from the microwave and measured in a heaping spoonful of instant coffee. As she stirred, the aroma wafted upward to her nostrils, doing a fair impersonation of real coffee.

She sighed. As difficult as it had been, she and Derek had both grown through the painful, tearful sessions with Tom and JoAnne Bennett, an older couple from their church who served as lay counselors. The Bennetts had weathered some storms of their own and their advice was offered with the authority only experience could bring. Olivia could finally say with conviction, "I'm glad we stuck it out. It was worth every agonizing minute."

She still wasn't sure about the babies part. Oh, sure, she wanted kids. Eventually. When she dared picture herself as a dotty old woman, she definitely envisioned herself a grandmother. But Olivia had been an only child, a much-longed-for baby born when her mother was forty-two and her father almost fifty. She hadn't been around children much, and frankly they scared the daylights out of her.

She and Derek had married when they were both barely twenty, and the ten years since had been eaten up with earning their degrees and launching careers. Now that Derek had his second master's degree and a job commensurate with it, they finally had some financial relief and time to enjoy each other.

They almost hadn't made it to this point. She took a sip of coffee and grimaced. A wave of nausea swept over her as she thought of the betrayal and anguish of the last two years. *Derek's affair.* She still almost couldn't make those words be true in her mind. It made her physically ill to consider the thought, the words choking her. She'd never dreamed something like that could happen to her. To them.

No one had been more in love than she and Derek Cline on their perfect wedding day. Sometimes she looked at their wedding album, studying their fresh young faces for a hint of what was to come.

She never found it. In the photos, their faces were luminous, their eyes only for each other. She felt she was looking at pictures of strangers. She still loved Derek, maybe more than ever. But she couldn't remember that innocent, giddy love they'd surely felt on that day. That once-upon-a-time fairy-tale day.

If there was a hint of the angst to come, it might have been found in the tight smiles worn by Derek's parents in their wedding portraits. Her own parents had died within a few months of each other while she was in her last year of college, and she had thought she would know the love of parents and family again in Bill and Carolyn Cline.

Unfortunately, Olivia Masden wasn't what the Clines had in mind for their only son. Derek's mother had been cold and distant from the first time they met. Olivia learned much later that Carolyn was still angry with her son for breaking up with his high school sweetheart and then daring to get married before he had a college degree.

Derek's father had actually accused Olivia—thankfully not to her face—of being a gold digger. The Clines had worn plastic smiles and behaved with civility the day of the wedding, but once the ink was dry on the marriage license, they'd made no bones about the fact they were less than happy with Derek's choice.

Olivia and her mother-in-law maintained a polite distance over the next few years. In the beginning, Olivia had made a valiant effort to bridge the distance. But she'd finally given up and learned to be grateful for the occasional tidbits of friendship Carolyn tossed her way.

Then five years ago, Carolyn had been diagnosed with breast cancer. Against Derek's protests, Olivia had reached out to her, even spending days at a time with her in the Clines' stately Oak Park home while Derek was on the road. By the time her mother-in-law died, barely a year after she was diagnosed, Olivia almost felt as if she'd lost a friend.

Bill Cline remarried less than a year later and retired to Florida to play golf every day. His new wife was even less interested in having a relationship with Olivia—or Derek, for that matter. Olivia sent birthday cards to both Bill and Doris, and Father's Day cards that she signed Derek's name to, but they hadn't spoken since the Christmas before last.

When Olivia and Derek had gone through counseling with the

Bennetts, the older couple speculated that Derek's affair was a delayed reaction to his mother's death—or more likely, to his father's quick remarriage, which Derek saw as a betrayal of his mom. Ironic that he'd chosen to deal with his pain by betraying his own wife.

Olivia's cell phone jangled in her purse on the counter, startling her. Derek had shut off their landline phone service before he left. The man was efficient, she had to give him that. She set down the nearly empty cup and rummaged through her purse. The caller ID displayed Parker & Associates.

She pressed Talk. "Hey, you… How's it going? Did you get everything moved in?"

"Almost. I'm leaving the heavy stuff for you."

"Very funny. So you're at work?"

"Yes, ma'am, I am. And it's great. I am sitting here with a stunning view of—" He lowered his voice. "Hang on a sec…."

A rustling noise came over the line and she shook her head, smiling. She could picture him casing the office, making sure no one overheard the consummate professional acting as excited as a ten-year-old in a video arcade.

"Okay." He came back on the line, his voice full of bravado. "I happen to be sitting here in a corner office at the *très* prestigious Parker & Associates with a gorgeous view of the lake…well, okay, it's more like a pond. But never mind that. Your old man is movin' up in the world."

She laughed. "Very cool, babe. I'm proud of you." She refrained from reminding him there was no place to go *but* up.

"Thanks. I'm kind of proud of myself, actually."

"You should be. You worked hard to get there."

"All I need now is to get you down here so we can start making babies."

"Whoa! Let me unpack my bags first, will you?" She feigned a pout. "Don't you even miss me?"

"Yes." Derek's tone turned serious. "I miss you like crazy."

"I miss you, too."

"But I'm dead serious about the babies, Olivia. Wait till you see the house. There's a perfect room for the nursery. It's got one of those—what do you call it?—turret things with a window seat and it's already painted baby blue. For my son."

She chuckled and hoped he wouldn't detect the strain behind her laughter. "It's called a dormer window. Turrets are for castles."

"Well, this is *our* castle, babe."

Her laughter turned genuine. "I can't wait to see it."

"It's just waiting for your magic touch—and a couple of babies—to make it perfect."

"Whoa, boy. One at a time." She knew Derek thought a baby would heal the ugly rift his affair had caused. He was still working through a lot of guilt. But she suspected he also blamed her somewhat for his indiscretion.

Maybe he had a point. Like him, she'd been caught up in building her career, unwilling to give up even a weekend for fear she'd lose momentum. She'd been scaling that proverbial ladder of success and *nothing* was going to stop her.

"You there?" Derek's voice broke through her thoughts.

"I'm here. You better get back to work. It'd be a real shame if you got fired before I even get down there."

"Ha! That's not going to happen. They love me already."

"I'm sure they do."

"I love you. Hurry home."

The words jolted her. He already thought of Hanover Falls as home. She hoped it would be as easy for her. "One more day of work and I'm there."

She heard him cover the receiver and speak in muffled tones to someone. "I gotta run, babe."

The dial tone trilled in her ear and she bit the inside of her cheek. He still didn't quite get it. This move wasn't all la-di-da joy for her. She was leaving a career she loved, a city that invigorated her, friends who'd become closer than sisters to her, especially over the past two years. She was giving up a lot to move to Missouri and have his babies. If she could even have a child. She'd been on the pill so long that sometimes she worried that it might not be so easy to become pregnant.

She pushed the niggling fear from her mind. She loved Derek, and she knew it was the right thing for them. She knew she would start getting excited about her new life—their new life—once she got there. But right now she wished he could just acknowledge that she needed to grieve a little for this life first.

And for what his affair had cost them.

Chapter Two

Reed Vincent woke up drenched in sweat, the dream vivid and suffocating. He sat up on the side of the bed, rubbing his temples, trying to focus on the clock on his nightstand. The giant digital numbers were blurry—maybe blurrier than they'd been yesterday—but he could still read them. Just barely. Seven-fifteen. The morning sun poured through the window and he squinted against its painful brightness even as relief surged through his veins.

His heart still stuttered like a jackhammer, but it had only been a dream. The stifling blackness, the coarse blindfold his fingers could not unknot. Gingerly, he touched his eyelids. The blindfold had been a figment of his imagination. *Ease up, Vincent. It was only a dream.*

But that was just the trouble. It wasn't a dream. One day…one day soon he would wake up and the numbers on the clock would no longer come into focus. And another day, their greenish glow might fade altogether.

He punched off the alarm clock and rolled off the bed. He grabbed the crumpled pair of blue jeans flopped over the ladder-back chair in the corner and pulled them on over his boxers. Experimenting, he left his glasses on the nightstand, and plodded through the kitchen and down the three wide steps that opened to the sunken studio.

The pine floor was cold beneath his bare feet, but sunlight already glowed softly through clerestory windows high on the north wall. He needed the light to paint by, but since his eyes had become ultrasensitive to it, he'd grown to prefer the dawn and dusk hours.

Inhaling deeply, Reed felt himself come fully awake. And fully alive. The mingled smells of oils and turpentine and stale coffee grounds never failed to invigorate him.

He grabbed a warped canvas from a stack of rejects behind the file cabinet and cleared off the easel. With skill and precision granted by years of practice, he clamped the canvas to the easel. He turned and started for the cupboard where his paints were stored. Halfway across the room he stopped.

He'd always told Kristina—back when they were on speaking terms—that even if he somehow lost his hands, he would still find a way to create art. He'd broken his right arm playing touch football in an alumni exhibition game a couple of years ago. While he was in the cast, he'd been able to do some rudimentary tasks with his left hand and it wasn't long before he could use the fingers on his right hand a bit. It had made painting a more laborious task than usual, but he didn't doubt that had the condition been permanent, he would have managed somehow, would have trained himself to work left-handed.

But he'd taken his sight for granted. It was one thing to think of painting left-handed, or even holding a pencil between his teeth, if that's what it took to continue producing art. But not to be able even to *see* what he'd created? He knew some talented abstract painters, but that wasn't how he'd made his name. Art buyers were notoriously discriminating. They didn't take kindly to a tried-and-true craftsman suddenly changing his style. Would Reed Vincent's paintings be worth a red cent if they were created without benefit of his sight?

Kristina hadn't seemed to think so. Reed didn't blame her for not wanting to risk getting stuck with a helpless invalid who might not be able to provide her with every good thing her daddy had supplied. Of course she was classy enough to never say it in so many words. He wondered sometimes if she had even admitted to herself why she'd broken off their relationship. But despite his failing sight, he could read the doubt—and worse, the pity—in her eyes from across the sizable rooms of the family estate.

Understanding Kristina's choice didn't make her rejection hurt any less. But he wouldn't take her back now, even if she had a miraculous change of heart. Back then, he'd been sure he was in love with the beautiful, talented Kristina Marie Hardesty. Thankfully, when her lack of loyalty and her self-centered bent revealed themselves, it took the edge off his adoration. His sister insisted it had also left him cautious and a little cynical. He didn't necessarily agree with Alissa, but if that's what it took to avoid a repeat performance, then so be it.

Squinching his eyelids shut, he stretched his arms in front of him and cautiously felt his way to the tall cupboard. Groping for the handle, he scraped his knuckles on the rough wood, but forced himself to keep his eyes closed. The door opened easily.

He ran his fingers slowly over the edge of the middle shelf that housed more than a hundred tubes of paint. Without faltering, he zeroed in on the box that held the small metal tubes. None of the small crimped tubes were stamped in Braille now. But when the time came, he'd find a way to label them. They were already filed alphabetically, and he could hire an assistant to help him select the right colors and even mix them on the palette if necessary. There were many aspects of painting that could be done by someone else—preparing the canvas, mixing the paints to his specifications.

Even with his eyes clenched tightly shut so the morning light didn't penetrate, he could visualize what a daub of alizarin crimson would look like on the canvas, or the cool hue that would result if he mixed Prussian blue with a dab of titanium white on the palette. He didn't suppose he would ever forget colors. They were too much a part of the essence of the artist, the essence of Reed Vincent.

Even as a child, he'd possessed a heightened sense of colors, discerning the violet and lavender in shadows, where others saw only gray; and differentiating the palest pink and yellow tints in shades most would have labeled simply "white." No, colors would be preserved forever in his memory. And hopefully the things he'd learned as he studied art over the years would enable him to instruct someone to mix them with the nuances in tone and hue that were so important to the outcome of a piece.

He mentally steeled himself to face the possibility of a future without his eyesight. If, in the process, he lost the gift of his art, he would grieve deeply. But it wasn't that loss he ached to consider so much as the possibility that he may never see the subtle changes in his precious niece and nephew as they grew up. His sister and her family were the joy of Reed's life. He wanted to witness the passing years crease Alissa's pretty face with smile lines. He wanted to watch little Ali and Mason grow into teenagers.

To think that he might never look into the eyes of his own future children was almost more than he could bear. Or that he might "see" the face of a wife he'd yet to meet only by tracing the contours of her brow with his fingertips.

He knew these physical things shouldn't matter. But they *did*. He was an artist. His very thoughts were visual…and vivid. Would a loving God take that from him? He had so much of life yet to experience.

He'd bargained with God more than once. He'd vowed to accept the loss of his sight graciously if only God would hold back the curse until he'd experienced the small blessings of life that others took for granted. A loving wife. Babies. The satisfaction of providing for a family.

But what woman could love him if the worst happened and he went blind? Besides, he would be a fool to father children he could never properly care for. He was dreaming, entertaining foolishness. He had to be realistic. He should be thankful if he could manage to provide for his own basic needs.

Shaking off the morbid thoughts, he opened his eyes and selected a few nearly empty tubes from the cabinet. He squeezed out carefully measured globs of cobalt blue, titanium white and cadmium orange onto a glass palette at twelve, three and nine o'clock, the way one might fill a dinner plate for a blind person.

He picked two flat sables from the bouquet of pricey paint-brushes that bloomed in a pottery jar on the taboret beside the easel.

Could he transfer what he saw in his mind's eye to the canvas? That had been a difficult enough task when his eyesight was perfect. He squeezed his eyes shut again, and leveled the palette over his left wrist and forearm. He felt for the edge of the canvas with his right hand. Planting his feet apart he flexed his toes, steadying himself.

It took supreme effort not to take a quick peek, but he felt for the edge of the palette and stabbed at it until he felt the brush meet resistance at nine o'clock. That would be the orange. He filled the brush and stroked the color onto the canvas, feeling the paint spread in a studied arc under the command of his wrist. It was a sensation as familiar to him as breathing.

Muscles he hadn't realized were tensed relaxed a bit as he visualized the texture of a burning sun. He emptied the brush in circular motions on the canvas. Finished, he aimed the brush in the vicinity of the jar of turpentine on the taboret, jabbing until he heard the telltale *blup-blup* of bristles hitting liquid. So far, so good.

He took the clean brush and loaded it with blue paint, working across the canvas from left to right, building a swell of ocean waves beneath his sun. He could "see" the canvas in his head far more clearly than he'd expected. Granted he'd chosen a simple scene, but this wasn't as difficult as he'd imagined. He relaxed further and began to enjoy his little experiment.

Reed continued to paint, feeling surprisingly optimistic. He measured off an invisible grid with his fingertips, and dotted whitecaps on his waves of paint. He could do this.

Ten minutes later he opened his eyes. He leaned forward, squinting to appraise his handiwork. His jaw dropped.

The canvas before him looked like something a kindergart-ner had painted—or a chimpanzee. He gaped at his awful crea-tion for half a minute, feeling the viscous bile of rage rise in his throat.

Unable to stop himself, he raked the canvas off the easel and in one motion, slammed the palette down on the uneven wood planks. The safety glass fractured with an earsplitting *crrrack*.

Reed sank to the floor and lopped his forearms over bent knees. It was all over. He was finished.

He hung his head in the crook of one elbow and watched the pine boards soak up greasy splotches of orange and blue.

Chapter Three

Olivia struggled to the surface, fending off suffocating blankets as her cell phone's mechanical tone played a sound track to her dream. She was walking down the street of a ghost town straight out of a B-western. Half a dozen people loitered on the dusty boardwalks that ran in front of the dilapidated buildings on either side of the street. Faceless names, they waved and beckoned as she passed.

There was Opal Something-or-other, the nice widow from church that Derek had told her about. The woman held out a cake, and though her face was obscured, Olivia somehow knew she was smiling. Derek's boss, Jay Brooks, stood on the other side of the cow-town street. His face, too, was a blur, but he was built like Olivia's uncle Jay—same middle-age paunch and balding pate.

The burr of her cell phone filled the room again, louder this time, and she came fully awake, groping for the phone on the bare floor beside her rented cot. She coughed and tried out her voice, the weird dream still thickening her brain. Without her reading glasses, she couldn't make out the display screen.

"Hello?"

Silence.

"Hello…" She waited several seconds before she folded the phone shut, annoyed. She pulled the blankets over her head and squeezed her eyelids together, trying to get back to the dream. Bizarre though it was, it had been interesting.

She'd always found it fascinating to trace a dream to its cause. This one wasn't too hard to figure out. Derek was already settled into the new world that would soon be hers. He'd talked enthusiastically about his new colleagues and the friendly neighbors in their subdivision. She had only names for these people Derek spoke of like old friends. And now that the day of her move was here, she felt more apprehensive than excited.

Wide-awake now, she threw off the covers and sat up on the side of the cot. She took her glasses from their perch on a stack of magazines that served as a nightstand, opened the cell phone again and scrolled through the recent messages. It was Derek who'd called. At 6:55 a.m. Had she actually managed to sleep a full eight hours on this lumpy cot?

She punched in his number only to get his voice mail. She sighed into the phone. "Hey, babe. Guess you're in one of those important company meetings wowing all your coworkers…never mind that it's Sunday morning." She giggled at her own joke. "But, hey, call me when you have a sec. I packed the car last night so I just have to drop the keys by the office and return the cot and I'm outta here. I'll call you when I get into town so you can guide me through the huge metropolis of Hanover Falls." She gave a little laugh. He'd get a kick out of that. "Okay…see you in seven hours and fifty-six minutes."

Derek had mapped out the route for her and knew almost down to the minute how long it should take her—as long as she didn't make too many stops or hit St. Louis at rush hour. Were there rush hours on Sunday? People racing to get to church? She doubted it.

She stripped the cot and folded the bedding, putting it in a neat stack by the door. When she'd wrestled the unwieldy bed into a neatly folded rectangle, she rolled it out to the front hall. It took her twenty minutes to dress and pack up the few belongings left in the house.

She took one last walk through the town house. This was it. Her stomach churned. This time tomorrow she'd be a small-town housewife waking up in Hanover Falls.

* * *

A summer storm bruised the Illinois sky as skyscrapers gave way to sprawling malls. By the time Olivia crossed into Missouri the sun glimmered on a lush green landscape dotted with farmhouses.

Traffic was light until Olivia got on I-44, but even with quick stops for lunch and gas, Derek would be happy that she was only fifteen minutes behind his ETA. The city limit sign for Hanover Falls boasted a population of just over ten thousand. Olivia tried unsuccessfully to fathom that number compared to Chicago's three million.

As she tooled down the town's Main Street, she had to admit this little burg had a lot of charm, set as it was in the foothills of the Ozarks. A nice place for a vacation getaway, but could a city girl like her be happy living here?

She dialed Derek's number. Correction: her number. *Their* number. It bothered her that she had trouble thinking of Hanover Falls as their new home. They were in this together, weren't they? She wanted to believe it. Why couldn't her heart seem to follow her head?

The phone rang four times before the answering machine picked up. That man. Derek had been in the house less than a week and he already had an answering machine hooked up and operational. No doubt she'd walk into a fully functional kitchen and rooms with all the furniture in place. Fine. Just so he didn't try to take over the decorating. That was her department and he knew it.

Decorating the house was the only thing that would keep her sane in the weeks to come. It was bad enough that Derek had picked out the house without her. But she'd been swamped at work, determined to finish up two big projects for clients before leaving the city.

She'd given her approval of the house based on some fuzzy photos on the Web site of the Realtor. It seemed nice enough. Spacious rooms with several built-in window seats, high ceilings with crown molding throughout, and a few other nice architectural details. And Derek had promised things looked even better in person. "It's move-in ready, babe. The whole place has been painted your favorite creamy white, and there's new carpet in the bedrooms. Oh, and you'll love the hardwood floors in the main rooms. It's practically a mansion."

"Are you sure it's not too much? I feel a little guilty spending so much, especially when I'm not going to be working."

"You deserve it," he said. "Besides, we need to get accustomed to some of the luxuries of life so Heaven won't be such a shock."

She'd laughed and let him prattle on, still in deep persuasion mode, knowing how reluctant she was to leave her beloved Windy City behind.

Now, she dialed their new home number again, this time leaving a brief message. He'd printed off a map from the Internet and sketched in a rough route for her to follow. She pulled it out of her purse now. The town was so tiny she could probably just drive up and down each narrow street until she came to the house.

She drove another half mile, trying to decipher street signs in the dusky light. She was surprised to look up and see a patchwork of green wheat fields and plowed earth on one side of the street and woods on the other. Even if their house was clear across town, they practically lived in the country.

Olivia turned the car around in someone's driveway, stopped to study Derek's map by the dim dome light, then started back down Main. Two blocks south and there it was—Glenwillow Road. The street sign was covered by a low-hanging elm branch, just beginning to bud. She turned right and found herself in a charming neighborhood of older homes with perfectly coiffured lawns and tidy landscaping.

She could see why Derek was so excited. She slowed the car to a crawl and bent over the steering wheel to check house numbers—227, 229, 333… There it was—335. The Realtor's sign was still planted in the front yard, a bold SOLD slashed across its face.

She turned into the driveway, peering up at the house through her bug-speckled windshield. She tooted her horn, excitement rising in her. If the inside of the house was as promising as the exterior, she could hardly wait to get her hands on it. She had to hand it to Derek. He'd picked a winner. A foreign emotion washed over her and she realized that she couldn't wait to see her husband. She'd missed him. A good sign. Maybe there was hope for them after all.

She tapped the horn again with the ball of her hand. Where was he? The driveway curved around to a double garage at the back of the house. She followed it and parked by the back entrance. There was a light on in one of the back rooms. That would probably be the kitchen.

Turning the key in the ignition, she opened the car door and was met by an amazing, almost eerie silence. No horns blaring, no sirens, no distant clatter from the El. This was going to be culture shock in a big way. How would she ever sleep in such utter silence?

She gathered her purse and bags from the front seat and went around to open the trunk. She thought Derek had brought her a key to the front door the weekend after he closed on the house, but she didn't have a clue where she'd put it. Hopefully he was home.

Juggling a stack of boxes and bags from the trunk, she rang the back doorbell with her elbow. A long minute went by. She tried again. Nothing. Groaning, she set her load down on the concrete patio and tried the door.

The knob turned easily and the door swung open.

"Derek?" She stepped into a small mudroom and called again. Her pulse quickened. What if she had the wrong house? She peeked around the corner into the kitchen. "Derek? You home, babe?"

The kitchen was brightly lit, and she breathed a sigh of relief when she saw the fire-engine red teakettle with its distinctive dent sitting on the stove. Derek's tea-stained UIC mug was beside the sink. At least she knew she was in the right place.

She put her bags down on the tile floor and walked through the large dining and living rooms, flipping on lights as she went. She roamed from room to room, viewing the house the way she evaluated a client's space when she did her first walk-through on a job. Her exhilaration escalated. She loved the house. And Derek was right. The paint and carpet were nearly new and exactly what she would have chosen herself. The hard part was done and she could concentrate on the decorating touches that would make the house her own. *Their* own.

Her mind reeled with ideas, visualizing window treatments and color schemes that would make the most of the home's architecture. The wooden floor in the guest room was in need of refinishing, and she made a mental note to consider a faux marble paint treatment she'd used with great success in a client's house last year.

As she'd guessed, Derek had arranged the furniture in the living room—if you could call his rigid rows of chairs and sofas "arranged"—and he'd set up their bed in the master bedroom. There were still boxes to be unpacked in each room, but he'd done the hard stuff, and the house itself looked great.

"Derek?" He must have run to the store. Or maybe he'd decided to go in to work this afternoon and just lost track of time.

She finished a quick tour of the house and unloaded the last of their belongings from her car.

She puttered around the house, scooting an overstuffed chair and ottoman to a new position in the living room and unpacking a few boxes. In spite of the fact that it was her own belongings she was pulling out of the pasteboard cartons, she couldn't shake the feeling that she was in somebody else's house.

Every few minutes she checked the clock Derek had hung in the kitchen—too high on the wall, she noticed. He might be efficient, but the man had no sense of design. An hour passed, then two, and still no Derek. His car wasn't in the garage, and he wasn't answering his cell phone or the phone at Parker & Associates.

She shivered, remembering too many nights in Chicago when he was supposedly "at work," yet couldn't explain why he didn't answer his office phone.

But he'd changed. She knew he had. She wouldn't have followed him to this Podunk town in the middle of nowhere if she didn't believe that with all her heart.

She dialed both numbers one more time and left messages. Maybe he'd misunderstood what time she was leaving the city. But she was sure he expected her tonight because she remembered him talking about having to skip the Sunday night church service so he'd be there when she arrived.

Maybe he'd changed his mind and gone to church services after all. They'd attended church sporadically before Derek's affair. But even after going through counseling and getting grounded in a new church, they'd never gone on Sunday night. Derek had been invited to this one—Community Something-or-other—by coworkers and had really connected. He could have at least left her a note.

Exhausted from the drive, she curled up on the sofa. She'd just rest her eyes until Derek got home.

She awoke with a start, feeling groggy and disoriented. The kitchen clock had ticked past 9:00 p.m. The irritation she'd felt earlier turned to genuine concern. Something was wrong.

She rummaged through the kitchen drawers until she found the phone book. The entire thing was no thicker than her address book, and the only map it contained was printed in such a microscopic font it was worthless.

She didn't have a clue who to call. This wasn't exactly the kind of thing you called the police about. A flush of shame coursed through her as she remembered the first time Derek hadn't come home from work and she'd done just that. The policewoman she'd spoken to had gently suggested the possibility of an affair, and Olivia had been foolish enough to be insulted by the accusation.

Six weeks later, the truth came out.

No. She would not call the police.

She flipped through the Yellow Pages and the church listings caught her eye. She ran her finger down the column. Cornerstone Community Fellowship. That was it. Tentatively—not sure what she would say if anyone actually answered the phone at this hour of the night—she dialed the number.

The phone rang half a dozen times before it sent her to a voice mail labyrinth. She placed the receiver in its cradle and covered her face with her hands. *Lord, what should I do?* Her stomach churned. *Oh, please…please, God. Don't let this be the start of another—* She couldn't finish the thought, even in her prayers.

She grabbed her purse and dug for her car keys on her way out the back door. Her house key still hadn't turned up, so she didn't dare lock the door behind her. She hoped this town was as crime-free as Derek claimed it was.

And she hoped this new beginning in a new town wasn't the beginning of the end for them.

Chapter Four

Streetlamps lit the rows of landscaped yards like a Thomas Kinkade painting as Olivia drove through the eerie quiet of the neighborhood. But when she turned onto the highway off Main Street, an inky blackness enveloped her. Derek had said the Parker & Associates offices were outside the city limits, but she wasn't sure which direction. At least if she saw his car there, she'd know he was at work. But why wasn't he answering his phone?

She flipped open her cell phone and started to dial 411 for directions before realizing she didn't have a signal. Great.

Taking a guess, she headed north on the highway. She drove for what seemed like miles without meeting another car and without seeing anything that looked like a prosperous business. When the road turned into a two-lane and snaked through a wooded area, she turned the car around in some farmer's drive and headed back into Hanover Falls.

She swung by the house, finding everything just as she'd left it, the windows dark and no sign of Derek's car. She backed out of the drive and headed to the other end of town.

Just past the city limit sign, she spotted a dozen or so cars clustered around a tiny greasy spoon diner. Somebody there would know where Derek's office building was.

She slowed the car and turned into the circle drive, parking in front of the building beside a row of cars. This must be the only place open in Hanover Falls.

The wind had picked up, and it flapped at her hair while she fought with the heavy door. Inside, raucous music played on a jukebox and a table of teenagers hovered over a large pizza.

An elderly couple stood at the cash register paying their bill. Olivia stepped to the side, waiting to speak to the cashier, who apparently was also the hostess. After she handed the couple their receipt, the girl grabbed a menu and came around from behind the counter. "We're only serving drinks and dessert now. We close at ten—"

"Oh, no…" Olivia put up a hand. "I'm not staying. I just wondered if you could tell me how to get to Parker & Associates. It's an engineering firm…"

The cashier eyed her. "You must be a reporter."

"Excuse me?"

"Oh. Guess not." The girl shrugged. "Sorry. I just thought… well, I've never seen you around here and the place has been swarming—"

"Do you know where Parker & Associates is?" Olivia worked to keep her voice even.

"I know where it *was*."

"Was?"

The cashier's eyes scrunched up and she cocked her head to one side. "You didn't hear about what happened?"

"No…" The word came out in a tight whisper.

"Oh, man, there was a huge explosion out there this afternoon. Something about a gas leak. This place was crawling with reporters earlier." She gave a smirk. "Most exciting thing that's happened around here in a long time."

Olivia sucked in a panicked breath and stared at the girl. "Was anybody…hurt?"

"I saw both the ambulances go by—that was probably about five o'clock. I heard one of those reporters say some guy got hurt, but he didn't think nobody got killed. That place is closed down Sundays, so nobody was in the—" She stopped abruptly and bent to look into Olivia's face. "Hey, are you okay?"

"Where…where would they have taken the—the one who got hurt?"

She shrugged. "The hospital—here in the Falls, I guess. Unless they airlifted him somewhere else. But I didn't hear no helicopter. Did you know him?"

Olivia reached out and clutched the girl's arm. "Where is the hospital?"

"Get back on the highway and head that way." She pointed through the plate glass. "There's a bunch of signs that tell you where to turn."

She nodded curtly and wheeled. Pushing past a small cluster of late diners, she shoved open the door and raced for her car.

The headlights caught a flash of blue surrounding the white *H* on the sign, and Olivia turned where the arrow directed. In a trancelike state, she followed the road, glancing constantly to the right, willing the next hospital sign to materialize.

"Oh, God, please don't let it be Derek. Please let him be okay." One prayer followed on the other's heels as the realization sank in. It *was* him. It had to be. There was no other explanation for him not meeting her at the house. Not answering her calls. Still she hoped against hope. And she prayed.

Maybe he'd heard about the accident and had gone to help out. That was something Derek would do. Especially the "new" Derek. The thought sent her hopes soaring and caused a warm, intense affection for her husband to well up inside her. But just as quickly that hope was dashed against the realization that Derek would have called her. He knew what time she was scheduled to get into town. If there were any way in the world, he would have let her know what was going on.

The signs led her on the winding highway that encompassed the town, and finally she saw the sprawling complex and the simple, lighted sign proclaiming Hanover Falls Medical Center.

She took the exit and turned onto the broad drive. The road forked. Her eyes darted between the signs and at the last second, she swung the car hard to the left toward the emergency room.

Parking in a space designated for the handicapped, she left the car unlocked and sprinted to the entrance.

The waiting room was empty.

The woman sitting at the nurse's station looked up as Olivia approached. Her name badge read Dorothy Berwyn, RN. "May I help you?"

"I'm looking for my...husband." The word opened the dam and she choked out the rest. "There was some kind of accident—an explosion out at Parker & Associates and I think my husband—"

The nurse slid her chair back and came around the desk. "What's his name?"

Olivia told her.

"Yes. He's here." The woman breathed out a stream of air. "Thank God they finally found you."

"Is...is he all right? Can I see him?"

The nurse turned sharply and studied her for a moment. She opened her mouth as if to speak, but then turned to the phone on the desk. "Let me call his doctor and let him know you're here. Then you can see your husband."

The woman seemed calm and unrushed as she dialed and spoke briefly with someone.

A flood of relief coursed through Olivia. Derek must be all right or they would have said something. They would surely be rushing her to the emergency room if he was critical.

A few minutes later, she followed Nurse Berwyn down the tiled hall, their footsteps matching in a steady cadence.

But instead of leading her to a patient's room, the nurse led her to a small sitting room off one of the main waiting rooms. She held the door and motioned for Olivia to have a seat. "The doctor will be with you in just a few minutes, Mrs. Cline."

The hum of the fluorescent lights overhead sounded like howling wind. She wanted to cover her ears, block it out. But she sat rigid, her hands clasped in her lap. Time crawled until the door finally opened and a tall white-coated man stepped into the room. He had a stethoscope looped around his neck and carried a metal clipboard against his hip.

He nodded and took a chair adjacent to Olivia. "Mrs. Cline, I'm Dr. Patton. I don't know what you've been told about your husband's condition, but I'll start from the—"

"I don't know anything at all." She held her hands out to him and her voice climbed an octave. "I went looking for him and when I stopped to ask directions to his office they told me about some explosion. What happened? Is Derek going to be okay?"

The man listened, his bushy eyebrows raised, then heaved a breath that smelled of stale cigarette smoke. "I'm sorry. I thought you knew." He folded his hands on his lap. "Apparently your husband was in the building at the time of the explosion. He was apparently thrown free of the fire that resulted, but the impact severely injured him, his brain. In effect, it caused what we term brain death."

Olivia gasped and grabbed the arms of the chair. "What is…the prognosis?"

"I'm very sorry, Mrs. Cline. But your husband didn't make it."

"I…I don't understand." Her hands began to tremble.

"Your husband is on a respirator." The doctor launched into an explanation about cranial nerves not responding and something about the interruption of the blood supply to the brain. "We'll do a series of neurological tests to ascertain the irreversibility of his condition, but…" His voice trailed off, and he shook his head, not meeting her eyes.

Olivia couldn't wrap her mind around the technical terms he tossed out. "But…if there's no hope, why is he on life support?"

"We've kept your husband on the ventilator because he had a card in his personal effects requesting to be an organ donor. The ventilator insures that his organs remain viable. But it's only his physical body that is functioning. I'm sorry, Mrs. Cline, there is no brain activity and we have no reason to hope—"

"No!" She covered her face with palms that were damp with perspiration. Swaying from side to side, she tried desperately to make the pain stop.

Dr. Patton reached out to touch her elbow. "I'm sorry. I can only imagine how difficult this is for you. But you need to understand that your husband's condition is irreversible. There is no hope for recovery."

"But can't you…can't you wait a while and see if he…responds?"

"As I said, we'll do extensive testing to be certain…. I understand you need time to absorb this news, Mrs. Cline. There are definitive tests to confirm brain death, and I can assure you every precaution has been taken. There is no room for error." He paused and his voice softened. "I assume you *were* aware your husband had signed an organ donor card, indicating he wished to donate his organs in the event of his death?"

She nodded, knowing it was true. But this man was saying they wanted to—to cut Derek open. Take his heart? His liver, his kidneys, his lungs, his eyes… It was too awful to absorb. She felt as if her entire body had been injected with Novocain. Numb, powerless to move one muscle, yet her thoughts were running a marathon.

"I know this is difficult. I'm sure you need a few minutes to absorb what has happened. Are there any questions I can answer about what happened?"

She had a million questions, but couldn't seem to form a coherent sentence.

"Can I call someone for you?"

Olivia stared at him blankly. Who would she call? Certainly Derek's father would have to be notified. But he wouldn't come, wouldn't help her. She could call Jayne, but she couldn't expect her friends to come all the way from Chicago. Her distant relatives had never been a part of her life. *Derek* was the only one she could think to call at a time like this. She let out a bark of bitter laughter and shook her head. "No. There's no one," she said.

The doctor stood silently across the room for what seemed like an eternity. Finally he cleared his throat and spoke quietly. "Mrs. Cline, we want to make certain that your husband's wishes can be carried out. I'm sure you are aware that time is critical, and of course, we want to make certain the organs are viable—"

"There's nothing else that can be done? Nothing?" She somehow managed to squeak out the words.

"We'll monitor things very closely for the next forty-eight hours, but…" The doctor shook his head, his expression somber. "I'm sorry."

"Can I see him?"

"Certainly. We can arrange that right away. You may speak with the organ procurement representative anytime after that. He will be able to answer any questions you might have, and help you make an informed decision."

Her hands started to tremble more violently. This couldn't be happening. It couldn't be true. Not Derek. Not when they'd just begun to heal from the agony of the past year. God wouldn't be that cruel. Would He?

"Mrs. Cline?" The doctor's solemn voice shook her from her thoughts. "Are you ready to go down to ICU now?"

She tried to stand, but her legs wouldn't hold her. Grabbing the arm of the chair, she steadied herself and finally gained her balance.

"This way," the doctor said, as if every day he led people to the death of their loved ones, the death of their marriages, the end of their hope.

Chapter Five

The door opened to a chill blast of air laced with a pungent anti-septic odor that turned Olivia's stomach.

Her gaze was drawn like a magnet to the hospital bed, then forced away as if the poles of the magnet now repelled it. Finally she forced her eyes to focus on the form that was Derek. At least they said it was Derek. She barely recognized the swollen, masklike face beneath the tubes and other apparatus.

Her breath caught and something inside her gave way. If what Dr. Patton said was true—if Derek really was brain-dead—it *wasn't* him lying in this bed. It was merely a shell. The man she was just learning to love was already walking the streets of Heaven.

A sob caught in her throat. This simply could not be happening. She'd already faced losing her husband to another woman. Why this? Why now? There had been times during those dark days when she'd honestly wished him dead.

Had she wished this on Derek? No. That was a silly, super-stitious notion. She hadn't meant it. Not really. But people always said "be careful what you pray for." Was God trying to teach her a lesson by giving her what she'd wished for?

A tumult of guilt crashed through her. And now she was supposed to make a decision about taking Derek off life support? She couldn't do it. She needed time. Time to make things right with him. To sort out her life…without him.

A nurse came from around the bed and eyed her, a question on her kindly face. "Are you Mrs. Cline?"

Olivia nodded.

"I'm so sorry. I know this is an incredibly difficult time for you. I'll leave you alone with your husband for a few minutes if you like."

Olivia couldn't think how to respond. Couldn't make a syllable form on her lips. She half staggered to the side of the bed. Then she fought the urge to run. Seeing Derek gray and puffy, with wires and tubes attached everywhere, terrified her.

She reached out and touched his arm. It was warm to the touch. He *felt* alive. The thought contradicted what the doctor had told her. Contradicted what she'd told herself all the way down the corridor. Did she have the right to make this decision for him? How could she be sure he wouldn't recover, might not live after all?

They were Christians. There was *always* hope. Wasn't there? *Dear God, I need You. Please, help me, Heavenly Father. I can't do this! I can't do this alone.*

The slow, steady beep of some monitoring device somewhere in the room marked time, along with the rhythmic suction and exhalation of the ventilator. Derek had always said he wanted to be an organ donor. Their driver's licenses had come up for renewal at the same time a couple of years ago and they'd both sat in the DMV office and signed the backs of their cards together. They'd even discussed it in the car on the way home afterward.

It had turned into a conversation that proved oddly prophetic. "What would you do if something happened to me, Derek?" she'd asked. "Would you find someone else?"

"Sure," he'd answered, a little too quickly for her taste.

"Wow, you sound like you already have her picked out," she joked.

"No. I'm just not the type to be alone." He'd smiled and chucked her under the chin.

But she had always wondered. Olivia didn't think he'd started the affair yet at that point, but she would always suspect that there was someone he was attracted to by then.

Derek had met Rachel Wyck at work. She was a sales rep who was in and out of the office. Apparently *in* long enough to flirt with Derek and start an affair. Olivia had never met the woman, but she'd seen her a couple of times when she dropped by Derek's office.

With her long auburn hair, petite build and bubbly personality, Rachel couldn't have been more different from Olivia. Maybe that was the attraction. Derek was outgoing and gregarious. They'd often fought about Olivia's penchant for staying home and "nesting" when he was itching to go out on the town. But didn't opposites attract? That's what he'd told her when they met. Apparently that only worked to a point. Eventually, he grew tired of the quiet girl, and the bubbly one won out.

Olivia forced the thought from her mind. That wasn't fair. She may not have been the one who had an affair, but she'd checked out of their marriage long before Derek had. She bit her lip, remembering.

She'd formed a circle of friends at work, and they started going out on the town together almost every weekend. She excused her neglect of Derek by claiming that it was important to her job security. Her boss, Elizabeth DiMartino, wasn't always part of the group, but often enough that Olivia could use her as an excuse. Until Derek pointed it out, she hadn't stopped to consider that, except for Jayne, her friends were all single. Elizabeth was long widowed, Lucy and RaeAnn were divorced, and the others were fresh out of college. She hadn't chosen her friends for their marital status—or lack thereof—but it did mean that she was the only one gallivanting—Derek's word—around town on Saturday night while her husband sat at home alone.

Well, Derek didn't sit home for long. And when she finally gave in to his request to spend more time at home, it was almost too late.

They had so many regrets. Both of them. So many things to try to forget. So many proverbial elephants in every room of their lives.

But then there had been that last weekend together in Chicago, when Derek had shown up at the town house with a dozen hothouse roses and a beautiful silver heart locket. Gifts he'd presented to her for no reason at all. "Just because you're my favorite person in the world," he'd said. Then he'd dipped his head in humility that was out of character for Derek Cline. "And because I'm so glad you gave us another chance."

They made love that night, and for the first time in a long time Olivia hadn't fought against visions of Derek's betrayal, hadn't thought once of the ugliness of his affair. Instead, their lovemaking left her feeling at one with her husband. Excited that they were off to a new beginning together. Brand-new.

The ventilator's mechanical hiss invaded her thoughts. Her fingers traced the heart-shaped locket at her throat. She pressed the tepid metal against her skin, then reached for the bed rail, steadying herself. Her gaze moved from her husband's pale, still form in the bed to the machines that pumped breath into him.

Now, somehow, she knew with certainty that it was not the breath of life the machine imparted. No. Derek was gone.

She needed to call his father. Let their friends know what had happened. Her brain started a frantic tabulation of everything she needed to do.

Finally the river of thoughts dammed up and her pulse slowed. There would be a lifetime to do all the tasks death required. Only one thing was necessary right now.

It was time to tell her husband goodbye.

"Mrs. Cline?"

Olivia started at the hand on her shoulder. "Yes?" The word came out like a scratchy recording and she cleared her throat, squinting against the bright lights in the waiting room. She didn't know if she'd been asleep for ten minutes or ten hours. How could she have slept at all at a time like this?

The doctor who stood in front of her wore a mixture of kindness and sadness on his face. It made her ache. "I wanted to let you know that…it's over. They've disconnected the ventilator. Your husband is gone."

She thought she'd already accepted the inevitable in the long minutes she'd sat in this chilled room, waiting for them to come and tell her what she already knew. She felt like a coward waiting out here. She should have stayed with him. Derek would have done at least that for her. The thought caused her to choke on a sob.

"I'm so sorry," the doctor said. He was the same doctor who'd talked to her about Derek's desire to be an organ donor. Martin Randall, M.D., his name tag said. An organ procurement officer, he'd called himself before. Such a serious title.

It all seemed surreal. She hardly knew how to make her thoughts line up with what was happening. "What…do I do now?" Her voice came out in a feeble squeak.

"You're free to go home for now. We will release the body to the funeral home as soon as they've taken the donor organs. I assume you designated which mortuary you wish to use?" He started leafing through the sheaf of papers she'd filled out earlier.

Olivia scrubbed her face with the palms of her hands. "We just moved to town. I didn't know the name of any place. I just left it blank…."

"There are only two funeral homes in Hanover Falls. I wouldn't hesitate to recommend either one."

"Could you…could you just choose one for me?"

"Certainly." He slid a ballpoint pen from the pocket of his jacket and scribbled something on one of the papers. When he was finished, he looked down at her. "Are you all right? Do you have someone to drive you home?"

She shook her head. She had no one. Her husband was dead. She was alone in a town she'd never visited before today. She'd called Derek's father earlier. He and his wife were flying in from Palm Beach tomorrow. For the funeral.

"I can have someone call a cab for you," Dr. Randall said. "I think the service is still operating this late on Sunday night."

"No." She shook her head and couldn't seem to stop. She wasn't even sure how to get back to the house. "I have my car here. Out by the emergency room. I'll be okay." It was a lie. How could she ever be okay again? She started down the hallway.

"Mrs. Cline? Mrs. Cline?" She turned at the sound of her name.

The doctor pointed with a corner of his clipboard. "The emergency room exit is that way."

She nodded and turned, wondering if she could possibly make it to the end of the corridor that stretched before her.

Somehow she managed to get in her car and retrace the path she'd taken hours ago, back to Glenwillow Road. There, she let herself into the house and locked the door behind her. She needed to make some phone calls.

Her husband was dead. There was a funeral to plan.

Chapter Six

Reed Vincent jerked to attention and sat up straight on the couch. The television blared in the background. He must have fallen asleep. But what had awakened him?

The answer came in the loud ringing of the telephone in the next room. He slid off the couch and knelt, squinting at the giant numerals that glowed from the DVD player. It was no use. They were a complete blur.

Groping for his eyeglasses with one hand and the remote with the other, he landed on the glasses first and shoved them on his face. He leaned toward the clock until his nose almost touched the front panel of the DVD player. It was six-fifteen in the morning. Wednesday.

This was getting to be a bad habit. He'd spent more nights on the couch than in his bed recently. The phone blared for his attention. He stumbled to the dining room, following the faint glimmers of light from the lamps he left on to guide him. At the desk, he fumbled with the receiver, putting the mouthpiece to his ear before he realized his mistake and flipped it aright. "Hello? Hello?" he said into the phone, realizing too late how loud he'd made his voice.

"Mr. Vincent?"

"Yes?"

"This is Dr. Shahzad's office."

He held his breath. They wouldn't call at this time of day unless—

"Sorry to call so early," the voice said, "but Dr. Shahzad wanted to let you know that he's had a surgery cancellation. We have donor corneas available. If you can get into the hospital by seven o'clock, he could do the procedure this morning."

His heart raced. His thoughts were wrenched back to the time he'd received a similar phone call. This was the call he'd been waiting for. The one that filled him with equal parts hope and fear. He'd already had one failed transplant.

Was it fair to try once more and risk being rejected again? Someone else could benefit from the donor corneas. Someone with a better chance than he had for a successful outcome. His ophthalmologist had continued to encourage him, insisting that it wasn't entirely unusual for a recipient to have an episode of rejection before a successful transplant.

Corneas didn't have to be exact blood type or tissue matches, and there were any number of donors he could be paired with. The wait hadn't been long.

He leaned against the wall and raked a hand through his hair. "I…I'll have to call my ride. And where do I go?"

"You have some time. The surgery isn't scheduled until nine o'clock, but we wanted to be sure you didn't eat anything. You can have sips of water, but you need to have an empty stomach when you arrive. You can come straight to admissions like you have before. We'd like to have you here as early as possible to fill out the paperwork and get you prepped. It will be outpatient again, assuming everything goes well. You know the routine." There was a note of excitement in the nurse's voice, as if she were delivering the best of news.

But was it? Or would this be just one more devastating disappointment? He'd thought he was prepared for this. He'd known they had him on the list of recipients, but now that the moment had arrived, he wasn't so sure.

With his head spinning, he stood and reached for the wall, following it to the hallway, then making his way into the bathroom without a misstep.

"Okay, Lord," he whispered. "I'm up for this if You are."

It was as though the words released his spirit from their prison cell, and the old hope soared within him. He was getting another chance. Another chance, perhaps, to be the artist God had created him to be. But more than that, a chance to see the ornery glint in little Ali's eyes, to watch his niece grow from a toddler into a young woman. To take measure of young Mason's height by something other than a hand on a broadening shoulder.

He would not turn down such an opportunity. No matter how guilty it made him feel.

The light that filtered through the plain cotton curtains was gray and heavy. But it was light. Morning. Olivia groaned and shook off the cruel spark of hope that fired in her just before she opened her eyes every dawn since Derek's funeral.

Ten days now. And each morning she woke with remnants of old hope clinging to her like cobwebs.

But this wasn't a dream. It had really happened. The accident, the terrible hours in the hospital. All of it. Derek was gone. And with him, the optimism they'd harbored. The new life they'd planned.

Still, as she had every morning for the past ten days, she padded into the living room and curled up on the plump chintz love seat where, at the Bennetts' advice, she and Derek had sat and prayed each morning in their old town house for the restoration of their marriage.

Here, Olivia had seen the first glimpse of hope that she might be able to forgive her husband and go on with him. Here, they had learned to laugh together again, here they had made love as husband and wife after a betrayal so great that neither thought their marriage could survive.

But it had. And their coming together had been sweet with promise as they clung to the fragile filament of faith that tied them to each other.

She hugged a sofa cushion to her chest and breathed in its scent, trying to capture some left-behind trace of Derek. But the fabric only smelled of dust and mustiness.

She tried to pray now, but her cries seemed not to reach past the ceiling. She felt abandoned. By Derek and by God. Left alone in this unfamiliar house where she couldn't even figure out how to work the thermostat to turn up the heat before she crawled between the icy sheets each night.

A familiar cyclone of nausea churned in the pit of her stomach and she clasped the cushion closer and curled into a ball in the corner of the love seat.

At least she'd slept last night. She had to make some decisions today. Wandering in this limbo wasn't an option anymore. There was nothing for her in this little town. Yet, Chicago had even less to offer now. Their apartment in the city was already rented and her job had been filled. She'd have to sell this house before she could move back. Derek had bragged about what a buyers' market real estate was in the small town. He'd gotten a bargain in this house. But would she be able to recoup the price if she put the house back on the market? She could kick herself for talking Derek out of the mortgage protection insurance that would have paid off the policy on his death. And because they had no children, and Olivia's job in Chicago had paid almost as much as Derek's, they had minimal life insurance policies.

She had a ten o'clock meeting with Jay Brooks, Derek's boss, this morning. Afterward she would go talk to the bank and find out just how dire her circumstances were.

Forty-five minutes later, she pulled into the parking lot of Parker & Associates. Yellow tape cordoned off a construction site at one corner of the building. Olivia swallowed hard and stepped out of the car, locking the door behind her. A few days earlier, she'd driven by Derek's old office almost accidentally, trying to find a grocery store. It hadn't been as difficult as she'd expected.

The wound in the building from the explosion had been neatly patched, and it looked as if the workers on the roof were finishing up the job already.

Macabre thoughts swirled through her mind—cartoonish images of Derek sailing out of his office and landing on the ground. She'd been told the whole accident was something of a fluke, but no one had said how her husband had sustained injuries that killed him, yet left his body intact, every organ healthy enough to offer life to someone else. She assumed it was a head injury. Her friends had urged her to sue. But she couldn't face that. She just wanted it to be over. The whole nightmare.

She shook off the thoughts and steeled herself to enter the building.

The receptionist's desk was ten steps from the front door. The woman behind the counter was all efficiency and zero warmth. "Mrs. Cline? Mr. Brooks is expecting you. Follow me, please."

She was ushered into Jay Brooks's office.

Olivia knew she'd met Derek's boss at the funeral, but apparently his face had been lost in the fog of grief and confusion, because she had no recollection of the man who rose and came around his desk to shake her hand.

"Mrs. Cline. Thank you for coming in. Let me say again how sorry I am."

"Thank you." She bit at her lower lip, irked at the tears that were always so close to the surface lately.

"Please, have a seat." He indicated a straight chair and went around to seat himself behind the desk.

She waited while he slid open a drawer and withdrew a sheaf of papers with a check clipped to the corner.

He pushed it across the desk to her. "Unfortunately, Mrs. Cline, your husband wasn't here long enough to accrue company benefits, however, we do want to offer something to help you with the transition."

She picked up the papers and stared at the attached check. Eight thousand, seven hundred and thirty-six dollars. The check was made out to Olivia Cline. It was barely two months' salary, and less than what they'd drawn together in Chicago for the same time period.

"What…what's this?"

"The board of directors opted to present you with a onetime payment, in spite of the fact that your husband was still on probation at the company. Of course, you'll be eligible to collect workers' compensation benefits."

She didn't know what to say. Part of her felt relief at finally having some cash in hand. But the rational part of her brain realized this was it. Workers' compensation would be minimal. There would be no generous insurance payment that would give her options. She'd done the math. One less mouth to feed did not translate to half the mortgage payment or electric bill.

The representative from Parker & Associates had assured her that the initial investigation of the accident, the result of a gas leak, clearly absolved the firm of any culpability. Maybe she would be forced to sue Parker & Associates, or the City of Hanover Falls. But what if she lost? She couldn't afford to retain an attorney.

She slipped the check from beneath the paper clip. "This is all he—Derek—had coming?"

The director's jawline tensed. "As I said, Mrs. Cline, your husband actually had...well, *nothing* coming...since this occurred during his probationary period, you understand." He stood and moved around the desk again, tapping his fingers on the edge of the polished surface. "This also includes salary for the few hours your husband had put in to date."

She nodded. "I see." But she didn't see. Didn't see at all how she would stretch this sum long enough to make the decisions she needed to make. She could sell Derek's car and come up with a little more cash, but they still owed several thousand dollars on that loan. Even then, until she sold the house there was no way she could make it more than a few months. Every penny of their savings—which wasn't much—had gone for the down payment and closing costs on the house. She would need to sell it quickly.

Mr. Brooks towered over her, seeming to dismiss her with his stare.

Numb, she stood and mumbled her thanks. Later, as she unlocked her front door, she couldn't remember exiting the building, couldn't recall one thing about the drive home. But she was home. She dropped the paperwork and the check on a kitchen counter and went again to seek the embrace of the love seat in the living room.

Chapter Seven

Reed took three short steps backward on the uneven floor and squinted, trying to focus on the painting. The sun streaming through the clerestory windows played off the still-wet crimson oil that matched the tip of the paintbrush in his right hand. It was hard to be objective, but he thought it was good. Through the gauzy veil of his vision, it looked at least as good as anything he'd done before the surgery.

He looked toward the clock on the wall over the worktable. His eyes were still sensitive to the light coming in the windows, but the clock's oversize face reminded him that it was time for his eyedrops again.

It had only been two weeks and his ophthalmologist had said his sight would continue to gradually change—hopefully improve—over the next few months. It might be six months or longer before he knew what the corneal transplant had actually accomplished. But if this was it, if this was as good as it ever got, he would live with it—and be immensely grateful.

Absently, Reed rolled the sable brush between his fingers and brought it to rest between them like a cigarette. He reached up to brush his pinky finger delicately across his eyelid. The pain was completely gone, as if the surgery had never happened. But the inner part of his eyelids stung now as salty tears erupted. He hated this part—being reduced to weeping out of sheer gratitude.

Because he could still paint. God hadn't taken away his gift. Reed could never say thank-you enough. He would weep every hour on the hour, if that would prove to God how truly thankful he was for this miracle.

He swallowed past the boulder in his throat and picked up his palette. The gallery in St. Louis had requested some larger framed pieces and he was long overdue getting a smaller piece framed for a longtime client. What he really needed was an assistant. He hadn't allowed himself to consider the possibility before the surgery. Hadn't known if he would even be able to work again until a couple of weeks ago. Now optimism buoyed him and made everything seem possible.

Yes. An assistant was just what he needed. Someone to select the paints and do the setup, cleanup and framing, all the tedious work, so he didn't strain his eyes any more than necessary. So he could save his best hours for putting paint on canvas.

If he didn't get his income up to its former level, paying an assistant might drain funds he would need later, but that was a risk he'd take. He would put an ad in the paper first thing in the morning.

Olivia parked the car in the potholed parking lot west of the church building and turned off the ignition. She pulled the keys out and dropped them in her purse, but made no motion to get out of the car. Gripping the steering wheel, her hands locked at eleven and one, she noticed her knuckles were white. Her fingers were actually shaking. She smiled in spite of herself. After all she'd been through, the thing that made her tremble with fear was walking into a church service by herself? How silly.

Derek would laugh at her. *He would have.* And she would have punched his arm and chided him for making fun of her. After all, she was doing this for his sake. She shook her head, trying to clear her mind. It irked her the way her thoughts twisted back on themselves ever since Derek's death. She'd start out thinking in present tense and in the middle of a word, she'd realize that it had come out all wrong. She'd try to correct it in her mind. *Derek is… Derek was… Derek used to be.* It was all too confusing.

She blew out a breath, trying to expel the sick feeling in her stomach. In one practiced motion she slung her purse over one shoulder and pushed open the car door. Might as well get it over with.

She locked the car and followed the clusters of people making their way through the parking lot to the entrance of the modest, steepled building.

An attractive couple just ahead of her swung a copper-haired little girl between them. "One…two…three. Whee!" They launched the child three feet off the ground before bringing her gently back to the sidewalk. Olivia guessed her to be about five or six. The girl's parents exchanged a smile that spoke a thousand words. Of love and pride and of belonging to someone special.

"Do it again! Do it again!" the little girl squealed.

The trio reached the door ahead of Olivia, and the man opened it, turned to allow his wife and daughter through, then held it for Olivia, as well.

"Good morning," he said when they were all inside. "Are you new to Cornerstone? I don't remember seeing you here before."

Olivia nodded. "Yes. We…*I*…just moved to town." She'd been correcting her pronouns since the day Derek died. We had become I. Ours had become mine. Us had become me. She wondered how long it would take her to quit thinking of herself as part of a couple.

"Well, welcome." The man put his arm around his wife's waist and drew her into the conversation, as he stretched out a hand to Olivia. "I'm Michael Meredith and this is my wife, Claire. And this—" he reached around his wife to put a hand on the little girl's head, as if to tame the wild abandon of copper curls "—is our daughter, Katherine."

Olivia forced a smile. "Nice to meet you. I'm Olivia Cline."

Michael wrinkled his brow. "Cline? That sounds…" He barely suppressed a gasp. "Oh… Are you Derek Cline's wi—?"

Olivia was grateful he stopped short of speaking the word *wife*… No, *widow*. She'd anticipated just such a moment, yet now that it was here, she couldn't think of a single reply. She nodded numbly.

Claire Meredith stepped forward. "Olivia," she said warmly. "It's so nice to have you here. We were just devastated to hear about Derek's accident."

"You knew him?" It surprised her for some reason.

"Derek attended our men's prayer group," Michael said.

"Oh. Yes, of course. He…talked about it. He really enjoyed it." She wondered just how much Derek had shared with the group about their troubles.

Claire put a gentle hand on Olivia's arm. "Would you like to sit with us?"

"Please," her husband seconded.

A strange warmth filled Olivia and she nodded again. "Thank you."

The Merediths led the way into the sanctuary and she followed them to a seat near the front. On the small stage in the corner, an ensemble played quiet music, but the people around them visited in soft murmurs, an occasional burst of laughter piercing the quiet. Olivia couldn't guess how many weeks it had been since she'd been in church. It felt almost foreign to her.

Claire turned to her. "So, do you plan to stay in the Falls? I'm sorry…I forget where you moved from…."

"Chicago."

"Oh, yes. That's right." Claire waited expectantly.

Olivia scoured her brain for the question she knew Claire had asked. Oh, yes…Hanover Falls. "I…I haven't decided yet—about staying. There are still some things I have to check into—insurance and the mortgage…"

Claire patted her arm. "If there's anything we can do to help, please don't hesitate to ask. I didn't know your husband well, but Michael thought so much of him. You've been in our prayers."

"Thank you." Tears were close to the surface. It seemed she was always on the edge of tears these days.

A young man with longish hair took the steps up to the stage two at a time and made his way to the microphone at the pulpit. The sanctuary quieted. Claire gave Olivia's arm a final pat, and turned to shush her young daughter and face the front.

Olivia was relieved to have her thoughts to herself again. But the little girl—Katherine—crawled around her mother's knees and scooted onto the pew beside Olivia. Trying not to smudge her makeup, Olivia turned and dabbed at her damp cheeks.

Katherine looked up at her with a quizzical frown, as if she'd never seen a grown lady crying in church. Olivia smiled and took a hymnal from the rack on the pew in front of her. The little girl did the same, watching Olivia and turning the pages exactly as Olivia did, then crossing her tights-clad legs when Olivia crossed hers. The imitation touched her in an odd way. She'd never really noticed children before, hadn't had much opportunity to interact with them one-on-one.

Like a cement truck plowing into her, an awful truth struck: she would likely never have a little girl or boy of her own. As skeptical as she'd been about Derek's desire to start a family the minute they were settled in Hanover Falls, she had slowly begun to warm to the idea. Now that dream was gone. Lost. Along with their chance to redeem the difficult years of their marriage.

A woman was singing a quiet worship song on the stage, and Olivia tried to concentrate on the words. But all she could think about was how she could be sitting in this sanctuary with four hundred people and still be so very, very alone.

Chapter Eight

"Come on in, Maggie!" Reed heard the front door slam and his neighbor's shoes clomping across the kitchen tiles. "I'm in the studio," he hollered again.

"There you are." Maggie Lenihan appeared at the top of the wide stairway that led to the kitchen. Her gray hair was cut short and her reading glasses dangled from a silver chain. She had a shoe-box-size package tucked under one arm. "This was on your front porch. Courtesy UPS."

"Oh, thanks. Just set it over there, will you?" He put a final flourish on an ocean whitecap and pointed with his elbow.

Maggie perched her glasses on the end of her nose and came around to the easel to peruse his work in progress. "Wow. That's gorgeous."

"Sorry. You can't have it...already sold."

She gave an exaggerated harrumph and raked heavily ringed fingers through her spiky hair. "Yeah, right. Like I could afford it anyway. Who's this one for?"

"Some bank in St. Louis. It's one the gallery in Taos contracted before I had the surgery."

"Well, it's beautiful."

"Is it really, Maggie?"

She moved closer and stood on tiptoe to look him in the eye. She tipped her head to one side. "You really don't know?"

"I *think* it's good. I hope it is. But I don't see as well as I used to."

"It's good, Reed. It's gorgeous." Maggie patted his arm and her voice wavered a little.

He couldn't see her expression well enough to tell if it was from emotion, or from the cigarettes she chain-smoked.

"You look good, too," she said. "Not so tired and pasty white as you did right after the surgery."

"Hey now, you don't need to go calling me ugly."

She laughed, but her voice quickly turned serious. "How are you feeling?"

He opened his mouth to answer, but she cut him off before he could get a syllable out.

"Oh, duh. Dumb question. Judging by that smile on your face— and the looks of that painting—I'd say you've never been better."

He stepped back and studied the piece with a critical eye. His style—blotches of paint that formed a mosaic of color—made it easier to see than the rest of his environment. He was adjusting, learning to reinterpret what his eyes saw.

And he was pretty sure his sight was still improving little by little. It had only been two months, after all. He looked up at Maggie. "You think so, huh?"

"It's gorgeous, Reed. Really. Some of your best work."

"You're not just saying that?"

She let out her trademark comical chuckle. "Since when has Margaret Lenihan ever softened the truth for anybody?"

He laughed. "Oh. Yeah. Good point."

The lines in her weathered face softened and she jabbed a finger in the general direction of the canvas. "This is good stuff, Reed. I mean it."

He flushed. "Well, thanks." He hadn't really been fishing for a compliment. But it was nice to know he wasn't just fooling himself that his work was up to par. "Hey, you don't want a job, do you?"

She eyed him suspiciously. "What job you talking about? I'm *not* cleaning your bathrooms."

Reed grinned. "No. Nothing like that. I'm thinking about hiring an assistant. For the studio."

"No kidding? What? You gonna teach somebody to paint 'happy little trees' for you? A Bob Ross gig?"

He laughed. "No, but I do need someone to help out with framing, shipping, deliveries…cleaning up the studio maybe, helping me prepare the canvases. My eyes get strained a lot quicker now. And I'm so far behind getting stuff to the galleries…but if I take time to catch up on all the business stuff, I'll be that much further behind on the art. You don't know anybody who'd be good, do you?"

She thought for a minute. "Not right off the top of my head. I'd take the job if I thought you'd pay worth a hoot."

"Ha! You wouldn't last a day working for me."

"Well, that's where you're wrong. I wouldn't last an *hour.*"

"Hey…" Reed feigned a wounded pout, and Maggie jumped at the excuse to give him a hug. She wasn't quite old enough to be his mother—not that anyone could have replaced his beloved mom—but Maggie was like a favorite aunt. And though he'd tried to express it, she would never know how beautifully she'd filled the empty spot Mom left four years ago when her heart finally gave out.

"I'll keep my ears open…let you know if I hear of anyone who'd be good. Maybe you can write something up and I can have my daughter put it on the bulletin board at her church."

"Sure. That'd be great."

She saluted him. "Now, I'd better get back and take that maniac dog for a walk." She hooked a thumb toward the kitchen. "There's a plate in the fridge for you. Just some leftovers. Zap it a couple minutes in the microwave and that ought to do it."

"Hey, thanks, Maggie. I appreciate it."

Reed was pretty sure Maggie's "leftovers" were fresh and homemade from scratch, but he wasn't about to let on that he suspected. She seemed to take great pleasure in keeping him ten pounds overweight, and if that's what it took to make the sweet woman happy…well, who was he to deny her the joy?

"Elizabeth? It's Olivia Cline."

"Olivia! How nice to hear from you. How are you, dear?" That familiar note of sympathy crept in.

Olivia hadn't seen her former boss since Derek's funeral. She'd forgotten how much of the native Bronx accent remained in Elizabeth DiMartino's voice.

"I'm doing well. Truly." She took a quick breath and plunged in, wanting to avoid the subject of Derek. "Listen, I know you already filled my position, but I was wondering if…if you're still looking to hire someone? I…I'm thinking I'll probably come back to the city if I can find work."

There was a long pause before she heard Elizabeth suck in a deep breath. "Olivia, I'd love to have you back…you know I would… But I just can't. Not now, anyway. You know how business was…still is, really. I'm cutting expenses to the bone as it is and—"

"It's okay, Elizabeth." Olivia cut her off, embarrassed to have put the woman in a position to have to make apologies. "I understand. Really, I do."

"I wish I could help, dear. You know I admire your work. I'll tell you what, leave your number with Joan at the front desk and if we have an opening you'll be the first person I call. And if you ever need a reference, you know I'll give a glowing one."

"Thank you. I appreciate that. I…I hope things pick up."

"Oh, they will. They always do. Well, I wish I could visit, but I'm already late for a meeting. Let me transfer you to reception. You take care, dear."

"I will—" The phone clicked in her ear and she knew she'd already been dismissed. She visited with Joan, the receptionist, for a few minutes, leaving her number at the house in Hanover Falls, as well as her cell phone number. But she wouldn't hold her breath. Jobs at Interior Ideas weren't easy to come by and it wasn't likely anyone would be leaving anytime soon.

What else did she know how to do? She'd started under Elizabeth DiMartino at Interior Ideas fresh out of college, happy to be an assistant to the woman who was Elizabeth's partner at the time. Olivia had worked her way up the ladder, until Elizabeth had finally turned her loose with a couple of clients. She'd loved her work and there had been a time when she'd entertained fantasies of starting her own firm. It only took a couple of years of witnessing the headaches Elizabeth DiMartino faced—with the building and the staff, not to mention finicky clients—to change her mind in a hurry.

Still, interior design was all she knew. Other than painting. And that was a pipe dream. One she'd never shared with anyone after the first time Derek laughed away any illusions she might have had. She winced, surprised by the pain she still felt thinking of his flippant dismissal of her artistic gifts.

But Derek had been right. It was anybody's guess how artists ever got to the point where they could make a living off their work. She put the phone quietly back in its cradle and slid the phone book back in the drawer.

Chapter Nine

Traffic was flowing smoothly and Olivia tapped the cruise control up a notch. She didn't know Jayne's neighborhood well, so she was anxious to get into Chicago before dark. She still wasn't sure what had possessed her to call her friend and former coworker and invite herself to stay the weekend, but Jayne Dodge had welcomed her and it seemed like a good thing to get back to the city for a couple days.

The countryside was lush with summer's green and it lifted her spirits as she ate up the miles along the interstate.

Jayne was sitting on the front porch waiting when Olivia pulled into the driveway just before six. Her friend wrapped her in a warm hug the minute she got out of the car. "How are you, sweetie?"

Olivia teared up at the endearment. "I'm okay. I think…"

"Well, I packed Brian and the kids off to his parents' for the weekend, so it'll be nice and quiet here." Keeping one arm around Olivia, Jayne steered her through the front door. "I've got a pasta salad in the fridge…or we can go out if you'd rather."

"Oh, no. A salad sounds good. I've been living on casseroles." She rubbed her belly absently. The thought of another bite of spicy food turned her stomach.

Jayne looked surprised. "You've been cooking?"

She shook her head. "The people from Derek's church…*my*

church…brought dinner every night for two weeks after he died. It'll take me months to eat all the casseroles in our freezer."

"How thoughtful…that the church would do that."

"It was." Olivia hesitated, not wanting to sound ungrateful. "It was just kind of weird having complete strangers show up on my doorstep serving up pasta and pity. I was tempted to hide and pretend I wasn't home."

Jayne clicked her tongue in sympathy. "How are you doing, Olivia? Really."

Olivia pressed her lips into a tight line. "I don't think it's really hit me yet. It feels like he's just away on a business trip. I keep expecting the phone to ring and he'll be calling from some hotel to tell me he misses me—"

"Oh, Olivia. I can't even imagine. I'm so sorry. You'll come back to Chicago, of course."

"I don't know if I can, Jayne. Derek didn't have any insurance and we've—*I've*—got the mortgage on the house. The Realtor says it's unlikely I could get what we paid for it."

"Didn't you have mortgage insurance?"

Olivia bit her lip. "No. Like a fool, I told Derek we didn't need it."

"Oh, no…"

"Yeah. Dumb, huh? But even if the house wasn't an issue, what would I do in Chicago, Jayne? When's the last time they hired somebody new at Interior Ideas?"

Jayne grimaced. "Good point. But what are you going to do in Missouri?"

"I don't know." Her voice trembled as she realized how hopeless her situation was.

"Do you…do you want to stay here for a while?"

Olivia stifled a mirthless laugh as she looked around the cramped combination living room and dining room. "It's sweet of you to offer, Jayne, but…" She shook her head.

"I just hate to see you stuck all alone so far away."

Olivia patted her friend's arm. "I'll be okay."

Jayne brightened. "Let's go fix something to eat."

She followed Jayne into the cozy kitchen, the knot that had sat in her stomach since Derek's death twisting tighter.

* * *

Reed wiped his hands, threw down the turpentine-soaked rag and stared at the cold pine boards. All day, he'd tried to ignore the niggling impulse that pricked at his conscience. He'd paid for ignoring it, too. He had two ruined canvases and a preliminary sketch that was mediocre at best to show for six hours of work.

He lifted his gaze to the high, beamed ceiling. "Okay, Lord. I get the message."

He washed his hands at the freestanding porcelain sink in the corner of the studio and went into the kitchen. He rummaged in the desk drawer for a decent piece of stationery. Settling for a lined gray sheet from a legal pad, he pulled out the chair and sat. He tested three pens before finding one that worked.

He still had to make his script large and bold to see it clearly, but his sight was improving day by day. His fear that the transplant would ultimately fail like the first one was one reason he'd hesitated to write this letter before. But it had been more than two months now and he was beginning to feel real hope that the surgery had been a success. That knowledge spurred him on.

He balanced the pen over paper, eager to let his gratitude spill onto the page. But ten minutes later, the paper was still blank. His mind whirred with ideas and pictures…every thought except the one that would give him the words he needed right now.

How did one express gratitude to the family of a person who'd had to die so that Reed's life could be returned to him? A corneal transplant wasn't a matter of true physical life or death, but without it, Reed knew his life would not have felt worth living. Were it not for the gift of some unfortunate person, by now he would no doubt be dependent upon others for his livelihood, and for who knew what other basic needs.

He touched the tip of the pen to the pad and forced his fingers to move the pen.

Dear Donor…

The words were impersonal and anemic on the page. He crumpled the paper into a ball and tossed it in the general direction of the trash can. He slid the desk drawer open, ripped another sheet of paper from the tablet and started again….

Dear donor family,
    First, let me say how deeply sorry I am for your loss. You will never know how much your loved one's gift of life has meant to me.

Every word seemed so trite and emotionless. He didn't know one thing that mattered about the person whose corneas had given him back his sight. Only that he had been a thirty-four-year-old man who'd been killed in an accident. Reed assumed a car crash. No doubt this man was someone's son, someone's husband, perhaps even some little boy's daddy.

If he thought about it too long, it overwhelmed him with guilt. Where was the justice when the recipient, Reed Vincent, had no ties—no one who depended on him for protection, for every financial need? Not even anyone who waited eagerly for him to come home from work every evening. If he dropped dead tomorrow, no one would know about it unless Maggie discovered him while delivering a plate of her famous leftovers.

Reed gave himself a mental kick in the pants—something he'd had to do too often of late. Didn't he trust that God knew what He was doing when He'd allowed the surgery that had restored Reed's sight? That's what he claimed. Then he would not be so ungrateful as to question the gift that had allowed him to resume working in his studio, to return to the life he loved and an income that was now greater than what he'd earned before the insidious disease had nearly robbed him of his sight.

His hands went up to rub his eyes, but he caught himself. Though his eyes no longer felt irritated, the doctors had warned him to take extra precautions. He still wore an eye guard at night and had been cautioned not to strain his eyes by reading or working too long.

He returned to his vain attempt at a thank-you, penning a few final, feeble words. The instructions forbade him from giving any identifying information or from signing his real name so he merely signed his initials.

That done, he went in search of the folder he'd gotten from the organ transplant agency that gave the address where a thank-you to the donor family could be sent. The information included sample letters and a list of phrases and "jump starts" for thank-you letters. Reed had purposely avoided reading them. He wanted his note to come from his heart, not sound like every other letter the family would undoubtedly receive.

But reading his note over one last time, he wasn't sure he'd succeeded. There simply *were* no words to express his gratitude. This would have to do. He folded the note and placed it in a plain white envelope.

"Lord, please bless this family," he whispered. "And help me to deserve the sacrifice they had to make in order that I could have my sight back."

As difficult as it had been to pen the note, it felt good to complete the task. He had to put the "survivor's guilt" behind him now and move on.

Anything less was a slap in the face to the God who had allowed this miracle in his life.

Chapter Ten

The pastor offered the benediction with outstretched hands and the organ music swelled along with the rustle and murmur of the congregation. Olivia tucked the worship program in her purse and slipped the bag over her shoulder. This was the hardest part. Getting through the gauntlet of sympathy and questions.

She looked up to see the Meredith family waving at her. She pasted on a smile and waved back. Claire Meredith worked her way through a knot of worshippers and hurried toward Olivia. Claire was probably planning to ask her to have dinner with them, since Olivia had turned down their invitation the last time she was here. She scrambled to think of an excuse. It was sweet of them to want to include her. But as much as she hated going home to an empty house, it was harder still to think of making conversation with people she barely knew. They would ask her about her plans, and plans were one thing she did not have.

"Good morning! We missed you last week."

"Oh…thanks." Claire's perky countenance roused a smile in Olivia. The upward turn of her facial muscles felt completely foreign. How long had it been since she'd had a reason to smile?

"I was visiting a friend back home—in Chicago, I mean."

"Oh? You're not thinking of moving back, are you?" Claire seemed genuinely disappointed.

"I don't think I can. My job has already been filled and I've got the house here…"

"Oh, I'm sorry. I love this town so much, I just expect everybody to feel the same. But it must be really hard being here… under the circumstances."

"Mommy?" Claire's daughter tugged on her mother's skirt, breaking the awkward silence that fell between them.

"What is it, Kati-did?" Claire put a hand on the little girl's cheek.

Katherine grinned shyly up at Olivia before turning pleading eyes to her mother. "Lindy wants me to go to Chuck E. Cheese with them. Can I?"

"*May* I. And did you ask Daddy?"

"He said to ask *you.*" She put a small hand on her hip and gave an impatient huff. "Can I? *May* I…please?"

Claire laughed. "If Daddy says it's okay, then it's fine with me."

The little girl squealed and raced for the door.

"Katherine Jean!" Claire called after her, her voice stern. But then she shrugged, rolling her eyes in mock aggravation. "Oh, well. I was going to ask if you wanted to go out to eat with Michael and me. This is even better—" She motioned with raised eyebrows in the direction Kati had run. "We can choose something besides pizza this way."

Olivia laughed and made a quick decision. It was time she stepped out of her self-imposed exile. "I'd love to have lunch with you."

"Oh— Great!" It was obvious Claire had expected to have to argue with her. "Let me find Michael and we'll meet you in the foyer."

Out in the entryway, Olivia turned away from the friendly but intent stares of other parishioners, pretending to inspect the collage of thank-you notes and activity notices posted on the large bulletin board near the front doors.

Her feigned interest turned real when she discovered a small notice posted in bold handwritten block letters:

WANTED—ARTIST'S ASSISTANT. PART-TIME. POSSIBLY PERMANENT. PREFER EXPERIENCE, BUT WILL TRAIN RIGHT PERSON. HOURS FLEXIBLE. CALL REED VINCENT.

There was a neat row of tear-off phone numbers at the bottom of the page. Olivia ripped one off and stuck the tiny scrap of paper in her purse.

"Oh, that would be a great job." Claire materialized at her elbow. "Have you met Reed?"

Olivia shook her head. "No. Do you know him?"

"I know his work. Michael and I drooled over a painting he had hanging in The Breadbox downtown a few months ago, but then we saw the price sticker. Ouch."

"Pricey, huh?"

"That's putting it mildly. I'd become an artist if I thought I could get that kind of money for every painting."

"He must be pretty good to command that kind of money."

"Well, I'm no judge of art, but I think he's fabulous. Michael does, too, and it's not often we agree when it comes to decor. Who knew that husbands were allowed to have opinions when it came to decorating the house?" She rolled her eyes, but couldn't hide the affection for her husband that flickered there.

"Derek and I used to go around about that, too." Olivia laughed. "I was the interior designer in the family, but that didn't stop him from having opinions."

Claire looked at her with a new spark of interest in her eyes. "So you're a professional interior decorator?"

"I am. Well, I was. I quit my job to move here. And now someone else has the position."

"You should call Reed Vincent. I don't know what an artist's assistant does, exactly, but if you have an eye for art, you should check it out."

Olivia dug the scrap of paper out of her purse. "Does he live here in town? It looks like a local number."

Claire nodded. "He has a studio in his home—at least he used to. We've never been there…we've just seen his work hanging around town. But someone told me he has stuff in galleries all over the country."

"Really?"

"You should call him, Olivia. Seriously."

"Maybe I will." She tucked the phone number safely in the side pocket of her wallet. She was a little intimidated by this guy's reputation, but she couldn't deny the spark of excitement that flared at the thought of working in an art studio.

Olivia parked the car at the curb in front of the large Tudor-style house. Her stomach was a churning ball of nerves and she popped another Tums in her mouth as she peered up through the windshield. Though the place had a slightly overgrown appearance, it appealed to her. Spirea bushes grew high around the brick and stucco facade, and their white flowers, now almost spent, made the steep pitched roof even more prominent. The front door had an arched top, with a tiny diamond-shaped window. A giant gingerbread cottage.

Inhaling a deep breath, she got out of the car and followed the lazy curve of the sidewalk to the front door. The door was partially ajar and the doorbell chime sounded back in her ears.

A blue-jean clad, barefoot man appeared in the doorway. He opened the screen door, squinting and shading his eyes against the afternoon sun. "Ms. Cline?"

She stuck out a hand. "Yes… Olivia, please."

"Come in, Olivia. I'm Reed."

She followed him into the house, her eyes struggling to adjust to the darkened rooms within.

"Why don't we go on back to the studio?"

She trailed behind him through a large, rather musty-smelling living room that was nearly vacant of furniture, and on through a lovely state-of-the-art kitchen. Here, sunlight streamed through the windows, illuminating sinks and countertops cluttered with dishes, half-empty drinking glasses and jars of murky liquid sprouting paintbrushes. A warning signal buzzed in her brain. His job description for artist's assistant better not include housekeeping.

But then she caught a whiff of turpentine. The pungent scent was like perfume to her. Her nerves untangled a little.

Without apology for the mess in the kitchen, Reed Vincent led the way through an arched doorway and down three wide steps into a spacious, light-filled studio.

"Oh!" She whirled slowly to take in every detail. "What a wonderful place!"

A pang of envy jabbed at her. The studio was an artist's dream. The space was neatly organized and tidy—in utter contrast to the kitchen they'd just passed through.

"Thanks," he said. "It works."

She went to the gallery wall to inspect the various frames that hung there. This guy was good. No doubt about that. She couldn't recall having seen his work before, but she hadn't kept up with the world of fine art after she'd gone to work for Elizabeth. Most of her clients had held definite opinions about the art they wanted to use in their rooms, and she'd always gone with their requests. She'd let her subscriptions to *Art World* and *Artist's Magazine* expire because it was too depressing to read about what she no longer had time to do. But Reed Vincent's studio brought the passion flooding back. If she ever had a studio like this, she had no doubt she could paint something brilliant.

She turned and started to see Reed looking expectantly at her, apparently waiting for an answer to a question she hadn't heard.

"I'm sorry. I got distracted. Your studio is so…wonderful."

He gave a wry smile. "If only people had that reaction to my art."

"Oh, I didn't mean…" Heat rushed to her cheeks. "It's beautiful, too. Your work is great. I mean, I haven't really looked at it enough to judge yet. Not that I know enough to judge it, but…" Good grief. She was a bumbling idiot. She was going to blow this interview before he even told her what the job was.

"You must be an artist."

"What?"

"To notice…to *appreciate* the studio," he explained.

"Oh, no… I mean, I used to do some painting, but it's been so long since I picked up a brush, I don't even know if I could remember how."

"You worked with oils?"

"Yes, and watercolor. A little of everything really. I...I just dabbled. I really haven't done anything in a while. Years, actually. My degree is in business administration. Southern Illinois University. But I took a couple years of art school," she added quickly.

"Oh?"

"Just a few classes. At Columbia College."

"Really? I graduated from the American Academy of Art in Chicago." He indicated a small table under the windows. "Have a seat."

Across from her, the artist straddled the chair backward, propping his elbows on the backrest. "Well—" his bare toes tapped out a nervous rhythm on the floor "—I guess I should explain what I'm looking for in an assistant."

She nodded, hoping to convince him that she did have a longer attention span than a two-year-old.

"It's a little hard to give you a job description because I'm not sure myself what I'm looking for. I've never had an assistant before. I'm having some—" He took off his glasses and kneaded the spot between his eyes before continuing. "I've had some problems with my eyes. I had surgery and that helped a lot, but I still have to limit my time. Save my eyes for the more tedious work."

He hesitated, as if he expected some response from her. She didn't know what to say, so merely nodded and tried to appear intent on what he was saying.

"I guess mostly I need someone to prepare canvases, organize my paints and supplies, clean up." He looked up with a rueful grimace. "It's not a very glamorous job I'm offering."

She waved away his apology. Though his manner was almost gruff, he had kind eyes—beautiful deep blue eyes—and something in them caused her to want his approval.

"And it's part-time," he said. "You did understand that? I can't promise it will turn into a permanent position."

"I understand. I'll take all the hours I can get, but you said in the ad that it was just part-time. I wasn't expecting more."

"Good. Have you done any framing? Putting stretcher strips together, mounting canvases?"

She chewed her bottom lip, then caught herself and took in a calming breath. "It's been a while, but I think I could catch on pretty quickly."

"Okay. Sure. I can train you." He raked a hand through his dark hair. The resulting mussed curls made him look vulnerable and boyish. "When could you start?"

"Right now?" Nervous laughter bubbled up. "I really need a job."

"I can't pay much. More than minimum wage, but not much. The whole starving artist thing, you know."

She nodded. "I understand."

"I usually paint in the mornings. The light is best in here around nine or ten o'clock, so you probably need to come in before that—at least for the first day or two—so I can get you started. You live here in town?"

"Yes. We…*I* just moved here. From Chicago."

"I bet this has been more than a bit of a culture shock."

She shrugged. "A little."

"So what did you do in the Windy City?"

"I was an interior decorator. I worked for Elizabeth DiMartino at Interior Ideas in Chicago for seven years."

His eyebrows went up. "What in the world brought you to the Falls?"

She hoped he didn't see her flinch. She'd wanted to avoid this question. "My husband's job."

"I see. Where does he work?"

She cleared her throat and studied the floor, willing her voice to come out steady. "Derek…my husband died in an accident shortly after we moved."

Reed seemed taken aback. "I…I'm sorry. I didn't realize…"

"No. Of course not." She scrambled to change the subject. "Do you…do you offer any kind of an insurance plan?"

He shook his head slowly, the lines of his face softening. "I'm sorry. I've never had an assistant before. And since it's not really a full-time position, I'm not set up for that."

"I understand. I'm still interested," she added quickly.

He nodded and pushed back his chair. "Well, I'm willing to give this a try if you are. You said you could start right away? How about tomorrow morning at eight?"

She had the job! "Yes. Sure. I'll be here."

He pointed in her direction. "You, uh, you won't want to dress up. Wear something you don't mind ruining."

She looked down at her crisp pleated black slacks and neatly pressed blouse. "Oh…of course."

She felt a strange elation as she followed Reed back through the house.

She had a job. In an artist's studio. A great studio. It was a start.

Chapter Eleven

Olivia knelt over the toilet, panting to catch her breath. "Lord, please. No! I can't be sick today."

For days—weeks really—she'd been feeling queasy, as though she were trying to come down with the flu. But today, of all days, it had finally hit her full force. Maybe it was just nerves over starting this new job, but she could not call in sick her very first day.

She struggled to her feet and wobbled to the sink. The splash of cold water on her face only made her feel worse. She dried her face and stared at her reflection in the medicine cabinet mirror. *Ugh.* The clock was zipping toward eight o'clock. She didn't have time to put on makeup, but if she didn't, Reed Vincent would probably send her packing before she even got through the front door.

She swallowed a couple of Derek's prescription-strength ibuprofen, then opened the drawers beside the bathroom sink one by one, searching for her makeup. She still felt as though she was living in somebody else's house. She located the blush and lipstick in the back of the second drawer and dashed a puff of peach-colored powder across each pasty cheekbone. She examined her reflection. A little better. The peach offset the green tinge of her complexion.

She'd always tended to have a nervous stomach, and it didn't help that she'd been existing on bananas and cold cereal since she'd thrown out the last of Derek's meager grocery supply. She hadn't unpacked the bathroom scales yet, but she could tell by the way her clothes fit that she'd lost a few pounds. Not that she couldn't afford to lose them, but why couldn't the weight have come off her thighs instead of her cheekbones?

Sighing, she went through the house flipping off lights. If she didn't leave the house this minute, she was going to be late for her first day of work.

Reed glanced at the oversize clock beneath the clerestory windows. He hoped his new girl Friday wasn't going to bail on him before she even worked one day. He'd thought the interview with Olivia Cline went well, and even though he was a little skeptical about how it would be trying to work with someone else in the office, he had left a whole laundry list of odd jobs for her to do. If she didn't show up, he was going to be a day further behind his deadline. He needed to get three new pieces to the St. Louis gallery and he'd promised to change out the art he had hanging in the Breadbox, a local eatery that showcased his work.

The doorbell chimed and he hurried through the house to answer the door. Olivia stood there with a wan smile, wearing jeans and a baggy denim shirt over a white T-shirt. Good. She'd come prepared to get dirty.

"Come on in," he said.

"Thanks."

She stepped inside, an expectant lift to her eyebrows. Even dressed for work, she was prettier than he remembered.

"Well, come on back and I'll get you started. You want a cup of coffee?" he asked as they passed through the kitchen again.

"No thanks…maybe later— Ooooh!" That same expression of awe Reed remembered from her first visit spread over her face when they stepped down into his studio. "The light is wonderful here this time of morning."

He smiled. "That's why I like to paint this time of day. I thought I'd have you prepare some canvases first. UPS delivered the supplies yesterday and I haven't even had time to open the boxes, but I think everything you need is here. You can work on the worktable over here. I think I've got all the tools you'll need laid out. The stretcher boards are in here." He gave some boxes a little shove with his big toe, and reached for a utility knife in the pencil holder on the table. "You've done this before?"

She nodded. "Here…I can do that." She took the knife from him and went to work slicing through the paper tape that sealed the smaller box. He watched as she pulled bubble wrap from the stretcher boards and began fitting pieces together.

Good. She was a self-starter. His sigh of relief came out louder than he intended and she looked up, a question in her eyes.

"All right then…I can see I'm not needed here." He motioned toward the box. "There should be enough for six canvases there."

"Okay."

"Well…" He turned hesitantly. "Just let me know when you're ready for the canvas."

She nodded and he resisted the temptation to go to the other side of the worktable and help her. He'd hired her so he could get some painting done.

He went to the small refrigerator where he'd stored yesterday's palette so the paints wouldn't dry.

He adjusted the easel and selected a brush from the pottery urn on the taboret beside him. But he was reluctant to dive in. He'd probably just get his brushes wet and she'd need his help with something. He stole a glance over the large canvas resting on the easel. Olivia labored over her project, seemingly unaware of him. He was all too aware of *her*. He hadn't thought about how ill at ease he would feel trying to work with someone else puttering around his studio.

Especially someone as attractive as Olivia Cline. Her dark blond hair framed delicate features. Her creamy skin was smooth except for her forehead, which was furrowed in concentration.

She glanced up and caught him watching her. He quickly looked away and prayed the heat rising in his face wasn't visible. He turned the knob on the easel, raising the mast and work tray enough to block his view of her.

Ten minutes later, after he'd gone through the motions of

tightening a canvas that was already taut as a marine's bedsheet, and mixed a blob of paint that was possibly the homeliest color ever created by any artist anywhere, he blew out a breath and headed to the kitchen for coffee.

Halfway up the stairs, he remembered his manners. "I'm getting coffee. Would you like some now?"

She laughed. "I've only been here fifteen minutes and it's already time for a coffee break?"

Did she know how uncomfortable she was making him? He shrugged one shoulder. "I'll bring it to you. You can keep working."

Her smile faded and she turned all business. "Sure. I'll take a cup. Thanks."

He must have sounded rude. He tried to think what he could say to smooth things over, but nothing witty popped into his head, so he simply asked, "Do you take anything in it…cream or sugar, I mean?"

"A little cream would be wonderful."

"Oh…um…is milk okay? I guess I don't really have cream."

She gave him a look he interpreted as well-then-why-did-you-offer? before smiling sweetly. "Sure. Milk is fine."

In the kitchen, he pulled two chunky mugs from the cupboard over the sink and poured the dark brew. He uncapped the milk jug and sniffed, deciding it had a day or two to go before it was officially sour. As he stirred milk into one mug, it hit him that something was wrong with this picture. He'd hired the woman so he could spend more time painting, and here he was, making *her* coffee?

This was *not* going to work. He'd made a huge mistake. There was no way he could work with this distraction. He was going to have to fire her before she'd even worked a day. He picked up the warm mugs. Well, the least he could do was let her drink a cup of coffee before he broke the news.

He set the milky coffee in front of her and was rewarded again with her warm, twinkly smile. *Twinkly?* Where had that come from? Since when did Reed Vincent even *think* the word *twinkly?* Good grief.

"Thank you." She took the mug from him and took a sip

before setting it on the far corner of the worktable. "Does this look okay?" She held up an assembled stretcher frame.

He took it from her and held it close, examining her workmanship. She was a perfectionist. "Looks good. Where did you learn how…?"

She dipped her head. "Like I said yesterday, I used to do a little painting—emphasis on the 'little.' I haven't done anything for a long time, but I learned to frame my own stuff because I couldn't afford to have it done."

"So you *are* an artist." He moved back to his easel, picked up his palette and balanced it on his forearm.

Her gaze lifted and panned the gallery wall behind him. "I wouldn't dare stand in this room and call myself an artist."

Though her face was a little blurry from across the room, he thought her cheeks had taken on a rosy flush. "I'd like to see your work sometime."

Her hand flew to her neck and she gave a warbly laugh. "Thanks, but I wouldn't inflict that on you. I just dabble. It's a hobby, really."

He ignored the comment and dipped a brush in paint. If they stood around chitchatting all morning he'd have a hard time justifying paying for an assistant. "Let me know when you have those finished."

"Oh…sure." She turned her back to him and reached into the box for another set of stretcher boards.

Chapter Twelve

The nausea was back, and with it, a terrifying suspicion. She'd felt fine when she went to bed last night, but now, for at least the third morning in a row, Olivia had awakened with a sour stomach. And along with it, a host of other symptoms she'd never experienced before, but had heard enough about from her girlfriends. It couldn't be. She and Derek had barely had a night together once he'd made the move to Missouri. And they'd been careful. *She'd* been careful. Her doctor had advised them to wait several months after going off the pill before they tried to conceive. She'd been grateful for that advice. She wasn't ready to jump into anything, and they'd both wanted to get settled in Hanover Falls before they got serious about starting a family.

Maybe it was just the old problems. She probably ought to go to the doctor and get back on some iron pills. Her cycle had always been somewhat irregular—part of the package of her particular ailment—but now that she thought about it, it had been a while since she'd had a period. In fact, she wasn't sure she'd had a period since moving to Hanover Falls two months ago. And she could barely remember the last time before that.

Another rush of nausea went through her, only this time its source was completely emotional. What if she was…? No. She couldn't even allow herself to think about the possibility.

She finished dressing and drove to Reed's house. She went

around to the back and let herself in the kitchen as he'd instructed her before she left yesterday.

She shut the door with more force than necessary, hoping to announce her entrance without surprising him. "Good morning," she chirped as she went down the steps to the studio.

Reed was at the easel already, brush in hand, full palette balanced on his forearm. "Hi. Be with you in a minute." He went right on painting without glancing up, but his greeting wasn't unfriendly.

"That's okay. I have these canvases to finish. Don't stop. I smelled coffee when I came through the kitchen. Can I get you a cup…or another cup?"

"Oh…yeah, that'd be nice." He dabbed a few strokes of paint on the upper half of the canvas with a flourish and dunked the paintbrush into the jar of turpentine. "My cup is over there." He motioned with an elbow.

"Got it." Olivia dropped her purse and jacket on a chair in the corner, retrieved Reed's mug off the counter and went to pour coffee. She found a fresh, unopened carton of half-and-half in the door of the refrigerator. "Hey, you got cream!" she hollered down to him.

"Oh, yeah. I thought you might appreciate that."

"Very much. Thanks." She carried the two steaming mugs down to the studio and set Reed's coffee beside him on the taboret. He glanced briefly her way, but went on working, seeming deep in thought.

She took a sip from her own cup and went to work with the stapler, stretching a length of canvas over a framework of pine strips.

A crash split the air and Olivia jerked her head up in time to see the contents of his mug splatter across the hardwood floor.

"Ouch!" Reed yelped, grabbing one bare foot and hopping away from the steaming puddle that crept across the floor.

A dark stain wet the flared bottoms of his jeans.

"Are you okay?" She jumped up to help him clean up the mess.

Growling something she couldn't understand, he grabbed a

roll of paper towels from beside the cleanup sink. He yanked off a too-small scrap and dabbed at the mess. "Where did *that* come from?" His voice was taut.

Was he blaming her for his clumsiness? She clenched her jaw, but pulled off a length of paper towel and knelt beside him, picking up the jagged pieces from the mug and sopping up the now-tepid liquid. "Be careful you don't cut your foot. Did you get burned?"

"I'm fine," he said tersely. "That's probably not a good place to set a cup of coffee in the future," he said, without looking at her. "I had no idea it was there."

Her hackles stood at attention. He *was* blaming her. She pummeled the floor with the soggy wad of paper, fuming, but she managed to sputter an apology. "I'm sorry."

He straightened and rocked back on his knees, meeting her eyes. "No. *I'm* sorry. Here…" He reached to take a piece of broken pottery from her hand. "It wasn't your fault. I should have explained."

She cocked her head, questioning.

"I still don't see very well…since my surgery. My peripheral vision especially isn't good. It's probably better if you don't put anything spillable near me without warning me."

Some of the steam went out of her. "I'm so sorry. I…I didn't know."

"Of course not." He gave her a guarded smile. "How could you know I'm an accident waiting to happen?"

"But how do you…" She motioned toward his easel, then bit her lip, regretting she'd started the question. If he hadn't explained by now, it was obvious he didn't like to talk about it.

But he shook his head. "I can see pretty well up close…thanks to the surgery. It's across the room that gives me trouble." He shot her a sheepish grin. "Or right next to my elbow."

His blue eyes held a charming gleam and she couldn't stay angry. "I'm really sorry. I didn't know." She should have warned him she'd put the coffee there. Even if she hadn't known about the problem with his sight, she could remember how engrossed she always became when she was working on a painting. Derek had often "materialized" at her side, sending her heart into a tailspin. She'd asked him a hundred times to warn her before he sneaked up on her. But he'd seemed to take a perverse pleasure in seeing her jump out of her skin.

"Hey." Reed's gentle tone drew her back. "I'm sorry I snapped at you. It wasn't your fault."

For some reason, the tenderness in his eyes, his tone, brought a lump to her throat. "Thanks," she murmured. But she turned her back to him and hurried up to the kitchen with the wad of broken pottery shards and soaked towels, afraid he would see the tears she couldn't explain to herself, let alone to him.

As she pulled into the garage that night, a fluffy, brown, tabby-striped kitten trotted around the corner of the house. She watched in her rearview mirror as it scampered into the garage behind her. She'd seen the little cat several times in the yard behind the house. At first, he'd shot under the fence the minute she opened the back door. But then he'd let her stroke him for a bit, and she was delighted by his ferocious purr when she did. She'd always liked houses with cats. Derek had been allergic to them, so they'd never owned one. But she enjoyed watching this one and had started leaving the milky dregs of her morning oatmeal on the back stoop for him.

She assumed the kitten belonged to one of the neighborhood children, but she'd asked a couple of kids playing in the yard behind her house and the elderly man next door, and no one seemed to know who the cat belonged to. She was terrified she would run over it some night driving into the garage.

She got out of the car and came around to pick up the kitten. His little motor immediately revved into gear. "Hey, little guy. Where do you belong?"

Tail twitching, he batted at her face with sheathed claws, his bright eyes challenging her to a boxing match.

"You little tiger, you. You think you're pretty tough, don't you, buddy?"

He squeaked as if in reply and Olivia laughed. But the soft weight of the kitten's paw against her cheek moved her unexpectedly. She could hardly remember what it was like to have someone touch her as tenderly as the little animal did.

She brushed away the thought and went on in the house, closing the door on the kitten's pleading mews. But when she opened it again a few minutes later to take out the garbage, he was still there, waiting with a comical expectant look on his expressive face.

"Hey, Tiger. What's up?"

The cat tagged along at her heels as she carried the trash bag to the bin in the garage. The birds were singing in the tops of the maple trees that towered over the house and a balmy breeze rustled the leaves overhead. It was a beautiful clear evening and it felt good to be out in the fresh air. As much as she liked the house, it was too constant a reminder of how alone she was here in this small town.

She went to the kitchen for the broom and took it back out to sweep the sidewalks and the patio outside the back door. Mr. Burnside next door was mowing his lawn. It looked as though it was all the elderly man could do to maneuver the old push mower across his yard.

Olivia winced when she saw the demarcation separating their lawns. The grass in her yard was a good two inches taller. She would have to deal with that someday soon. They'd had a groundskeeper in the town house in the city, but Derek had purchased a new lawn mower when he moved and the yard had been immaculate the day Olivia arrived in Hanover Falls.

Michael Meredith had come over and mowed the lawn for her a couple weeks ago, but already it was overgrown with splotches of dandelion and some other weed she couldn't identify towering even higher than the turf.

When Mr. Burnside spotted her, he turned off his old push mower and shuffled to the sidewalk where Olivia was standing. Tiger scampered over to investigate and Mr. Burnside poked playfully at the cat with the toe of his boot.

"Looks like that cat's adopted you."

"You haven't heard anyone asking about him, have you? I still don't know who he belongs to."

"Nope. Haven't heard anything. I'd say he's yours if you want him."

"Oh, I don't know if I can keep him." She didn't want to tell him that she couldn't afford her mortgage, let alone pay for shots and neutering. And then there was cat food and kitty litter and who knew what else a cat required.

"Well, I think somebody better claim him," Mr. Burnside said. "He's been making a racket at my window the last few nights. Three o'clock in the morning he comes, crying to get in, I 'spect. I wouldn't know why. I've sure never encouraged him. Never fed him or let him inside…"

Olivia colored at the obvious hint. Apparently the man had observed her feeding Tiger.

But he didn't wait for her to defend herself. He gave a wave of his age-spotted hand. "I better get back on the job. Sun'll go down before we know it."

Olivia went back to her sweeping, but she watched surreptitiously as her neighbor finished mowing, noting the way he followed a spiral path, overlapping the swath the machine cut each time. If she could figure out how to start the mower, she could probably get the job done.

Tiger played just out of reach, batting at a fat beetle crawling on the driveway, then loping over to chase Olivia's broom. She accidentally swept him off his feet, and he tumbled head over paws, like a clown performing a perfectly orchestrated pratfall. He righted himself, looking dazed, and Olivia laughed until tears blurred her vision.

She leaned the broom against the house, scooped the kitten into her arms and cradled him under her chin. "Kitty cat, you'd better go back where you belong before I get too attached to you."

His low *meow* seemed to say smugly that it was already too late for that.

The next day, while they sorted through a paint cabinet and organized hundreds of tubes of oils and acrylics, Olivia told Reed about her new feline friend. "I don't know who he belongs to, but I wish they wouldn't let him run loose. I'm afraid he's going to get run over."

Reed held a tube of paint close to his face, squinting. He shook his head and handed it to her. "Can you read that? Does that say vermilion?"

He'd told her that he'd had eye surgery, but other than the spilled coffee that day, she hadn't seen other evidence of his vision problems. She took the tube from him and read the tiny print. "It says viridian."

He shrugged. "No wonder I couldn't make that look right." He dropped the paint tube in the spot marked with a large capital *G* in the paint caddy they were organizing. "So you adopted a cat, huh?"

"More like he's adopted me."

"Well, whatever you do, don't feed it or pet it or pay any attention to it, or you'll never get rid of it."

She stopped and stared at him. "What makes you think I want to get rid of him?"

"Cats are nothing but a nuisance. Oh, sure, they're cute when they're little, but I never did have much use for them after they pass that fur ball stage."

"I've always wanted a cat. But Derek—my husband—was allergic, so we never could have one."

He gave a little snort, shrugged and walked over to his easel. "Looks like you've got that pretty well under control. I better get started here."

Not knowing quite why, she felt chastened. Maybe Reed just didn't feel like talking. They'd made small talk most of the morning. And she'd enjoyed every minute. She hadn't realized how starved she was for someone to share the little everyday things with. But it was true that Reed wasn't getting much painting done with her yakking away at him.

She bit her tongue and finished organizing the paints in silence, then started in on the matting project he'd assigned her.

This job didn't pay much, but it was all she had right now and she couldn't afford to lose it. Derek's retirement account was dwindling at an alarming rate and the house payment was due in another week.

And with her telling physical symptoms, another unthinkable possibility was becoming more certain every day.

Chapter Thirteen

There was a new Hy-Vee grocery out on the highway on the outskirts of town, but Olivia wasn't in the mood to run into anyone. Not that she knew more than a handful of people in Hanover Falls well enough to do more than say "hello." Still, tonight she just wanted to get what she needed and get out of there.

She steered the wobbly cart through a wide aisle of the little food market three blocks from her house. She'd put a carton of milk and a bag of salad greens into the cart, but they were decoys. Her real mission was on the aisle near the pharmacy. Even though the chances of running into one of the three people she knew in town were nil, she glanced furtively around before stopping in front of the display of pregnancy test kits. She grabbed two different brands from the shelf and steered the cart around the corner.

She figured she would attract fewer curious gazes reading labels in the cosmetics department than standing in front of the birth control and feminine hygiene products. She compared the packages and tucked the cheaper one under the bag of lettuce.

The clerk at the checkout had to try twice before the box scanned and Olivia had a comical vision of him requesting a price check over the store's public address system. But it finally scanned and she made it out of the store without running into anyone. A bitter taste rose in her mouth. She should have been on Derek's arm, whispering excitedly about this purchase, and going home to await the results together—disappointed if they were negative, an unforgettable celebration if the little blue line said a baby was on the way.

Instead, she felt like a guilty teenager. She hadn't done anything wrong, but if she truly was pregnant, she was going to feel every bit as desperate as an adolescent mother-to-be.

She stuffed the change in her wallet and crossed the parking lot to her car. For a town where it only took four minutes to traverse one end to the other, the drive home felt like a cross-country road trip.

The kit's instructions said the results might be more accurate if used first thing in the morning, so she put the box on the counter in the bathroom where she'd see it as soon as she woke up.

As if she would forget. What if she *was* pregnant? She almost couldn't breathe at the thought. The morning queasiness had abated somewhat, but now other symptoms had taken its place. Symptoms that were hard to pin on any other ailment. What would she do if she was going to have a baby? The check from Derek's company would be gone in a matter of weeks, just paying monthly bills, and the amount his workers' compensation death benefit provided was a drop in the bucket. She didn't have health insurance. She had no idea what obstetrical services cost, but snippets of pregnant friends' conversations came back to her now, accompanied by visions of the pained expressions their faces had held while discussing the financial cost of giving birth. She would barely be able to scrape together enough to make the next mortgage payment. How was she supposed to pay for a doctor, let alone a baby?

She grabbed the newspaper from the front porch, spread it out on the kitchen table, and began to search the classified ads for a job that paid better.

A night of thrashing and weird dreams did nothing for Olivia's state of mind. At 4:00 a.m., she finally got up and went into the bathroom. The ominous box sat on the counter where she'd left it. She opened it and spread out the instruction sheet, following it to the letter. There was no room for error here.

Ten minutes later, she sat on the side of the bathtub staring at the faint blue line on the test stick. The line was a much paler shade of blue than the example on the box, but there was no denying it was a positive reading. She scanned the instruction sheet again, grasping onto one promising sentence: "In rare instances a false positive indication may result…"

Please, God, let that be what this was all about. A single clammy bead of perspiration trailed down the crevice between her shoulder blades.

She couldn't be pregnant. She just couldn't. What would she tell Reed? She needed that job. But more than that, Reed had become a friend. Besides the casual acquaintances she'd met at church—and they were really Derek's friends—Reed was the only ally she had in this town. If she were honest, he was the reason she hadn't hightailed it back to Chicago weeks ago.

She wondered what his reaction would be if she told him. She chewed her bottom lip. If she truly were pregnant, there was no if. She had to tell him. It wouldn't be fair for him to train her only to have her leave when the baby came. If she even stayed in Missouri.

But she'd wait until she'd at least seen a doctor. She would be even more mortified if she told him, and then the pregnancy test turned out to be wrong. Still, she found herself praying harder than she'd ever prayed for exactly that to happen. "Please, God. I'm begging You. Just this once, answer my prayer. Please let this all be a mistake."

Reed walked through the hall by the open bathroom door, through the kitchen, and back to his studio for a second time, calling Olivia's name. Her car was in the drive, but she was nowhere to be found.

He went back to the window. Maybe she was in the car and he just hadn't seen her. Those shaded windows sometimes played havoc with his unpredictable eyesight. She'd probably sat in the car waving and wearing that winsome smile of hers and he'd rushed by, ignoring her. He'd hid his handicap from her pretty well, he thought. Not that he was trying to deceive her. After all, she knew she'd been hired to be his "eyes." Even so, he tried to be as independent as possible. He didn't need her feeling sorry for him or rushing to do for him what he could and should do himself.

He pulled the curtains back and looked out on the drive. The blue Intrepid was still there and this time the sun's angle was such that he could make out a figure through the driver's-side window. It almost looked as if she was huddled over the steering wheel. Was something wrong? Maybe she was just listening to the tail end of a radio broadcast or a favorite song. Kristina had been funny about that, never letting him turn off the car until the end of whatever song was playing on the radio. He smiled to himself, thinking of her quirk, then felt the muscles of his brow twist into a frown.

Where had that come from? He mentally brushed away the painful cobwebs of memory.

He watched the street through a split in the curtain, expecting Olivia to emerge from the car at any moment. But when he checked again five minutes later, the doors were still tightly closed and he didn't see any movement inside the car. Was she okay? He opened the door and strode across the lawn to her car.

He tapped on the window of the driver's-side door. "Olivia?"

Her head jerked up at the sound of his knuckles on the safety glass. Through the darkened window, he saw her swipe at her cheeks. Was she crying?

Before he could think about the implications of his action, he pulled open the car door. "Olivia? Are you okay?"

She turned away, but not before he saw the dampness on her cheeks.

"Is…is everything all right?"

She turned and flashed a smile, sliding out of the car as she did, avoiding his eyes. Something was definitely wrong, but it was obvious she wasn't going to let him in on it.

A frisson of regret coiled through him. Why had he even

come out to her car? What was he supposed to do now? He couldn't pretend he hadn't noticed she was crying.

"Are you okay?"

She recreated the plastered-on smile from a minute ago. "I'm fine. Sorry I'm late."

Okay. She didn't want to talk about it. He let relief replace regret. He could pretend, too. "I'll be inside," he said. "No hurry. Whenever you're ready."

She reached for her purse on the passenger's seat, and with one smooth, feminine motion, shut the door with one hip and pressed the keyless entry to lock the car.

She led the way to the house and he watched her, trying to interpret the reason for her tears from her demeanor. Whatever it was, she seemed perfectly fine now.

"What's on the agenda for today?" she asked as they passed through the kitchen. Was he imagining it, or did her voice hold the vibrato of recent tears?

"Are you sure you feel okay?"

She sniffled and turned to face him, her hands raised like a shield. "I'm fine. Do you want me to cut some more canvas?" She walked across the room, tossing her purse in its usual corner before pulling down the roll of canvas she'd been working with yesterday.

He hesitated. He'd wanted to show her how he kept his inventory with the galleries, but he sensed she'd rather keep to herself today. He gave himself a swift mental kick. The inventory was what needed doing most. He was starting to resent having Olivia in the studio, but it was his own fault. He made a terrible boss, worrying too much about his employee's feelings or whether she'd feel put upon if he asked her to do something he considered grunt work. He was paying her a decent wage. Maybe after he wrote out her first check today, he wouldn't feel so guilty about the work he assigned her.

As if she'd read his mind, she straightened and put her hands on her hips. "I can do whatever you want. If you want me to clean the studio or something, I don't mind. Really."

That settled it. "Would you mind making some phone calls?

I need to check in with my galleries and see what they need. I'll show you the inventory lists and contact information. They're over here on the computer."

He sat down on a high stool to one side of the computer desk and pulled out the chair beside him, motioning with a toss of his head for her to sit with him.

She slid into the chair and gave the mouse a click. The computer screen flickered to life and she leaned in to study the array of files scattered haphazardly atop the desktop wallpaper. The desktop picture, a dusky landscape, faded and morphed into a sunny nautical. He'd set slides of his own favorite artwork as screen savers. In her presence, it suddenly seemed a little vain, but her reaction put the thought immediately to rest.

"Ooh, I haven't seen this piece before." She turned to him with admiration on her face. "It's gorgeous. Is it a real place?"

"Sort of. It was a port of call on a cruise I took with my grandparents when I was a teenager. I don't even remember which island we were on… Saint something… St. Thomas maybe? This is how I remember it. I'm sure the reality is even more beautiful than I remember."

"Oh, we were on St. Thomas once." A faraway look glazed her gold-flecked irises, and she absently fingered the heart-shaped locket she always wore around her neck. "On our honeymoon."

"How long ago was that?" The words were out before he could think better of speaking them. She'd always been reticent about discussing her marriage. This was the first time he'd heard her use the intimate *we*.

Olivia shook her head as if coming out of a trance. "A long time ago. Ten years. I suppose everything is different now."

Her raised brow and sad smile told him that she, too, had caught the obviously unintended double meaning of her words.

He looked at the floor and rubbed at an imaginary smudge on the smooth pine board. "That must have been really hard—" he dared to meet her eyes "—losing your husband, I mean."

She swallowed hard and closed her eyes, but not in time to hide the sheen that had come to them.

He dropped his head. *Vincent, you idiot.* Why did he have to go and bring that up? And how could he even wonder what she'd been crying about in her car a few minutes earlier? The woman had lost her husband just two months ago. Why wouldn't she be crying? He could only imagine how she must be feeling. And then he had to open his mouth and insert his big fat foot.

He put a hand on her arm. "I'm sorry. I didn't mean…"

She gave a little nod. "No…it's okay." She took a deep breath and leaned into the computer screen. "Now which file do I open for the inventory?"

He opened his mouth to apologize again, then thought better of it and bit his lower lip. He pointed to a file among the half dozen lined up on the computer's desktop. "Open this folder first," he said, making his voice all business.

Chapter Fourteen

The antiseptic smells of the doctor's office took Olivia by surprise, bringing back disturbing memories of that terrible night at the hospital after Derek's accident.

She sat on the edge of the examination table, twisting the hem of the too-short gown until it looked as though it had been through a wringer washing machine. A week ago it would have driven her crazy to look so unkempt, but now all she could think about was the verdict she would get today.

The door opened and she started at the sound of her name.

"Mrs. Cline?"

Dr. Bennington was a pretty blonde who couldn't have been a day older than Olivia. Yet something about her demeanor made Olivia feel she could confide in her. She'd never had a female physician before, but now she was glad she'd chosen a woman.

The doctor bent back the cover of a folder and looked at the lone sheet of paper it held before glancing up at Olivia. "Well, your suspicions are correct. You are indeed pregnant." She quirked a thin, penciled eyebrow. "That's good news, I hope?"

Olivia couldn't answer. Her head suddenly felt too heavy for her neck to support. She dropped her chin to her chest, struggling to fill her lungs with air.

"Not such good news, I take it?"

She tried to shake her head, but her neck muscles felt paralyzed.

The doctor put a hand on Olivia's shoulder. "It's okay. I understand. You need some time to think about it."

She forced her head to bob up and then down.

"Would you like to call someone to take you home? Is your husband…?" She let the words trail off, obviously hinting.

"My husband…died."

She didn't see the shock on Dr. Bennington's face, but rather felt it in the tightening of her grip. "I'm so sorry. Then the father of this baby isn't…involved?"

Olivia looked up, startled. "No. Oh, no. The baby is my husband's," she said with more force than she intended. "He's only been gone a few weeks…ten weeks, I guess. Or twelve…" She shook her head. Had Derek really been gone that long? She stared at the advertising calendar hanging behind the small cabinet in the corner. Derek had died March 14. The glossy page was turned to the month of June. How could that be? Three months? It seemed like only yesterday.

A mortifying thought struck her. Would others assume this baby had been conceived after Derek's death?

"Mrs. Cline? Mrs. Cline, are you all right?"

She forced herself back into focus. "I…I'm okay." Her voice came out in a squeak. "Just give me a few minutes."

"You take all the time you need." The doctor's tone turned gentle. "We don't want you driving if you're upset. You can stay right here until you're ready. I won't need this room for a few minutes. Are you sure you don't want me to call someone for you?"

"No. I'm fine."

Dr. Bennington gave Olivia's shoulder a pat and left the room, closing the door quietly behind her.

"I'm fine," Olivia whispered to the empty room. But she wasn't fine. She was pregnant. She was pregnant without a husband, without a real job, without medical insurance, with a mortgage she could barely pay. She could try to sell the house. But it had been on the market for over a year before she and Derek bought it. What were the chances she could sell the house at all in this little town, let alone sell it before she had to default on the loan?

She tried to inhale, but her throat constricted and her lungs seemed unwilling to inflate. Sheer panic ran through her veins and she clawed the air for her next breath. It came, involuntarily, and she forced her shaking hands to steady. She had to get out of here.

She slid from the table and pulled on her clothes. She had to talk to someone. But who? Reed Vincent was the only person she really knew in Hanover Falls. This wasn't the kind of thing you talked to a man about—even if he had become a friend. Besides, he didn't need to be worrying that she couldn't do her job. This job was more important than ever now. She'd just have to tough it out.

The streets of the little town seemed extra quiet for a Tuesday afternoon. Olivia pulled into the driveway and got out to open the garage door. The automatic door opener had broken the second week she'd been here and she hadn't dared to even have someone come out to look at it.

She pulled into the garage, then got out to close the door behind her. The pulleys creaked and groaned as they crept down the track, but just before the heavy door met the concrete floor, the little tiger cat scampered underneath. Olivia gasped and stuck her foot out, trying to stop the door. She and the cat squealed in unison as the door smashed her toe and his tail.

Hopping on one foot, she reached for the cat, but he scuttled to the corner of the garage to lick his wound. Olivia's toe throbbed, but she welcomed the pain that matched her emotions.

She rocked from side to side, then tested her step. Her toe didn't seem to be broken, but she'd probably be limping for a couple of days. She hoped the cat had fared better. Approaching him gingerly, she reached out a hand and stroked his head. "You okay, Tiger? I'm sorry, buddy, but you can't just go running under stuff like that."

He wrinkled his nose and nuzzled her hand. Olivia inched closer and sat down on the garage steps where she could rest her foot, but still reach the cat.

"What am I going to do, Tiger?" She felt silly talking to a cat, but he pricked his ears and nudged her hand, seeming to say, "Go on. I'm listening."

She scooped the kitten up onto her lap. His warm, furry body and the cadence of his purring soothed her more than she would have thought possible. The garage was airless and stuffy with the odor of lingering exhaust fumes, but for the next twenty minutes, she poured her heart out to the little feline.

Somewhere in the midst of giving voice to her fears and grief, her words turned into a prayer. She drank in the comfort that praying had offered her in the past, and she was grateful that today her Heavenly Father had provided a living creature to offer the physical presence she so longed for.

She hugged the cat to her chest. "Oh, thank You, Lord, for bringing this little fellow here tonight. I don't know what to do…who to turn to, but I know You're there. Thank You for showing me that. I don't know how I would have handled this news, Lord, without You in my life."

Cradling the cat in her arms, she rose and carried him inside. She hoped Tiger's owners—if he had any—wouldn't miss him or worry about him. Tonight she needed a friend.

Reed watched Olivia from behind the protective veil of his canvas. She was going about her work as usual—affixing wire hangers to the back of several large canvases today. She worked in silence, her brow furrowed as she twisted the copper wire with the pliers. But the lines around her eyes weren't just from concentration. She was upset about something. He could discern that much from her posture, even though her head was turned so he couldn't see the expression on her face.

He felt prompted to ask her what was wrong, but the words wedged in his throat. Twice he opened his mouth to speak, but ended up choking out a nervous cough and hiding again behind an unfinished painting. And a miserably bad painting at that.

Olivia had been coming here for a month now and he had completed one lousy painting in that entire time—and wasted canvas on three other pieces that were total garbage. He wasn't blaming her. Not really. But somehow she unnerved him to the point he couldn't seem to work. It wasn't just her creamy complexion and those sultry gold-flecked brown eyes, or her womanly figure—though there *was* that. It was something more. It was the way she went about the odd jobs he gave her with such purpose and resolve, yet always managing to amuse him with her wry comments and playful laughter. Even if he tried not to let on that he found her delightful.

He didn't dare entertain romantic thoughts about her. Well, okay. He did dare. Several times a day. That she was so recently widowed should have been reason enough for him to banish those thoughts from his mind. But if he were honest with himself, his real reasons had far more to do with his own self-doubts. For all he knew, he might yet go blind. Yes, this last transplant seemed to have been a success. He was seeing more clearly every day. Sometimes he had to slap down the elation he felt when he looked out the window and took in the crisp outline of a leaf, or when he caught Olivia's eye across the studio and could discern the minute nuances of her expression. Her face had been a blur from that distance only a couple of weeks ago.

Still, the surgery came with a lot more warnings than guarantees and his doctors were only cautiously optimistic about the end result. He had no business counting on such a future, thinking about what it would be like to have Olivia as his wife.

Wife? Where had that come from? Olivia still saw herself as another man's wife. He was reminded of that nearly every day when she corrected *us* and *we* to *me* and *I*. He had no right to fantasize about her belonging to him. *Give the woman time to grieve, Vincent. Good grief! What is your problem?*

He jabbed a dry brush at the canvas, not caring if he ruined another painting. She glanced over at him, but quickly looked away when their eyes met. Almost as if she'd read his thoughts. He felt the heat creep up his neck. But watching her for another minute, his foolish thoughts were pushed aside. For the first time, he realized that she was upset. Hurting deeply about something. He saw it in her eyes. Something more than the haunted expression he'd attributed to her grief over her husband's death. How long had this new pain been there without him noticing?

He cleared his throat, working up his nerve. "Hey... Is everything all right?"

She froze, a deer-in-the-headlights sheen in her eyes. "Why do you ask?"

"I don't know. You just...you're awfully quiet today."

She yanked a length of picture wire from the large coil on the framing table. "I just don't feel like talking."

"Oh. Sorry."

"No. I didn't mean..." She shrugged. "Never mind."

"What? You were going to say something...."

"I didn't mean I didn't want to talk to you. I...I just meant I don't really have anything to say."

He grappled for what to say next. "How's your cat?"

That coaxed a smile out of her. "He's not mine."

"Oh, yeah. Did you ever find out who he belongs to?"

"No. But I confess I haven't been trying too hard. I—" She dipped her head. "I brought him in the house last night. He slept on the foot of my bed."

"Uh-oh."

She quirked her mouth in a guilty-looking grin. "What?"

It was good to see her smiling. "You know what. He's your cat now. Whether you want him or not."

"Maybe I do want him."

He shook his head, but offered a smile. "I wouldn't have a rodent in *my* house."

She gave a frustrated yelp, glaring at him. "Cats are *not* rodents! Where did you study biology?"

He was grateful to see a hint of teasing replace the pain that had been in her eyes. Good to see some of her spunkiness back. Maybe she was just lonely. He'd be more than content to be a listening ear. "Okay. Maybe I was harsh with the rodent comment." He shot her an impish grin. "I meant varmint."

"Varmint? *Varmint?*" Her blond hair bounced as she tilted her head, frowning comically. "Now there's a hillbilly word if I ever heard one."

"Hey! Who're you calling a hillbilly?"

She shrugged. "If the shoe...er, *clodhopper* fits..."

He roared with laughter and she seemed to derive great pleasure from that.

But a minute later he cocked his head and studied her. "You don't much like living in this little town, do you?"

The smile faded from her face as quickly as it had appeared. "I don't have much choice, Reed."

"What's stopping you from going back to Chicago?" He regretted the words the minute they were out of his mouth. His question sounded cruel in retrospect.

She turned back to the strands of braided wire filament, twisting several together with far more tension than necessary.

He waited for a long minute. Silence. "Olivia?"

"What?" Her voice was a whisper.

"I'm sorry. It's none of my business. I shouldn't have pried."

She waved him off. "Don't worry about it." That sorrowful glaze was back in her eyes.

"Something's wrong. Is there anything I can do? I'm sorry—"

To his horror, she burst into tears.

Without thinking, Reed slid from the tall stool he'd been perched on and crossed the studio in three long strides. Before he could think about the implications of his actions, he put an arm around her shoulder, pulling her to him. "What is it, Olivia? What's the matter?"

She shook her head against him, but she didn't try to pull away.

"Come on. You can talk to me. Maybe I can help."

"No," she sobbed. "I can't. I can't." She struggled free from his awkward embrace, knocking over the coil of picture wire.

Reed caught it and set it upright. "Olivia, please…I—"

But she was halfway across the room. She took the three steps to the kitchen in one stride and seconds later he heard the front door slam.

He started to go after her, but remembering how Kristina had been, he decided it would only make things worse. He was worried about her, but he'd give her some time. Maybe it was just a hormone thing.

Still, the emptiness he felt after she'd gone from the room revealed the truth. He'd barely known her for a month, but he was falling hard for Olivia Cline.

Chapter Fifteen

Olivia drove away from Reed's house trembling, praying she wouldn't have a wreck. She could scarcely see through the curtain of tears that seeped from beneath her eyelids. But she had to get away.

Her head swam remembering how she'd felt in Reed Vincent's arms. So warm and safe and—no! Stop. It was wrong to be thinking this way. She never should have let him touch her. She knew he didn't mean anything by it. He was only trying to be a friend. But the way it made her feel— It was wrong. She was married— No. Of course not. Derek was gone. But she was in mourning. She had no right to be feeling the things she was feeling. Longing for someone to talk to, someone to share her secret with.

This was too much to bear alone. She simply couldn't hold things in another minute. But it couldn't be Reed. That she knew. Not the way he made her feel.

The sun ducked behind a cloud and Olivia pulled onto a side street and parked the car in front of a derelict building.

She rummaged in her purse for her cell phone and dialed Jayne's number.

A childish voice singsonged a greeting. "Dodge residence. This is Jeffrey speaking."

"Hi, buddy. Is your mommy home?"

"She can't come to the phone right now. Who is this?"

Olivia swallowed back a panicked sob. But then she heard Jayne's voice come faintly over the line. "Jeffrey! Who are you talking to? That's not polite. Hello? Are you there?"

"Jayne?"

"Olivia! How are you? Are you in town?"

"No…I'm in Missouri. Do you… Can you talk?"

"Sure. What's going on? You don't sound too good."

"I'm not good."

"Oh, sweetie. What's wrong?"

"I'm pregnant, Jayne."

Jayne's gasp of horror told her that things really were as bad as she feared. Until she realized that Jayne had misunderstood.

"It's Derek's baby, Jayne. But I just found out. I'm probably four months along—maybe more. You know how messed up my system has always been. I didn't even think about it until…well, you know what that's like."

Jayne's voice was thick with concern. "What are you going to do?"

"I don't know. I have no idea." She slumped against the steering wheel. Her little flip phone suddenly felt like a rock in her hand.

"How can I help?"

"I don't know, Jayne. I don't know why I even called. I just…I had to talk to somebody."

"Oh, of course you did! I'm so sorry. Is there…is there anybody there? Have you gotten to know anyone yet?" She answered her own question. "Probably not well enough to talk about something like this, huh?"

Olivia nodded into the phone. "Not exactly. There're a few people from church who've been friendly, but they were more Derek's friends than mine."

"Oh, but if they knew Derek, I know they'd help you if they could. Are you still in the house?"

"I am, but I don't know how long I can keep up with the mortgage. It's over fifteen hundred dollars a month. I'm making twelve dollars an hour, Jayne, and Derek's check is nearly gone."

"Have you called Elizabeth? Maybe they're hiring again and—"

"She doesn't have anything. Even if she did, I wouldn't be any better off in the city than I am here. I'm having a baby, Jayne." Her voice climbed a crescendo of fear and frustration. "I'm sorry… It's not your fault. I shouldn't have bothered you."

"Olivia, stop. It's not a bother. I'd do anything to help. You know that. Do you need some money? We don't have much, but maybe we could give you a loan…get you through the next couple months…."

She sighed. "That's sweet of you, Jayne. I know you'd help if you could. I don't even know why I called. I'm just feeling a little desperate."

"You sound like you've made up your mind to *have* the baby."

"You know how I feel about that." She'd wondered when Jayne would get to that. They'd disagreed sharply on the subject in the past.

"I'm just saying that if there was ever a time when people would understand—"

"No, Jayne. That's not an option for me. It just isn't."

"Okay. I respect that. And you'll keep the baby?"

Olivia closed her eyes and chewed her lower lip. She could never end the pregnancy, but she had begun to entertain the idea of giving the baby up for adoption. It might be the best for everyone. She had nothing to offer a child. She wasn't sure she would even have a place to live once November rolled around, let alone a job. And she'd be a single parent. It was no way for a child to start life.

But every time she tried to imagine placing a baby—her baby, Derek's baby—in another woman's arms, she shut down. She didn't know if she could do it. Frightened as she was by the prospect of becoming a mother, there was something terrifying about thinking of giving up the rights to this child forever. What if she found later that she couldn't have any more children?

Jayne cleared her throat softly and Olivia shook herself back to the present. "I need to go, Jayne. I…I'll keep in touch. And I do appreciate your offer to help. I'll think about it. You'll let me know if you hear of anything opening up there?"

"Of course I will. You take care of yourself now, okay?"

"I will."

The cellular connection went silent and Olivia sat staring at her flip phone for a long minute.

Finally, she drove home. But as soon as she'd parked the car, she went straight to the kitchen and rummaged in the drawer beneath the telephone for the thin Hanover Falls phone directory. Derek had scratched some telephone numbers in the back—people from work and church.

She ran her finger down the list until she came to Michael Meredith's number. Michael and Claire had been the first ones to reach out to her. She'd felt comfortable with Claire, and Olivia remembered that the couple had known Derek. Somehow that seemed important to her right now. She lifted the phone from its hook and punched in the number.

The burr started on the other end and she frantically pressed the keypad, disconnecting the call. She'd missed church more often than she'd attended after those first few weeks. Claire Meredith would probably barely remember her. And even if she did, she wouldn't be interested in playing counselor to some stranger.

The jangle of the phone startled her. Michael Meredith's name was on the caller ID. Oh, no. She hadn't hung up in time and now they were calling to see what she wanted. Her throat constricted.

She let it ring half a dozen times before she picked up the handset. "Hello?"

"Olivia? This is Claire Meredith." Olivia could picture the pretty redhead on the other end. She had a voice that matched her cheery disposition. "I saw your number on our caller ID. I was up to my ears in laundry and must not have heard the phone until the last ring. It looked like you just called a minute ago, though…" Her voice trailed off in a question.

"Oh, it's okay…" She scrambled to think what to say, but Claire beat her to the punch.

"I was just thinking about you Sunday. Michael and I have missed seeing you in church. I've been wondering if you'd like to come over for coffee some morning. I'd love to visit…if you have time."

Olivia was surprised by the uncertainty in Claire's voice. Almost as if she was as afraid of being rejected as Olivia was. "I'd like that." She blurted out what amounted to an acceptance before she could think of an excuse to decline Claire's invitation.

"Oh, that's great. How about tomorrow? Katherine only has a half day of school, so I'll have to pick her up at noon, but if you could come around nine or so, we'd have plenty of time to visit."

Reed had asked her to go to one of the galleries in St. Louis tomorrow, and she didn't dare cancel, as tempting as it was. She'd forgotten how much she liked Claire. "I wish I could, Claire, but I have to work in the morning. I guess maybe you didn't hear that I got that job with Reed Vincent…you know, the artist. I usually get off around two o'clock, though."

"Oh, that's wonderful! No, I hadn't heard. Well, maybe we can find an afternoon that works. I'll see if I can arrange a play date for Katherine or else we won't get a word in edgewise. Is everything going okay?"

Olivia's throat constricted and she swallowed back sudden tears. She tried to answer, but she was afraid her voice would give her away.

"Olivia? Are you there? Is…is everything okay?"

"It's been kind of a rough week."

"I'm so sorry. I'm sure it's not easy. You must miss Derek terribly. I can't even imagine…"

"It…it's not just that, Claire." She took a deep breath. "I just found out that…I'm pregnant."

Silence, then a thready sigh. "Oh, Olivia. Do you know yet how far—?"

"I'm about four months along…I think. They'll do a sonogram at my next visit. But I just found out for sure yesterday. Derek…he wanted kids so badly."

"I don't even know what to say." Claire's voice came out in a whisper. "Such wonderful news, but how sad that Derek won't—" Her voice broke.

That opened the floodgates for Olivia, and for a long minute only the sound of their tears filled the line.

"Oh, Olivia," Claire finally said. "Is anybody there for you? Do you have someone to talk to?"

She sniffed back the tears and tried to compose herself, but she couldn't do more than shake her head into the phone.

"I'm coming over." Claire's voice held determination. "You should not have to be alone at a time like this. You're still in the same house, right? On Glenwillow?"

"Yes," she managed to squeak.

"I'll be right there."

Suddenly Olivia found her voice, but the phone went dead in spite of her feeble protests.

Her gaze panned the house. Things were a mess. She'd barely unpacked a box since she'd arrived. But she didn't care. All she felt was tremendous relief that she could finally share this terrible burden with someone—someone who believed that this baby was wonderful news. It was a foreign idea to her, but remembering the inflection in Claire's voice when she'd said it, a spark lit in Olivia, and she felt hopeful for the first time in a very long while.

Chapter Sixteen

Olivia was waiting on the front porch steps when Claire pulled into the driveway. Olivia had worried that she might have Katherine with her, but she was alone. It would have been awkward to share what she needed to with the little girl there.

The sun was warm on the painted porch floor, but before she could invite Claire in, the young woman plopped down beside Olivia on the steps and put an arm around her shoulder as if they'd been friends forever. The sun played off Claire's apricot-colored hair and set a halo behind her. Indeed, she seemed like an angel, come to Olivia's rescue.

She almost cried again at the warmth of her new friend's arm draped over her shoulder like a favorite sweater. It had been so long since she'd felt the gentle touch of another—

She stopped in midthought, remembering Reed's embrace. But that had been fraught with too many conflicting emotions and too much guilt. She didn't know Reed well enough to accept his comforting hugs, and besides, he was her boss.

Claire clicked her tongue in a soothing rhythm, much the way she probably comforted Katherine when she skinned her knee or lost a favorite doll. Olivia felt the tension go out of her shoulders.

"So what can I do?"

"I don't even know what I'm going to do, Claire, let alone tell anyone else how they can help."

"Do you have family who can help?"

She shook her head. "Derek and I were both pretty much alone in the world. Maybe that's what drew us to each other in the first place."

"I understand. I lost my grandmother a few years ago. She was my last living relative." Sadness glazed her eyes briefly, but then she smiled. "Katherine's named after Nana."

"Oh, how special. I never knew my grandparents." She forced cheer into her voice. "Katherine is adorable. She looks so much like you."

A grin lit Claire's delicate features. "She's our joy. She's a little bit spoiled. I'm not ashamed to admit it. But we love her like crazy. She needs a brother or sister to share the limelight with, I think. We've been trying for a couple years, but…" She shrugged.

Olivia gave a wry smile and pointedly looked down at her still-flat belly. "I'll trade you places."

Claire gave a little gasp. "Oh. I didn't even think of that. Oh, my."

"Funny how God works, don't you think? I've been trying to understand how in the world He could let this happen to me, and frankly, wishing it weren't true. And here you sit wishing just the opposite."

Claire shook her head. "I know. There are an awful lot of things that don't make sense in this world. But I have a feeling we'll see things from a much different perspective someday."

"You mean Heaven?"

"Well, that, too, but also just getting older and looking back on life. Seeing how far God has brought me, all He's led me through." The sadness returned to her eyes. "Michael and I went through some pretty rough things when we first fell in love. Things that didn't make any sense at all…."

She glanced up with a soft smile. "It all worked itself out. In fact, God knew what He was doing all along. We just couldn't see it at the time. I sometimes think He does that on purpose, just to keep us dependent on Him."

"Well, I'm sorry, but I don't much like that part of His plan."

"Oh, but, Olivia, when you hold that baby in your arms, I really think it'll all make sense."

She sighed. "You really think so?"

"I'd be willing to bet the farm on it." She giggled and clapped a hand over her mouth. "Oh, wait…the sermon Sunday was about gambling. Let me rephrase that."

Olivia smiled. "I hope you're right, Claire. But it's a little hard to see from where I'm sitting right now."

"I understand. Let's just take one day at a time. What do you need today?"

The plural of Claire's "let's" warmed Olivia's heart and suddenly she didn't feel quite so alone in the world.

"Today? Today I need a friend."

Claire grinned and snapped a sharp salute. "Reporting for duty."

Reed pulled out of the car wash and flicked on the wipers, watching the last of the beaded water sluice off the windshield. The dashboard of the Ford Escape was dusty, but he didn't have time to do anything about that now.

His appointment with the gallery owner was in less than an hour, and he still had to figure out where Olivia lived.

She'd come in at the usual time yesterday morning, apologizing for running out the day before. She hadn't volunteered any more than that, but she seemed to be all right. He hadn't wanted to push it. They'd have a long ride in the car together today. Maybe he'd ask her about it.

He swiped at the dust on the instrument panel. Why had he never noticed how badly in need of a good detailing his vehicle was? He ripped a tissue from the almost-empty box on the console and tried to get the worst of the grime off. He only succeeded in making cloudy trails through the dust. Well, she'd just have to overlook the dirt.

At the stoplight, he took time to put in his eyedrops. He'd gotten lax about using them as often as he was supposed to. Today, the sun reminded him. Even with his darkest sunglasses, the bright June sunlight stung his eyes. The light changed and he hurriedly put the lid on the bottle of eyedrops. He squinted against the glare, wiping away the moisture from the corner of his eyes with one finger. Maybe he should ask Olivia to drive today. His vision was probably better than half the people on the road. Scary thought. Still, he didn't want to take any chances. But just thinking about explaining such a request to Olivia stung his pride.

He'd been looking forward to this day all week, but now that it was here, his palms were damp and he fought back a tangle of nerves. It was two hours to St. Louis, and then they had to come back, too. That was a lot of time to fill with a woman who didn't say a whole lot. It wasn't like in the studio when they could pretend to be absorbed in their work. He'd never worried about what to talk about for a minute with Kristina. She'd always managed to fill every waking second with conversation—even if she was talking to herself half the time.

He turned onto Glenwillow Road and craned his neck to read the house numbers. There it was. On the right. He brought the Escape to a slow stop as he took in the place. Nice house. The yard was a little overgrown and the planters on the porch were empty, but he could see the potential. Maybe he should offer to mow the lawn for her. With his new riding mower, it wouldn't take him more than half an hour. But he didn't want to insult her.

He pulled into the narrow drive and put the car in Park. He had the door open and one foot on the driveway when she appeared at the back door. Instead of her usual jeans and baggy shirt, she was wearing black slacks and a dressy, silky-looking blouse. She looked great.

He shut his door and leaned over to open hers. "Good morning."

"You found me."

He nodded. "Kind of hard *not* to find someone in the Falls."

She smiled and climbed in. He watched her as she buckled her seat belt. She was wearing pale pink lip gloss and her cheeks had a rosy glow.

He backed the car out of the drive and headed out of town. Okay, he was seriously going to have to keep his eyes on the road. The last thing he needed was the distraction of a beautiful woman sitting the perfect distance from him for his vision to be its sharpest. Funny…though he'd thought Olivia attractive before, he never would have described her as beautiful. But there was just no other word for her today. The idea of letting her drive was looking better all the time. More time to take in the view.

"Or do you know yet?" Her mellow voice jolted him.

He rubbed the place between his eyebrows. "I'm sorry. What'd you say?"

She gave him a funny look and for a minute he was afraid he'd been thinking out loud.

"I just wondered if you knew what time we'd get back."

"Oh. I'm sorry… I zoned out there for a minute." He looked at his watch. "Unless we have to wait on Gavin, I don't expect to be at the gallery for more than an hour. But I thought we'd catch lunch before we start back. There's a great Mexican restaurant I try to eat at every chance I get."

Olivia didn't say anything.

"If that's okay… But if you need to get back sooner, we don't have to do lunch."

"No. That's okay."

Oh, great. She was going to be as talkative today as she was lately in the studio. He reached for the radio. "What kind of music do you like?"

She seemed surprised that he'd asked. "I usually listen to classical at home, but I like just about anything. Except country."

He grinned.

"Don't tell me. You like country?"

His grin widened. "Well, four of the six dials are set pretty far west, and the other two are talk radio, but hey, I'm flexible. Why don't you find a station you like."

"No, that's okay. I can handle whatever."

He dropped his hand. "How about we don't listen to the radio right now."

"No, seriously, country is fine. Maybe I'll develop a taste for it."

"It is an acquired taste, they say. I wouldn't know, since I grew up on it."

"Really?"

"My dad played in a band."

"A country band?"

He nodded, letting a slow grin spread across his face.

She cringed. "Oops. Sorry if I insulted the family business."

He laughed at the hangdog expression on her face.

"It's okay. My mom wasn't a big fan, either."

"Really? Even though that's what your dad played?"

"I suppose she liked it at some point, but Dad was on the road a lot…traveling with the band. I think that soured her a little. She and my sister and I spent a lot of time with my grandparents while he was on the road."

"Oh. That would be tough."

"I don't think I realized until after Dad died what a bone of contention it was between them."

Olivia fell silent, and he started to regret that he'd brought up the subject. For once he wouldn't have minded the distraction of trucks and semitrailers on this stretch of I-44. But traffic was light and he drove on.

"Reed…I think…"

He turned to see Olivia grasping the door handle. Her face had a greenish cast to it, and a glint of panic lit her eyes.

He tapped the brakes. "What's wrong? Are you okay?"

She shook her head and gripped the door handle tighter. "Please…stop the car."

Reed rode the brakes until he came to a place where the shoulder was wide enough to pull over. The Escape had barely come to a full stop when she yanked at the handle and threw open the door.

He sat in a half stupor behind the wheel, listening to her retch in the ditch, out of his view. He opened his door and started to get out, then thought better of it. There wasn't much he could do for her. Probably best to leave her in peace.

He looked at the clock on the dash. Why didn't she tell him she was sick? Now he'd have to take her all the way back to the Falls. They'd come a good forty miles and he had appointments he couldn't break.

He was just about to jump down from the vehicle and go see if she needed help, when she climbed back into the passenger seat, looking embarrassed, but far less green.

"Are you okay? Do I need to take you home?"

"I'm fine now." She pulled her door shut, buckled her seat belt and stared straight ahead.

"You sure? You didn't sound fine a minute ago."

"I'm fine."

Traffic whizzed by them. He waited for an opening and eased back onto the highway. After setting the cruise control, he pulled the last few tissues from the box on the console and handed them to her. "Here."

"Thanks." She took them, not meeting his eyes, and dabbed at the corners of her mouth.

"I can take you home if you want." He hoped she didn't detect the insincerity of his offer.

"No, Reed. I'm fine. This is…" She eyed him, as though weighing whether she could trust him. "This is a morning thing. I'll be fine now."

"A morning thing? I don't get it…"

"Morning sickness. It passes. I'll be fine…until tomorrow morning."

"Huh?"

She sighed and closed her eyes briefly as if she were gathering strength. "Do I have to draw you a picture, Reed? I have morning sickness."

The light finally went on. He tried to keep his jaw from sagging, but he could see from her expression that he wasn't succeeding.

"You're…?" He stared pointedly at her belly, which denied what she seemed to be trying to tell him.

"Yes. I'm pregnant. With my husband's baby."

He dog-paddled through the confusion of her words. "I didn't… I didn't think it was anyone else. I mean, I didn't even know you were… I had no idea."

She gave an odd smile. "I just found out myself. I'm sorry."

He stared at her. "What are you apologizing for? This is…it's a good thing, isn't it? I'd think you'd be…" He let his voice trail off because he truly had no clue how this news would make her feel. But it was her husband's baby. Surely it was a gift to be left with a part of the man she'd loved. A way for her husband to live on, in a sense.

He looked over to find her glaring at him.

"Why does everyone think this is such wonderful news? How am I supposed to take care of a baby? I can't even pay my mortgage!" Her voice cracked and she put a fist to her mouth.

"I'm sorry. I just…I didn't know." He was starting to sound like a broken record. *God, give me the right words.*

Boy, had this trip turned out differently than he'd planned. He'd set out intending to woo the lovely Olivia Cline, and suddenly he was counseling a nauseated pregnant woman who wasn't even sure she wanted to be pregnant. He wished his sister were here. Alissa would know exactly what to say.

He took a deep breath and shot up another prayer. "Olivia, I don't know what your circumstances are, but I do know that God wouldn't have put you in this kind of a situation without already knowing exactly how it was going to work out. I guarantee He has it all figured out, even if we don't."

"We?"

"Well… I just mean… I'll help you however I can. You've got a job with me for as long as you need it. I can even give you a small raise if that'll help." *Lord, I'm really going out on a limb here. I need good news at the galleries today or I may not be able to keep Olivia on, let alone give her the raise I just promised.*

"Reed… You don't have to do that. I would understand completely if you need to let me go after…"

"No. Of course not. There's no reason you couldn't bring the baby to work."

"Have you ever been around a baby?"

"Sure. My niece and nephew." He shrugged. "All they did was eat and sleep."

"For the first few months, maybe. But babies turn into toddlers. If you think I was bad spilling your coffee, you don't have an inkling of what a crawler could do to your studio."

He hadn't thought of that. Ali and Mason weren't allowed in his studio even now that they were in school. "We can worry about that when the time comes," he said lamely.

Olivia put her head against the window, kneading the space between her eyebrows with two fingers.

He slowed the car. "Are you sick again?"

She didn't look at him. "I'm fine. I really don't want to talk about it anymore." She sounded near tears.

"Okay." He reached between the seats for the jacket he kept there. Wadding it into a messy lump, he handed it to her. "Here. Use this for a pillow."

She smiled wanly and took it from him. "Thanks."

He flipped the radio on and tuned to a station that played classical music. It wasn't exactly his style, but he had to do something to fill the silence.

She looked over her shoulder and smiled again. "That's nice. Thanks."

"No problem." *No problem?* He smirked to himself at the ironic words. Olivia was pregnant. He'd meant everything he said to her. God probably did know how this was all going to work out, but it had sure put him in an awkward tailspin.

Chapter Seventeen

Olivia washed her face at the tiny sink in the stylishly appointed restroom and dried her hands on a towel from the basket beside the sink. She leaned into the mirror and studied her face. She was feeling much better after her little nap in Reed's car, but her pale complexion didn't reflect that fact.

She rummaged in her purse for some blush, but had to settle for a daub of lipstick smudged into her cheeks. She checked the mirror again. A little better.

Smoothing her blouse, she took a deep breath and then opened the door. Reed was bent over, inspecting a marble carving—a Pegasus-like creature—perched on a pedestal in the lobby.

She walked up beside him. "Very nice. Do you know the artist?"

He shook his head. "I've always wanted to try carving. Marble would be a challenge, though. Maybe I could work in sandstone…." He ran his hands over the smooth surface of the sculpture. His eyes were unfocused, and she wondered if he'd forgotten she was even in the room with him.

"Reed?" A voice from behind startled them both.

Reed straightened and turned to greet the graying, ponytailed man coming toward them with hand extended.

Reed reached to shake his hand. "Hey, Gavin. How's it going?"

"Going good, bro. I hope you brought me some work."

"I did."

"Good, because as soon as I hang it, it's sold."

"Really? Well, that's good news." Reed turned and put a hand on Olivia's arm, drawing her into their conversation. "Gavin Chambers, I'd like you to meet my assistant, Olivia Cline."

"Well, now I didn't know you'd gone and got yourself a partner."

Olivia shuffled her feet and cleared her throat. "Oh, no… I'm just Reed's assistant."

Gavin winked at her. "Well, you must be the best assistant he's ever had because this guy's work is flying out of here."

She grinned. "I'm pretty sure I'm the *only* assistant he's ever had."

"Well, then you *are* the best, aren't you?"

Reed laughed politely and changed the subject. "Gavin started The Chambers—what is it, six years ago now?"

"Eight. You were just a pup back then."

"I'm still just a pup compared to you."

Olivia enjoyed the men's banter. It struck her that she'd never seen Reed interact with others. Every minute they'd spent together had been in the studio, just the two of them. She saw a side of him now that surprised her. She'd never pictured him as outgoing and fun-loving. But he was holding his own with the gregarious gallery owner.

Gavin gave them a quick tour of the gallery, pointing out new pieces to Reed, and cuing him in on what was selling in the St. Louis market. "Your nautical stuff is good. I'd like to see more of that. Maybe some smaller pieces…things we could price a little lower, yet still let people own an original van Gogh…er, I mean an original Vincent." Gavin laughed at his own joke.

Olivia could tell Reed was embarrassed by the comparison, but he humored the older man, laughing softly. "We'd better get down to brass tacks," he said finally. "I promised Olivia I'd have her home in time for a nap."

She didn't exactly appreciate his condescending comment, but she merely smiled and followed the men into what appeared to be Gavin's office. The smallish room held a desk with a couple of chairs positioned in front of it. But the chairs were stacked high with framed art and boxes bearing FedEx labels. Gavin cleared off one of the chairs for her, stacking the artwork carefully against one wall, but Reed waved off his offer of a chair and leaned against the doorjamb.

Gavin perched on a corner of his desk, crossing an ankle over his knee. "So what can you bring me and how soon can you get it here?"

"Well, I've got a couple larger pieces—seventeen by twenty-four—that I can deliver as soon as Olivia gets them framed." He turned to her. "Would you mind driving down with them some day next week?"

"Sure. That'd be fine."

"But it'll be a while before I can get some smaller ones to you."

"I'll wait, but not very patiently. You're in demand."

Reed's raised eyebrows told Olivia he was pleasantly surprised by this news. A full-time artist, no matter how talented, didn't live in a house like Reed's with that fabulous studio unless he was either selling well, or had inherited a fortune. From what he'd said about his parents, she'd assumed the former. But maybe business hadn't been so good recently. Maybe that eye surgery he'd mentioned had put him behind schedule.

But if things were tight, he'd have been looking for an excuse to lay her off, not offer her a raise. She wasn't sure what to think about that. It had touched her, his offer. But even if he doubled her wage, she couldn't raise a child on that kind of income. *Lord, what am I going to do?*

"How's your stomach?" Reed gave her a sidewise glance from behind the steering wheel.

"I'm fine." She really didn't want to talk about it anymore.

With every mile, she was regretting that she'd revealed her pregnancy. She'd thought he would probably regret that he hired her, and instead he was going all mushy on her. It was sweet of him, really it was. But she didn't need someone fawning over her. Her emotions were too tentative for that. She was afraid she might dissolve into tears if he showed one more speck of concern.

"Would you want to stop and get some lunch?"

She glanced at the clock on the dashboard of the Escape. It was almost one-thirty. The poor man was probably starving. "I didn't realize it was so late. Sure. We can stop whenever you want to."

"Would you rather just hit a drive-through?"

"If you don't mind." She didn't feel like going in anyplace, and somehow it seemed easier to avoid making conversation in the car. She hated that she'd made herself so vulnerable. All she wanted to do now was get back home.

He took the next exit and drove slowly past a frontage road with a smorgasbord of fast-food places. "What do you think? Sandwiches, a burger…?"

"I really don't care, Reed. You choose. The only thing that doesn't sound good is Mexican food."

Reed turned into a sandwich shop's drive-through lane. "This okay?"

She nodded.

He got in line behind two other cars. "See anything on the menu you like?"

"I'll just have a turkey sub, please."

Back on the road, she opened the bag and arranged their drinks on the console. She laid a napkin on Reed's knee under the steering wheel, unwrapped his sandwich and handed it to him.

He took it with raised eyebrows and a surprised smile. "Hey, now this is dining in style. I'll have to bring you with me more often."

She flushed, realizing that without thinking, she'd catered to Reed the way she always had to Derek when they ate in the car.

She peeled the wrapper off her own sandwich, and stuffed a bite in her mouth to avoid comment.

He pointed to the fries she'd balanced between their drinks in the cup holder. "Help yourself. I can't eat all those."

She nodded her thanks. But she wasn't the least bit hungry. In fact, her stomach was feeling a little queasy again. She choked down half of her sandwich and tucked the rest of it back in its wrapper, hoping Reed wouldn't notice.

She leaned her head against the window.

"Here…" Reed produced the jacket she'd used for a pillow earlier.

"Thanks." She pretended to nap, but the thoughts careening through her brain wouldn't let true sleep come. She replayed Reed's words: *I'll help you however I can. You've got a job with me for as long as you need it.* Could he mean that? Or would she bank on it only to have the rug pulled out from under her?

The tires droned on the highway, lulling her into a sort of stupor. Soon she realized that soft classical music was playing over the sounds of the road. She couldn't help but smile at that.

Still, one prevailing notion mixed with the churning worries. Reed was pampering her, doting on her. And she liked it more than she cared to admit.

Chapter Eighteen

Reed rubbed at his eyelids, then forced his hands into his lap. His eyes had been bothering him all morning, itching and burning and playing tricks on his vision. But rubbing them would only complicate things. In the beginning, right after the surgery, he'd been warned sternly that rubbing could damage the tender newly transplanted corneas. That danger was probably past, but he didn't want to take any chances. Besides, he knew what the remedy was. He needed to put away his paints, go lie down and rest his eyes. Invariably, that did the trick.

But he had gallery requests to fulfill, and Olivia would be here any minute. He couldn't very well be in bed when she arrived.

As if on cue, the door opened and he heard her moving through the front rooms. He picked up his paintbrush and went back to work, but his heartbeat ratcheted up a notch as it always did in her presence. He'd learned to push back the feelings and ignore the impulse to express his growing feelings for Olivia.

He hadn't pried about her pregnancy, except to ask how she was feeling and to insist she take a break each afternoon. She seemed to appreciate his concern, but she hadn't said any more about her plans or her feelings toward the news that she was carrying her husband's baby.

Maybe she'd taken his words to heart...that God knew her circumstances and had everything under control. He hoped so. It killed him to think of her alone and frightened. It made him want to take her under his wing. But he couldn't exactly do that under the circumstances.

Why did he even torture himself thinking about her? Even if she weren't pregnant, it would be too soon on her part for him to pursue a relationship. She was still grieving. He had to remember that. He had to be patient.

"Good morning." Olivia appeared in the doorway, looking cheerful and even prettier than usual in a loose robin's-egg-blue T-shirt.

He reined in the desire to simply stare at her, and turned back to his easel, forcing his voice to sound normal. "Hi."

She put her bag down and went back to the kitchen. They had a comfortable routine by now, and he waited for the sounds that had become his morning music over the last few weeks—the clatter of cups and saucers, the hiss of the coffeemaker. Sometimes he wondered how he'd gotten through his days without Olivia's presence in his house.

"Hey, where'd these come from?" she yelled from the kitchen.

"Oh, you found the cinnamon rolls? Maggie made them. My next-door neighbor," he explained.

"Yummy. Are you offering?"

"Only if you bring me one, too."

She appeared on the top step. "Oh, so now I'm the maid?"

He jerked around. For a split second he'd thought she was serious, but she wore a playful smirk. He played along. "Yeah, and could you do the laundry while you're up there?"

She gave a very unladylike harrumph and disappeared back into the kitchen, humming a tune he couldn't identify. Probably opera.

He smiled and picked up his paintbrush. Something had changed between them that day in St. Louis…the day she'd told him she was pregnant. They were easier with each other now. More like old friends than employer and employee. They joked around more, and she had started humming while she worked—sometimes even if there was no music on the CD player. If it had been anyone else, it probably would have driven him nuts. But he liked hearing her voice. Liked hearing her sound happier.

She brought plates with rolls warmed in the microwave, then went back for coffee. She set his mug carefully to the side, out of range of his elbow. "Coffee on your right," she warned.

A few minutes later, he glanced across the room. Olivia had brought in the load of paint rags he'd put in the dryer last night. She appeared to be deep in thought as she methodically folded and stacked them on the worktable.

He went back to painting, but a minute later, he looked up to see her watching him.

"Are your eyes bothering you?"

He hadn't realized he was rubbing at his eye again. He pulled his hand away from his face. "I'm okay." He never had explained the details of his surgery to her, but she seemed to instinctively watch out for him and sense when he was struggling. It was unsettling—and touching at the same time.

"Do you want me to pull the blinds?"

"I'll get it." He hated to sacrifice the light, but it did help to slant the blinds slightly. He slid from the stool and crossed the room. The sky outside the wide bank of windows matched Olivia's shirt. He would rather have been outside today than stuck in the studio. Olivia probably felt the same way. If the weather was like this tomorrow, he should take advantage of it and get some photos.

Before his surgery, he'd often loaded up his easel and scouted new scenes to paint on location, but the light that was conducive to plein air painting was too harsh for his eyes now. He'd been toying with the idea of painting from photographs. The new digital camera he'd bought did an amazing job of capturing the light. If he could shoot some new reference material, he'd be set for the winter.

He thought about the idea again that afternoon, just before Olivia left for the day. "Hey, if the weather holds would you want to go out on a photo shoot with me tomorrow?"

He'd issued the invitation almost without thinking, and cringed inwardly at a sudden flash of memory. He had taken

Kristina on a photo shoot once. It wound up being a disastrous medley of bug bites, sunburn, snagged clothing and a twisted ankle. Maybe this wasn't such a good idea.

But Olivia merely shrugged. "Sure. As long as I don't have to run the camera."

"Oh, no. I'll do that. But I could use someone to tote my extra equipment and hold the reflector, maybe help me find some good subjects. You have an eye for composition."

She acknowledged his compliment with a lift of one shoulder. "Where are you going to shoot?"

"Maggie said the roses are still in bloom at the county park out west of town. I thought I might try to get some photos before everything's done blooming for the year."

"Oh, I love florals. You haven't done many of those, have you?"

"That's what I started out with actually, but it was the landscapes that sold first, and now the nauticals. But I'd like to get back to flowers. I've been wanting to try some transparent glazes."

"We worked with glazes a little in one of the art classes I took, but I never had much success."

"They can be tricky to work with. I've had the best luck applying them a little deeper than I want and then softening them back with a rag or stipple brush."

"Maybe that's what I was doing wrong."

"I've got a couple books on the topic that you might find interesting. I'll try to find them and bring them when I pick you up tomorrow. If you're agreeing to go, that is."

"Sure."

"Um…there's only one hitch." He gave a comical grimace.

"Uh-oh. What did I just commit to?"

"Well, we need to get out while the light is right. Early morning is the best for what I'm trying to capture."

She eyed him suspiciously. "How early are we talking?"

He ducked. "Five-thirty?"

"You would really get a pregnant woman out of bed at five-thirty in the morning?" she groaned.

It was the first time she'd spoken so casually about her condition. He hoped it meant she was coming to terms with the coming baby. "Okay, okay. How about we make it six?"

"Oh, wow, thanks for that generous half-hour reprieve." Her voice dripped with sarcasm, but her smile let him know she was willing.

"I'm not making it mandatory." He laughed, then turned serious. "Really, if that's too early, I understand. But if we go any later, by the time I get set up the sun will be too high. I've done photos solo before so it's—"

"No. I'll go. I'm sure I'll survive."

"Tell you what. I'll let you go home early today and take a nap…rest up."

She rolled her eyes. "Oh, that's big of you."

"Tomorrow's Friday. You'll have the whole weekend to sleep. Do I need to give you a wake-up call?"

"I have an alarm clock, thank you very much," she said with a droll smile.

"Okeydoke." He gave a comical salute. "I'll pick you up at six." He turned back to his easel, suddenly feeling more at home in his house, in his studio, than he'd felt in months.

The blare of Reed's horn sliced the early-morning stillness and Olivia grabbed another saltine from the box—and a plastic "airsick" bag, just in case—before running out the door. She hadn't thought about the morning sickness when she agreed to go with Reed this morning. The queasiness had abated somewhat over the past week, but early morning was definitely *not* her best time. She hoped the poor guy didn't have to pull over to the side of the road for her again.

She locked the front door behind her and jogged down the driveway to where Reed's Escape was parked.

He leaned across the seat and opened her door for her. As soon as she was buckled in, he handed her a coffee cup dressed in a cardboard sleeve.

"Ooh, what's this?"

"Skinny decaf cappuccino, with whipped cream, just like you like it."

"Hey, you're good."

"I still don't get ordering skinny with whipped cream. That makes no sense to me."

"The skinny is for me, the whipped cream is for the baby." She patted her belly, which was starting to pooch out a little.

His eyes twinkled, bluer than ever. "Oh, *that's* a good one. Wish I had such a good excuse."

She didn't reply. Reed had been asking about the baby and her pregnancy recently, and while she'd shared with him some, she still wasn't completely comfortable talking about it. The subject of her pregnancy always brought up the specter of Derek.

Specter. She stopped short. Why had that word cropped up? Why couldn't she find joy in memories of Derek, in the prospect of giving birth to his baby? Reed and Claire seemed to think this child was a gift, that she would have this living memorial of her husband. They didn't realize that the good memories were few. After their first honeymoon year, the only good in her marriage to Derek had lain in the hope of a future together, something to redeem the past. But that hope had died with Derek. As long as she lived, she would never understand why God had taken him from her just when they'd begun to work things out.

Reed rolled up to a stoplight and Olivia watched out the window as two sparrows took turns dipping their beaks into a muddy puddle, their rhythmic motions like the pendulum of a clock. It was how she felt. Just going through the motions. Up one minute and in the mud the next. She couldn't allow herself to think too deeply about her situation or she would fall apart. The only bright spot in her life was sitting beside her in the driver's seat. She flushed at the thought. What would Reed think if he knew she felt this way about him?

"You okay?"

She started at the sound of his voice but nodded, groping unsuccessfully for a reply.

The light turned green and he drove on. "You're awfully quiet."

"I'm fine. Just thinking."

"Do you want to tell me what you're thinking…?"

Had he read her thoughts? She squirmed at the mere idea. "I…I don't really think you'd be interested."

"Try me."

She turned to study his expression. What she saw there was utter sincerity. It was all she could do not to pour out every question that plagued her. Instead she took a more generic tack. "I just wish I knew where I'd be this time next year."

"With the baby, you mean?"

"I guess. The baby, the house, my job... I...I don't know. Sometimes I wonder if it's even fair to this child for me to—" She clipped off the word. She couldn't finish. It was the first time she'd dared to give the thought a voice.

"Would you...could you really do that? Give your baby up?"

She bent her head and stared at her lap. "I don't know..." The truth was, giving her baby up for adoption was no more difficult to picture than keeping it was. Raising a child? She could not imagine.

"Olivia..." Reed pressed his lips into a tight line, as though trying to decide whether he should say something.

She waited for him to continue.

Apparently he took her silence as permission, and when he finally spoke, it was like a floodgate opening. "I know this is none of my business. You didn't ask my advice, but I can't *not* say something."

"Okay..." As much as she wanted to shut him up, to change the subject, she also hung on every syllable. She couldn't make this decision alone. She longed for someone to tell her what to do.

"I know it won't be easy to raise a child on your own. I know you're worried about how you'll provide for your baby. If you were fifteen years old, I'd applaud a decision to put your baby up for adoption. Heaven knows there are plenty of people who would give anything to have a child to love. But you...if you did this, I think you would regret it for the rest of your life. This is your husband's baby, Olivia."

Again, her eyes found her lap. She felt like a child being chided for something she hadn't even done.

Reed slowed the car and turned onto a narrow county road. They bumped along in silence for a minute before he spoke.

"Listen, it's not my decision to make, but I just can't let you do it without—"

"Excuse me," she huffed in exasperation. "And just how exactly are you going to stop me if I make that decision?" What had happened to the happy-go-lucky mood this morning had started with?

He held up a hand, a look of genuine contrition in his eyes. "I'm sorry. It's not my business."

"No…I'm sorry." She massaged her forehead. "I shouldn't have snapped at you."

He reached out and touched her arm. "It's okay. I'd probably be snapping at people, too, if I were in your shoes."

"It's just…I don't know yet what I'm going to do. It's just all too confusing…."

"Can I say something?"

She shrugged. *Might as well,* she thought. *You haven't hesitated to say what you think so far.*

"I know I mentioned this the other day, but I just want to be sure you knew I meant it. It looks like my work is taking off, so I can give you as many hours as you need. I've got plenty of work that needs doing. And starting with your next paycheck, you'll have a raise. When I hired you I thought I'd have to do a lot more training than I did."

She was skeptical and must have looked it, because he went on. "You've been a big help in the studio, Olivia, you really have. I'm not just saying that."

Why was he acting this way? Was she just some charity case to him? A way to make him feel good about himself? He always seemed so sincere, but that's what bothered her. People didn't just make offers like Reed had made without a reason. When she'd started to suspect Derek of running around, Jayne had accused her of being overly suspicious. Well, look how that turned out.

Reed put a hand over hers on the edge of her seat. "If there's anything I can do to help, I'm here."

She slid her hand out from under his, resisting the urge to rub it, to rub away the conflicting emotions his nearness made her feel. "Why, Reed?" In spite of her efforts to quell it, her voice rose. "Why are you doing this? You don't even know me. You don't owe me anything."

He had turned off onto a side road several minutes earlier and now he pulled over to a rutted trail that ran parallel with the road. "I drove out here the other morning and scouted out some sites," he explained, easing the Escape to the side of the trail and setting the parking brake. "The light is perfect this time of morning. But we need to hike into the woods a little ways. We can talk while we walk, okay?"

"I'm done talking," she said, opening the passenger door and sliding down from the seat.

He grabbed his camera bag and tripod from the backseat and followed suit. He slammed the door behind him and came around to her side of the vehicle, holding out his camera bag. "Would you mind carrying this while I get my tripod set up?"

She took the bag from him and trailed him as he led the way through the brush into the dense woods. Cars whizzed by on the highway to the north, but as they walked farther into the underbrush the sounds of motors were replaced by birdsong and the spongy squish of wet leaves beneath their tennis shoes.

They walked a few feet in silence before Reed hooked a thumb in the general direction of where they'd parked the car. "I didn't mean to cut you off back there. I hope you didn't think—"

"No." She shook her head, feeling like a broken record. "I really don't know what else to say, Reed. You don't owe me anything."

He stopped in his tracks, then whirled to face her. "Why do you think it's about me owing you anything? Why can't you just accept it as a friend helping a friend? I think you'd do the same thing if the tables were turned."

"Well, that's not exactly possible." She grinned in spite of her raised hackles.

He didn't return her smile. "You know what I mean. You know, you led me to think that you believed in God."

"What?" Where had that come from? "Of course I believe in God. What does that have to do with anything?"

"Then why don't you seem to understand the principle of helping a friend in need?"

For some reason, she wanted to wipe the smug look off his face with a slap. But then that would have only proven the point he was trying to make. She took a deep breath and forced a smile. "Listen, I appreciate what you're trying to do. I'm just not sure you've thought it through. I'll think about it. I promise. Right now, let's shoot some pictures before the light shifts and we've wasted the whole morning."

He pulled out one leg of the tripod, then another, telescoping each to its full length. "Okay," he conceded. "But remember, you promised to think about it. This discussion is not over."

Chapter Nineteen

Reed lay prone on the forest floor, his digital camera on the ground in front of him. Olivia couldn't help but think how cute he looked in that position.

"Can you give me just a little more light, Olivia? Tilt the reflector a bit to your left?"

But he didn't sound cute. He sounded frustrated. Reed indicated with hand motions which direction he wanted her to move.

Olivia inched to her left, holding the giant Frisbee-like device with both hands.

He flapped his hands the other way. She moved right.

But from the look on his face at the moment, apparently she wasn't reading him right. Wouldn't be the first time.

He'd given her the seemingly brainless job of aiming the reflector at a fern in an attempt to soften the harsh sunlight. But the job was proving more difficult than she thought, and the look in Reed's eyes told her his patience was waning. Not that she had an endless supply, either.

Olivia's muscles ached from trying to hold the stupid thing steady. The wind attempted to wrest the unwieldy reflector from her hands as if it were a kite. She tipped the reflective surface a few degrees, trying to deflect a ray of light onto the object of Reed's attention, a delicate fern frond growing out of a rock.

"Whoa…whoa… Not quite that much." He laid the camera

down carefully and scrambled to his feet. "Here," he said, coming to her side and taking the frame from her hands. "If you hold the frame at ten and two you'll have better control of it. It helps if you kind of plant your feet wide, too." He demonstrated, then handed the reflector back to her.

She placed her hands on the device as if it were a steering wheel and attempted to mimic his stance. "I've got some issues with balance, in case you hadn't noticed." She looked pointedly at her rounded stomach.

"Oh, I noticed all right." He laughed.

Just then, a breeze caught the reflector from behind, practically lifting her off the ground. She struggled to hang on to the fabriclike disc, no doubt an expensive piece of equipment, and in the process, she stumbled over a rock.

Reed reached out to steady her and instead fell into her, sending the reflector sailing, and knocking her to her knees. The empty tripod somersaulted over them both and Reed ended up sprawled on his back on the spongy floor of the woods.

Olivia's giggles were squelched when she saw the look of horror on Reed's face.

His voice quivered as he scrambled to his knees, reaching for her. "Are you okay? Are you hurt?"

"I'm fine. Just clumsy," she huffed, taking his hand briefly to steady herself. She sat back on her haunches and brushed the dirt from her palms.

Reed straightened and gently placed his hands on her shoulders, looking her up and down. Then he ran his hands down her arms, as if feeling for broken bones. "You're sure? The baby...? You're both okay?"

"Reed Vincent. *Quit* worrying. Babies are well cushioned in here." She placed a hand over her stomach. "It takes a lot more than a little tumble to hurt a baby." It felt strange to refer to it as a baby. She'd thought of it only as a pregnancy so far—and an unwanted one at that—but those words had tripped off her tongue.

Reed stroked her arm, then slid his hand up behind her neck, cradling her head. "You're sure."

His gaze searched hers and he was so close she could smell his spearmint chewing gum.

"I…I'm positive." She tried to lean out of his reach, but he twined his fingers through her hair. For one alarming second, she was afraid he was going to kiss her. "I'm fine." Her own voice warbled and her cheeks flamed at the tenderness of his touch.

He shook his head, as if sloughing off a bad dream, and let his hands fall to his side.

She pressed shaking hands to the rocky ground and tried to get to her feet.

"Here." He reached out his hand. "Careful. You're sure you're okay? Walk around a little, make sure you didn't sprain anything."

If she hadn't been so unsettled by his gentle attention a few seconds ago, she would have almost found his mother-hen doting humorous. But she was trembling inside, too. And she knew why.

She'd *wanted* him to kiss her. She had leaned away, resisted, but if she were honest, she knew that she was only doing so for Derek's sake.

She flung off the thought and looked around for the reflector. It had blown into a copse of trees and was fluttering between two white-barked trunks. She trudged through the dense overgrowth to retrieve it, grateful for something to do besides looking into Reed's eyes.

"Here… Let me get that."

He was beside her again. Too near for comfort. She felt his eyes on her, but she didn't dare look up.

"I've got it. I hope it didn't get torn." She made a show of inspecting the reflector for rips.

"It looks okay. Here…I'll take that."

"I've got it." Olivia moved away and looked up between the massive branches overhead. Her heart thrummed and beads of perspiration had broken out on her forehead. "Is the sun too high now? For pictures."

He followed her gaze. "Not if we hurry."

They both fell into business mode. Reed picked up the camera and fiddled with the settings. She took her place a few feet behind the spot where he'd been shooting. Reflector in hand, she looked down. Then she saw the fern. Or what was left of it. In their scuffle, the tender plant had been trampled beyond recognition.

"Oh, no! It's ruined."

His eyes went to where she was pointing. His shoulders slumped when he spotted the wilted fern. Olivia put a hand to her mouth. "Well, that was a whole lot of work for nothing. I'm so sorry, Reed."

He looked askance at her. "What do you have to be sorry for? It's not your fault." He smiled. "Besides, it wasn't exactly all for nothing."

The nuance of his smile brought warmth to Olivia's cheeks, and though a part of her thought she should look away, she didn't.

As if he'd just realized the underlying meaning of his words, Reed looked down. "Besides, there are other fish in the sea…so to speak."

She studied him, wondering why he'd chosen that particular turn of phrase. *Other fish in the sea…* Was he trying to make a point that had nothing to do with ferns or photos? But the expression on his face seemed innocent. Far more innocent that he'd been a minute ago with his fingers toying with her hair so appealingly.

Stop it, she chided herself. She changed the subject to force her own thoughts down a different path. "Do you want to look for some other scenes to shoot, or is it too late?"

He glanced at the sky. "Let's walk a few more minutes and see what we find."

He picked up the tripod, and tamped off the worst of the mud and grass.

Olivia started on through the woods, but Reed's voice behind her halted her.

She turned to see a pained expression on his face.

"You know," he said. "I think we'd better head on back."

"Oh?"

He didn't respond, but did an about-face and started back through the woods.

She shrugged. "Okay."

Reed was strangely silent on the trek back to the car. He loaded the equipment into the back of the vehicle, climbed in and turned the key without a word.

But as soon as the engine sputtered, he switched off the ignition. He sat there for a minute, then turned the key and started the car again.

Please, God, don't let there be anything wrong with the car. After what had happened, Olivia couldn't think of anything more awkward than being stuck out here alone with Reed Vincent.

But he revved the engine and it roared to life. He put an arm across the seat behind her and skillfully backed several hundred yards down the trail toward the main road.

"What happened?" she asked when they were back on the highway.

He knit his brow. "What do you mean?"

"Is there something wrong with the car?"

He dropped his head and flashed a sheepish grin. "The car is fine."

"Oh." She turned to look out her window. Reed was acting strange.

"Olivia?"

She turned again to face him.

"I…I owe you an apology."

"Reed, I am fine. Would you quit worrying about me?"

"No. You don't understand. I…I don't know if you get what happened out there—" he jutted his chin in the general direction of the woods "—but…well, I owe you an apology."

She tensed, waiting for him to continue.

He studied his lap for a moment, then trained his eyes on the road and let out a low sigh. "I don't know whether to just let this go or try and talk it out."

She froze. "I…I don't understand." But she was pretty sure she *did* understand.

"Olivia, the only reason I hightailed it out of there is because I wanted to kiss you so bad I wasn't sure I could help myself."

Whoa. She hadn't expected such subtlety. In spite of her misgivings about Reed's confession, she almost giggled.

"What's so funny?"

She hadn't realized she was grinning "out loud." But thinking about facing Reed's question quickly erased any hint of a smile. "Nothing's funny. I…I don't know what to say." What *could* she say? How in the world was a woman supposed to respond to a declaration like that?

"You don't need to say anything. I just… I want to apologize. It won't happen again." He stared out the windshield.

A chill went up her spine. Was he trying to tell her that he was letting her go? After he'd just promised she could work for him as long as she needed to? "I…I really need this job."

He looked up, a question in his eyes, then understanding struck. "No…no, I'm not firing you. I'll just…" He grinned, looking like the proverbial little boy caught with his hand in the cookie jar. "I'll just have to try and keep my balance next time."

He flashed a winsome smile—a smile that made her think maybe she preferred Reed Vincent a little off balance.

Reed closed the door behind Olivia and trudged back to the studio. He was a fool. What had he been thinking, opening his big mouth and all but declaring his everlasting love for her? He'd hoped getting things out in the open might clear the air between them. And yes, if he was honest, he'd hoped it might open a door for her to confess that she reciprocated his feelings.

But that was just the problem. She obviously didn't. She wasn't ready. It was too soon. He knew that. Why did he have to go and force the issue? Why couldn't he just be patient and let nature take its course, so to speak? But nature *had* taken its course, and look where it had almost landed him. He'd put them both in an extremely awkward position, made an employee he did not want to lose miserably uncomfortable even setting foot in his studio, let alone his house.

She'd be home in five minutes. He needed to call her and try to explain. But his pathetic explanations were what had gotten him in trouble in the first place. When would he learn that a man didn't have to say everything that popped into his mind?

As he passed through the kitchen, he slapped the palm of his hand hard on the kitchen counter. His elbow caught on an open cabinet door in the process. *Ouch.* Pain shot through his arm, an electrical current kind of tingling that told him he'd hit his "crazy bone." *Grow up, Vincent!* The last thing he needed was to injure his arm or hands. He was hopeless.

He reached for the telephone and punched in the memory code for his sister's number in Indiana. Alissa would let him bellyache and then she'd make him laugh and nothing would seem quite as bad as it had before. Maybe she'd even give him some good advice about how to handle this whole thing with Olivia.

On the third ring a squeaky voice answered. "Wobinson Wesidence."

"Hey, munchkin, it's Uncle Reed. Is your mommy home?"

"Uncky Weed! Hi! I'll get Mom."

The phone clattered in Reed's ear. He smiled. Ali was in kindergarten, but she still bore the tail end of a speech impediment that Reed privately hoped she wouldn't outgrow for a good long while.

He hadn't had a munchkin fix in a few months. He needed to take some time off and go see his niece and nephew. But it was a five-hour trip one way and it was getting harder to find a good time to visit now that Ali and Mason were in school.

"Hey, bro!" Alissa's cheery voice came on the line. "What's up?"

"Oh, nothing… I just hadn't talked to you for a few days. Thought I'd call…"

"Oooh-kay." Alissa drew out the word and a thick thread of suspicion crept into her voice. "Let's try that again. Hey, bro. What's up?"

He sighed heavily into the phone. He never could get anything by his big sister.

"Reed Vincent, if I didn't know better, I'd think that sigh was a sign of girl trouble."

How did she *do* that? The woman could practically read his mind.

"Well… *Is* it?" He could almost see her wide eyes and surprised expression. "Reed?"

He grinned into the phone, feeling better already. "Man! Don't bother making small talk before you cut to the chase."

"Aha! It *is* a girl. I knew it!"

"Um…at my age, I think they're referred to as women, but yes, I guess I've got woman trouble."

Alissa's squeal of delight made him hold the phone at arm's length. His sister had tried to hook him up with a parade of her friends ever since he and Kristina had broken up. He'd only taken her up on her long-distance matchmaking services once and that had been a disaster of epic proportions.

He put the receiver back to his ear.

"…so tell me, tell me," Alissa was saying. "What's the scoop?"

"I don't know if there is a scoop. I met someone."

"And…?" He could almost see her jumping up and down.

"Well, I like her. A lot."

Another squeal. "So tell me about her. What's she like? Have you asked her out? What's her name?"

Reed laughed. "Lissa, Lissa, one at a time. It's Olivia. You know, my assistant. She's gorgeous. She's an artist—well, a decorator, really. She's incredible…."

"But you told me her husband just died a few months ago."

"He did—and she…she found out she's pregnant with their baby. That's the woman trouble. How can I ask out a woman under those circumstances?"

That managed to leave Alissa utterly speechless.

He didn't blame her. Laying the truth out like that had shocked him a little, too. And made him sound mildly insane.

Finally his sister found her tongue. "Um…you want to run that by me one more time?"

"See? Now you understand my problem."

"Reed. Are you serious? She's *pregnant?* What have you gotten yourself into?"

He pulled out a bar stool and perched on it, resting his elbows on the counter. This was going to take a while.

"Working together, we've gotten to know each other really well. She's…she's someone special."

"I figured that."

"What? How did you know?"

"Reed, she's all you've talked about the last few times I've called."

He hadn't realized. "Oh. Well…I like her, Lissa. A lot. I don't know how to describe it. There's just something about her that—"

"Reed, I don't want to sound skeptical, and granted, I don't know Olivia yet, but… How can you be sure she's not just using you?"

"Why do you say that?"

"Think about it, Reed. She's a single, pregnant woman. You're a rich and famous artist."

"I'm not famous."

"Whatever. It just makes me very nervous."

"Oh, it's not like that. Not at all. She didn't even know I had feelings for her until today. And she was uncomfortable with it."

"Oh."

"That's why I called you." He slid a notepad from the end of the counter and started doodling. "I think I might have scared her off."

"How pregnant is she?" Alissa was still in skeptical-big-sister mode.

"She just found out a few weeks ago. I think she's due in November."

"Good grief, Reed. Her husband couldn't have died too long ago. Unless—"

"He died this spring," he interrupted, "March, I think."

"March? Reed. She's not ready to start seeing someone else."

"I know that. I know… But she needs help. Her husband didn't leave her with much of anything, and she's got a big mortgage and now a baby on the way…."

Alissa's sigh whooshed in his ear. "I think you're getting way too involved. Even if you do like her, you've got to give her time, Reed. She needs to grieve. And figure out what she wants to do. Doesn't she have family to help out?"

"Not that she's close to. She just moved here from Chicago. Her husband had just started working here in the Falls when he was killed."

"Well, she may not even stay around then. Reed, don't get too involved. She'll probably go back to Chicago."

"I don't think so. She doesn't really have anything to go back to. And I told her I'd hire her full-time. She's a little desperate for a job under the circumstances." He pressed the pen harder to the paper, retracing the abstract lines he'd sketched.

"Reed. Listen to yourself. She's desperate? Even if she's not taking you for a ride, it's just too soon. She can't possibly be ready to have someone else in her life."

"I know that, Lissa. We're just friends right now." He could have kicked himself for even bringing it up with his sister. But what really irked him was the fact that she was right. It was too soon for Olivia to entertain the idea of him being anything more than a friend. He kneaded his temples. After today, he'd be lucky if she could even think of him as an employer. Why did he always rush ahead without thinking things through?

Without consulting the Lord.

The words stunned him. That was the real problem, of course. It was exactly what he'd done with Kristina. He saw something he liked and he went after it. Never mind that he hadn't whispered so much as a prayer about it. Let alone cracked his Bible in search of guidance.

"Reed? Are you there?"

He sighed. "Yeah. I'm here. You're right, sis. As always. I'll give it some time. Pray for me, would you?"

"I always do."

"And tell Mick hi."

"I will. I love you."

"You, too, Lissa."

"Be good." He heard the worry in her voice and wished he could relieve it.

But he didn't want to make promises he couldn't keep.

Chapter Twenty

Olivia slipped on her sandals and headed down the driveway to the mailbox. She hadn't checked it in several days. The only thing she ever got were bills. And Derek's mail. Nearly four months after his death, it still startled her to see Derek's name boldly printed on a magazine or credit card offer. As though he were still a part of this world. Sometimes she thought he was. His presence had seemed to hover awfully close yesterday afternoon in the woods with Reed.

Shaking off the thought, she pulled down the arched door and slid out the bundle of mail. Three bundles actually, each neatly secured with a wide rubber band. She removed a band and thumbed through the first batch as she walked back up to the house. Nothing worth saving. She deposited the stack in the trash bin in the garage.

Before closing the garage door, she checked for Tiger. The little cat had become a permanent fixture in her backyard. Usually he greeted her at the garage door the minute she pulled into the drive, but she hadn't seen him today. He'd probably be meowing at the back door as soon as she sat down to eat.

She went in through the kitchen and plopped down at the table. She slit an envelope and pulled out a hefty electric bill and another containing a late notice for the trash and sewer service. She filed the bills in Derek's desk. She needed to sit down later tonight and pay them. But she dreaded the job. It was depressing to see how fast her funds were dwindling.

She stripped the rubber band off the last bunch of mail and leafed through the catalogs and envelopes, culling the first-class mail out of the pile for the trash. The return address on a plain white envelope caught her attention. It was from Mid-America Transplant Services. She slipped a fingernail beneath the glued flap and ripped it open. Inside was another smaller white envelope. The front was blank, but the envelope was sealed.

She stared at it for a long minute before opening it. She knew what it contained even before she opened it.

She took out a single sheet of lined paper and read the words penned in bold letters.

Dear donor family,

First, let me say how deeply sorry I am for your loss. You will never know how much your loved one's gift of life has meant to me.

It's difficult to write this, knowing that you are grieving a terrible loss, while for the first time in a long time, I have hope. I'll never understand the unfairness of it, and can only pray that you find some small comfort in knowing that your loved one's decision to be an organ donor gave another man a new chance at life.

This quote by Albert Schweitzer that I found in some of the literature from the Mid-America Transplant Services seemed as if it was written for me:

"Sometimes our light goes out, but is blown into flame by another human being. Each of us owes deepest thanks to those who have rekindled this light."

You see, I have my eyesight back because of your loved one's donation.

As I read back over this note, I'm tempted to tear it up and start over. My words seem so inadequate. But I don't think another attempt to say what's in my heart will make

any difference. All I can say is a very simple, humble thank-you. May God bless you and comfort you.
Sincerely,
A grateful man

Below that, the note was signed only with initials—a flourish that looked like *REN* or *REV*.

Olivia spread out the creased page on the table and read it again. She'd never considered that she might receive a thank-you note from one of the recipients of Derek's organs. Her breath caught as the crushing emotions of that time came roaring back. What a horrible, agonizing decision it had been. And yet, she'd received some comfort in the knowledge that some measure of good would come from the tragedy. Knowing that it had been Derek's wish to donate his organs, she'd felt a sense of purpose in making the difficult decision. Rereading the letter now, her breathing steadied and she felt comforted all over again. It had been the right thing to do. She felt sure of that now.

She wondered about the man who had written the note. She picked up the page and looked at the signature again. *REV?* Did that mean reverend? Was he a pastor, or was Rev—or Ren—a nickname of some sort? She remembered the doctor in the hospital telling her that the whole process would be anonymous. It was probably just a made-up name, or maybe the letters were purposely obscured so she couldn't make the signature out.

Still, she found herself wondering who this man was that had taken the time to let her know that his life had been changed because of Derek's death. She skimmed the page. It said he had his eyesight back because of Derek. Strange. She'd envisioned someone receiving Derek's heart and liver and kidneys—the main organs—but she'd never considered that someone had gotten his eyes—the corneas, she assumed.

It was a little morbid to think about. The recipient must have meant he'd undergone a corneal transplant. Did that mean they'd actually taken Derek's eyes? She shivered at the thought.

Derek had been gone for four months now. In that time, she hadn't once considered the people—real men, and likely some women, as well—who had been recipients of his organs. She'd been too busy grieving his death, and coming to terms with her pregnancy. Just trying to get by.

Now it jolted her to know that somewhere out there someone was probably walking around with Derek's heart beating in his chest, someone—maybe two someones—had his kidneys and his liver and… Who knew what else they transplanted these days. It was eerie to consider, and yet it made her glad to know that something good had come out of his death.

Somewhere, a man had his sight back, simply because she had signed on the dotted line that night, according to Derek's wishes.

She folded the letter and slid it back in the envelope. Would she be receiving more notes like this in the days to come? Or would this be the only one? If she had been the one to regain her sight—or her life—because of a stranger's generosity, would she have written to say thank-you?

It wasn't an easy question. She'd always found it difficult to know what to say to the bereaved. Always afraid that mentioning the loved one's name would stir up grief anew. It was a foolish presumption. As if there were any way she could forget about Derek now.

Especially when she had the reminder that was growing more insistent every day. She placed a hand lightly across her belly, something she did almost unconsciously many times a day. This morning, lying in bed, she'd thought she felt the baby move. *The baby.*

She gripped the envelope tightly. Maybe someday, she would show it to her son or daughter and tell them their daddy had been a good man.

Unbidden, Rachel Wyck's face loomed in her mind's eye. The woman Derek had cheated on her with. She tried to shake the image from her head. Why couldn't she get over that? Derek had asked her forgiveness. He'd tried to make things right with her and with Rachel. Slowly, their marriage was healing. *Had been* healing. She corrected the tense.

Was she living in a fantasy world, wishing things had been different than they were? Did it count if your husband asked forgiveness, then died before you had time to rebuild your life together?

She didn't know. She'd had such hopes for them. Hopes that someday they could put all the ugliness behind them, even laugh at what they'd been through. But now, sometimes she wasn't even sure she'd forgiven Derek. If she had, why did she still sometimes rehash the terrible arguments they'd had because of his affair?

Dropping her head in her hands, she scrunched fistfuls of hair between her fingers, tugging at the roots. The physical pain almost felt good—dulling the pain in her heart.

She stared at the envelope on the table. It seemed to be silently demanding something of her. Something she wasn't yet ready to face.

Squeezing back the tears, she pushed her chair away from the table and scooped up the letter. She walked to Derek's desk and stuffed the envelope beneath a stack of insurance documents.

Chapter Twenty-One

The wood floors felt like concrete beneath Reed's bare feet as he paced back and forth in front of the studio windows, one ear tuned to the doorbell.

He wondered how Olivia would be with him today. Or if she'd even come to work. Even though it had gotten him into trouble in the first place, he'd decided that one last time he was going to speak his mind. That had to be better than leaving things unsaid between them. He thought it would help her to know where he stood, but if he were honest, he was doing it as much for himself as for her.

He turned to stare at the canvas propped on the easel. If the sorry excuse for a painting that sat there now was any indication of how this whole incident was going to affect him, he was in trouble. He'd promised Olivia that she could have a job with him, and he would keep that promise. He would have no trouble keeping her busy. But they had to clear the air first or he wouldn't have a job to offer her.

He heard the doorbell chime. She'd had her own key to let herself in for several weeks now, but she always gave him a warning ring before coming in. His heartbeat quickened when he heard her shoes on the kitchen tiles. He shot up a prayer. *Lord, please give me the right words to smooth things over.*

She appeared in the doorway a few seconds later. "Good morning." She didn't meet his eyes.

"Hi, Olivia."

"You want me to finish those frames?" Her tone was tentative.

"Yes, but…can we talk first?"

She nodded and leaned against the worktable, her arms folded protectively across her midsection.

He went back to the easel and picked up a paintbrush. He was too nervous to use it, but it felt better to have the canvas as a barrier between them. "I just want to apologize again about…about Friday."

She held up a hand as if to stop him, but he plowed ahead.

"Olivia, I just want you to know that I realize how foolish it was for me to say those things to you. I don't know what I was thinking." He dipped his head. "Well, yes, I do know." He looked up with a guilty grin. "But I did not need to say everything I was thinking. I realize that it's way too soon for you to think about… being with someone else. I respect that and I just want you to know that you don't have to worry about me. I promise I'll be a perfect gentleman."

He couldn't read her face as she waited for him to go on, but he plunged back in. "Things are going really well for me right now and I can use all the help you can give me. If you can give me full-time hours, I'll have no trouble finding work for you, and as I said, you have a raise coming on this next paycheck."

Eyes downcast, she whispered his name. "Reed…I…"

Reed swallowed hard, waiting for her to look at him.

She lifted her head and met his gaze. "Thank you. I…I appreciate it. I think, though, before you make too much of an investment in me—in me working here," she added hastily, "you should know that I'm not sure I'll stay in the Falls after…after the baby."

So Alissa was right. "I understand," he said. "Let's just take it one day at a time, can we?"

She waited wordlessly.

"Right now, I need your help and you need a job. Can we just both be grateful for that?"

She nodded. "Thank you," she said again.

The knots in his shoulders relaxed for the first time since Friday. *Thank You, Lord.* He reached out to adjust a clamp on the canvas. "Okay then. Let's get to work."

Her smile conveyed her own relief.

The queue at the pharmacy was only three people long and Olivia gave a sigh of relief. Small-town life had its perks.

When it was her turn, she handed the prescription slip to the teenage girl behind the counter.

The teen glanced at the slip, then at Olivia. "Congratulations. When are you due?"

"This fall…November," she stammered, taken aback by the girl's straightforward question.

"Oh, my sister's due then, too. November 15. You morning sick, too? My sister's sicker than a dog."

Olivia was aware that the ears of every customer in the tiny combination gift shop-pharmacy were tuned in to their conversation. "I'm fine," Olivia said. "Um…how long do you think it will take to fill this prescription?"

"Oh, it's just vitamins. Don't even have to count 'em. I'll get them." She disappeared into the maze of shelves behind the counter.

Could teenagers dispense medicine? Olivia smiled an apology at the elderly woman in line behind her.

"A little one on the way, huh?" The woman beamed at her. "That's exciting. Is this your first?"

She nodded. She should have figured out by now that a smile was an invitation to conversation in this little town.

"My Ernie and me—we raised six children. People don't cotton to big families these days, but we would've had six more if I hadn't had to have the surgery." She leaned in with a stage whisper. "Female surgery, you know."

Olivia squirmed and nodded again. She craned her neck, praying that the girl who was supposed to be filling her prescription would reappear.

"Is your husband excited? I know my Ernie was just beside himself every time I told him I was in a family way." The woman waited for an answer with a sweet smile on her face.

Olivia grasped for a reply. "My husband…passed away."

The woman gasped and a frail, blue-veined hand flew to her throat. "Oh, you poor thing! What happened?"

"An accident. He was killed…in an accident." She cleared her throat and shuffled her feet on the worn carpet in front of the checkout. The woman probably meant well, but Olivia would have been happy for a trapdoor to open in the floor about now.

"Here you go, ma'am." Ah, the next best thing. The girl handed a red-and-white striped package over the counter. "The pharmacist will be here in just a minute to speak with you and answer any questions."

"Thank you. That's okay. How much do I owe you?"

The girl punched in the amount. Olivia paid cash and a sixties-style cash register spit out a receipt.

Fortunately, when she turned to leave, the elderly woman was gossiping with another woman in line. Olivia ducked into the greeting card aisle and made a beeline for the door.

Back home, Tiger was waiting for her in front of the garage. Olivia watched in her rearview mirror as he followed the car inside. The minute she opened her door the cat jumped up on her lap, purring and nudging at Olivia's chin.

"Stop that, you silly cat." She giggled as his whiskers tickled her neck. "Let's go get you something to eat. Is that it? Are you hungry?"

She was tempted to let the cat inside. As Mr. Burnside had said, Tiger had practically adopted her. But judging by the feline's slick coat and plump belly, she suspected someone else was feeding him and she didn't want to kidnap him. Or catnap him, as the case may be. She snickered again at her own silly joke.

She stroked the cat's soft fur, then scooped him up and took him to the back patio where his dish was. She took her things inside and came back with a scoopful of Cat Chow. She'd been feeding Tiger table scraps—her leftovers—but after doing a little research at the library one day last week, she discovered human food probably wasn't good for him, so she'd picked up a bag of cat food at the grocery. It hadn't been as expensive as she'd expected, but Tiger was going through it at a pretty good clip.

Still, she understood now why studies showed that cat owners managed stress better and had lower blood pressure and all the other benefits she'd seen touted. The little cat had become a real bright spot in her life. She had to admit she would be disappointed if Tiger turned out to belong to someone else. But she couldn't afford to take him to the vet. Besides, she didn't even know how long she'd stay in Missouri.

She had a lot of decisions to make in the next few months. She'd settled the decision to have the baby. There had never been any other possibility for her. But although she'd begun to accept that there was a baby growing inside her, she was no closer to making a decision about that child's future than she had been the day she'd discovered she was pregnant.

"Hey there, neighbor!" Mr. Burnside from next door hobbled across the lawn.

She waved and went to meet him halfway. "Hi, Mr. Burnside. How have you been?"

"Oh, I don't have any complaints. Well, now, I take that back. I have one complaint."

"Oh, what's that?" She enjoyed her visits with the old man, even if he could be a little crotchety at times.

"That dad-blamed cat of yours has taken to yowling under my window again."

"Oh, he's not my cat," she said, then quickly added, "I'm sorry he's been bothering you. Maybe I should put an ad in the paper…to see if we can find out who he belongs to."

"Well, *you* may not think he's yours, but I think he has different ideas." He glanced pointedly past her.

She turned to see Tiger, contentedly licking his paws over an empty bowl. She grinned guiltily. "He was looking a little scrawny. I thought he needed a little extra food…"

Mr. Burnside harrumphed, but Olivia thought she detected a hint of a smile behind his rheumy eyes.

"Well, if you're going to keep the animal, you're going to have to do something about his prowling."

She sighed and shook her head. "I really can't afford to keep him, but—"

"Well, I can't miss much more of my beauty sleep." Mr. Burnside screwed up his face and closed one eye in a comical wink. She smiled another apology and made an excuse to go in the house.

She flipped on the kitchen lights and looked around the house, trying to use a critical eye. Except for the plants and a few things she'd brought from Chicago, the house looked virtually the way it had that day she'd first walked through the back door. Derek had arranged the furniture in neat lines against the walls, and centered the rugs on the floors, but the knickknacks and paintings were still in boxes in the bedrooms and the coat closet in the hallway.

With a sudden burst of energy, she decided that tonight she would begin to unpack and try to make the house look like a home. Even if she decided to go back to Chicago, she would need to sell the house. In her business, she knew all too well that most people had trouble seeing the potential of an empty shell of a house. A beautifully appointed, lived-in home sold far more quickly.

She brushed off her hands and went to the broom closet for her tool kit. Her first project would be to hang her painting in the foyer. In spite of her intentions to hang it in a place of honor as soon as she moved, after Derek's death, she had lost all desire to try to make this place a home. The painting had languished against the back wall of the walk-in closet in their bedroom—*her* bedroom now. She went and got the painting and held it against two different walls in the airy foyer, leaning back as far as she could to gauge the effect. The sun had almost gone down outside the windows, but remembering how the light played off the west wall in the mornings, she decided that was the best spot.

She worked for twenty minutes tightening the canvas where it had buckled. Then she measured down from the ceiling and across the breadth of the wall and pounded a nail through the picture hanger, anchoring it in place. She hung the picture and stepped back to view her handiwork.

It looked good. But then, she thought of Derek's comments about the painting, and a surge of defiance straightened her pos-

ture. Just as quickly her shoulders slumped. She had no reason
to defend her right to hang her painting in a place of prominence.
Derek was no longer here to defy. A wave of sadness tinged with
guilt swept over her.

She stared at the painting. Slowly, her pastoral scene with its
open sky, rolling pastureland and pond and languid cows grazing,
started to soothe her as it always had. She could almost feel her
blood pressure drop and the tension in her muscles ease. She had
work to do.

She couldn't invest any real money in fixing up this house,
but a lot could be accomplished using the things they'd brought
with them from Chicago.

Unsuccessfully, she tried to picture their town house in the
city, to disassemble the rooms in her mind and see what decorative items might work in this house. She'd just have to unpack
some boxes and see what was there. She rubbed her hands together and tackled the first box, taking inventory of what she had
to work with. Maybe she could weed through their belongings
and put together enough castoffs for a garage sale. In their lean
newlywed years, that had always been one way she could come
up with a little extra cash.

She could sell some of the art they'd collected, too. She'd
always told Derek it was like a small insurance policy. She
wasn't sure if it would even bring what they'd paid for it now.
But that would be a last resort.

One by one, she unpacked boxes and tried out artwork and
linens and decorative items in the various rooms. Though money
had been tight, she and Derek had collected a few nice things.
Each object seemed to have a memory attached to it—the vintage
Shaker basket they'd found for a quarter at a garage sale, the delft
candlesticks he'd bought for her on the Riverwalk in San
Antonio. She found herself in tears several times after pulling
some memory from a pasteboard box. But it was a blessing to
be reminded that they *had* had some good times together. Their
marriage hadn't been all conflict and betrayal.

She found a half-empty bucket of saffron paint left in the garage by the former owners, and on a whim, she painted one wall

at the end of the dining area. Her excitement grew with each successful rearrangement of furniture, and each pleasing tabletop vignette she composed. For the first time in weeks, she felt the passion, the exhilaration she always felt when she used her gift for design.

She worked until after midnight and fell into bed in a satisfied state of fatigue.

When she woke up the next morning the first thing that greeted her blurry eyes was the cheery arrangement of books and candlesticks and clunky old costume jewelry she'd arranged atop a linen scarf on the oak dresser. Amazing how a few simple items could give her so much joy. "Thank You, Lord," she whispered.

She climbed out of bed and headed for the bathroom, whistling. She ate her bagel and coffee at the dining-room table, delighted with how her freshly painted golden wall reflected the morning sun. It made a worthy backdrop for the framed print she and Derek had spent half a month's salary on in a gallery along the Mag Mile one Saturday morning. Never mind that it might soon have to be sold to make a house payment. She really should get in touch with the Realtor and see about listing the house. She shook off the thought. Not today, when this house was finally starting to feel a little like home.

Why hadn't she wrought her homey touches on the house weeks ago? She ripped off a bite of bagel. No, that was a foolish thought. She'd been in the throes of grief then. She could no more have thought about decorating this house then, than she could think of kissing Reed Vincent now.

She sucked in a breath. Where had *that* come from? And why was she sitting in the privacy of her own kitchen blushing?

Olivia took a swig of coffee, stuffed the discomfiting thoughts of Reed in a hidden recess of her mind, and shook her head, as if the physical action might clear the muddled slate of her brain.

She fiddled for a minute with a simple floral centerpiece she'd left unfinished last night, then cleared her dishes off the table. Tiger would be waiting by the back door, meowing for his breakfast. She gathered her things for work, along with the bag of cat food, and went out the back door.

Tiger was nowhere in sight, but usually a gentle shake of the bag brought him running. She filled his dish and freshened his water bowl, but still no cat.

"Here kitty, kitty…" She tiptoed through the dewy grass behind the garage, calling for him. The backyard was empty. Yesterday morning, Tiger had presented her with a dead ground squirrel that was almost as big as he was. Maybe he'd given up on her and decided to hunt down a mouse for breakfast.

She checked her watch. It was almost nine-thirty. She couldn't wait around for a silly cat. She rolled down the top of the bag of cat food and put it away in the back entryway, locking the door behind her.

Next door, Mr. Burnside's garage door rolled open and Olivia watched his old Plymouth turn into his driveway. He was out and about early. He tooted his horn at her and waved his arms broadly over the steering wheel. Did he want something?

She walked over to the fence that separated their yards and waited for him to crawl out from behind the wheel.

"Good morning." She smiled, and gave him a questioning glance. "You're up early."

He reached out and put a veined hand on the side of his vehicle to steady himself. "Wanted to take care of our little problem right away," he said, opening the back door and pulling an empty cardboard box from the seat.

"Oh?" She had no idea what he was talking about.

"That cat. He yowled half the night again." He scowled and flapped the upside-down box, as if emptying it of something vile. "I saw him waiting by your back door when I went out to get the paper this morning and figured I'd nab him while I could."

Olivia held her breath, managing to push a strangled "Oh?" through her lips.

"Good thing the pound opens early. They took him right in."

Her breath hitched. "You…you took him to the pound?"

"The Humane Society, actually. I figured if anybody's looking for him, that's where they'd go first." Mr. Burnside looked so proud of himself she wanted to smack him. He'd taken Tiger to the pound? Olivia could only stare, speechless.

The old man cocked his head, studying her. "You did say you couldn't keep him, right?"

"Well, I did, but… Yes. I did." She was afraid to say anything else. She turned quickly, mumbling over her shoulder. "I need to get to work."

Chapter Twenty-Two

Olivia crawled into her car and lurched down the driveway in Reverse, a sudden fury fueling her. How could he? Tiger wasn't his to dump at the pound. And he'd taken the cat before he even had anything to eat that morning. She gripped the steering wheel and gnawed at the corner of her bottom lip. She should have given the man a piece of her mind. How could he be so cruel? He hadn't even asked her!

Wait a minute, Liv. She talked herself through another wave of fury. Mr. Burnside *had* asked her if she intended to keep Tiger. Just last night he'd let her know that the cat was still causing him trouble.

She pounded the steering wheel with the flat of her palm. But she didn't know he was talking about taking the cat to the pound! He'd never said that!

The tears came and she permitted herself a good cry all the way to Reed's house. By the time she turned on to Reed's street, she was beginning to come to her senses. As much as she'd enjoyed having Tiger around, maybe it was for the best that Mr. Burnside had taken him away. And he'd said it was the Humane Society he'd taken Tiger to, not the city pound. They didn't destroy animals there, did they? At least not right away. Maybe someone would claim Tiger.

Tears pooled behind her eyelids, but she tried to listen to her practical side. She had no business spending money on cat food. And if she had taken responsibility for Tiger, she would have had to pay for his shots and the vet bills. Already the expenses had added up to more than she'd expected.

Still, the little cat had been one of the few bright spots in her life. She'd come to look forward to seeing him at the end of a long day at the studio. It might not make sense to a financial planner, but as far as she was concerned, Tiger was worth every penny she'd spent on him.

She didn't dare think too long about what would happen to him if no one claimed him in a few days.

She parked in front of Reed's house and dried her tears, checking her makeup in the rearview mirror before getting out of the car.

A gray cat darted through the yard across the street. Olivia pictured Tiger, caged and meowing pathetically at the pound, and the tears started afresh. Poor little kitten.

She forced the tremor from her voice and let herself in. But her falsely cheery "good morning" to Reed didn't fool him.

He looked up and studied her for a minute, concern in his knit brows. "Olivia? Is everything all right?"

She waved him away. "It's nothing."

"Well, it doesn't look like nothing. What's wrong?"

She hurried to the worktable and turned her back to him, wishing she could just go home and have a good cry.

"You want to talk about it?"

She took a deep breath. "You'd just laugh."

"What? Why would I laugh?"

"Because…" Her voice came out in a broken sob that made her laugh at herself in spite of the genuine ache in her heart. She whirled to face him. "Because I'm crying about a stupid cat."

He dropped his paintbrush into a jar of turpentine and leaned back on his stool. "Tiger?"

She nodded. "My busybody neighbor took him to the pound last night."

"Why?"

The tears were close again and she bit her lip, willing her voice to remain steady. "He was crying under the window at night and—"

"Your neighbor was crying under the window?"

The quirk of Reed's mouth told her he was only trying to inject some levity in the situation. It was apparently working, as she found a smile tugging at her lips.

"No, silly. Tiger. He meows at night and it keeps Mr. Burnside awake. So he took Tiger to the pound."

Reed's eyes flashed. "Well, that was a low-down, dirty-rotten thing to do. He didn't even ask?"

Olivia couldn't help but giggle at the incensed pitch of his voice.

"It wasn't his fault, really. I made the mistake of telling him I couldn't keep the cat. Nobody else claimed him, so…" She shrugged. "He took him to the Humane Society. I'm sure he was just trying to help."

Reed's harrumph reminded her of Mr. Burnside's reaction when she'd told him she thought Tiger looked a little scrawny.

"But why *can't* you keep him?"

"I couldn't afford the shots he'd need…and I'd have to get him neutered. And cat food and kitty litter aren't exactly cheap."

"Kitty litter? You mean he'd be a house cat?"

She shook her head. "Well, if I could keep him, he would."

"Well, then, you wouldn't have to worry about him bothering your neighbor…if he was inside."

"It doesn't matter, Reed." Her voice rose. "I can't keep him. I don't even know if I'll be—" She stopped short. Reed didn't need to know that she was still entertaining the idea of moving back to Chicago.

"But you'd keep Tiger if you could?"

She shrugged, then nodded vigorously. The tears started again. It didn't help that Reed was being so sweet about it. She swallowed the lump in her throat. "I thought you didn't like cats."

He grinned. "I don't. But I like *you*. I'm sorry, Liv. Do you want to just…go home for the day?"

"No… No." She turned away, strangely touched by his use of

the nickname no one had called her by since childhood. She opened the file drawer and found the inventory sheets she'd been working on yesterday. She was being ridiculous, crying over a dumb cat. "I'm fine," she told him, when she had control of her voice.

Reed was quiet the rest of the morning, but Olivia sensed his eyes on her several times, and she felt all the more foolish for making such a scene. She went out for sandwiches at the deli down the street and brought them back to the studio. Reed was in the middle of a painting, so they worked while they ate, making small talk. Reed didn't bring up the subject of Tiger again, but Olivia thought about the kitten several times throughout the day and hoped he wasn't too scared and lonely at the shelter. She comforted herself by imagining that Tiger was making all kinds of new feline friends.

Reed left the studio around four to run some errands. He wasn't back at five, so she cleaned up the studio and locked up his house behind her. She drove home, wishing she'd kept her mouth shut, and her tears to herself.

Chapter Twenty-Three

Olivia dreaded going to her empty house and all the reminders that Tiger was gone—the empty yard, Tiger's food and water bowls and the catnip toys she'd bought for him. She drove downtown, hoping to pick up a few things at the tiny office supply store, but it was already closed. She still wasn't used to this town that closed down before sunset. She wasn't hungry, but decided she ought to eat for the baby's sake. She drove out to the diner on the edge of town and ordered a salad at the drive-through window. She'd only been inside the diner once since that awful night she'd gone there trying to find Derek. But Reed had sent her there to pick up burgers for their lunch one day. Of course he'd had no way of knowing the traumatic memories the diner held for her. And she'd never told him.

A few weeks ago the owner had installed a drive-through window and a big neon sign out front. The restaurant held a big grand opening and sent coupons to all the businesses in town, including Reed's studio. They'd used the drive-through for lunch there several times since. It didn't even seem like the same place to her now. In fact, the diner held some rather enjoyable memories now.

She thought about taking her food to the park to eat. Anything to put off going home tonight. Funny how all her cozy decorating touches couldn't make up for the fact that her little feline buddy was gone and the house seemed empty again. But eventually, she'd have to face putting away the things that reminded her of Tiger. She briefly entertained the thought of getting another kitten. But right now it would be foolish. Her money would best be spent on trying to get the house ready to sell.

She tried to get psyched about finishing the decorating projects she'd dived into last night. If the house was going to sell, she needed to get things spruced up. And it would be something to occupy her mind. But her enthusiasm from last night had waned. Sighing, she turned the car toward home.

As she rounded the corner onto Glenwillow Road, she was surprised to see Reed's Escape in her driveway. What was he doing there?

She pulled in the drive, but Reed wasn't in the car, nor was he up on the front porch. Curious, she parked beside his vehicle and got out, calling his name. No answer.

Strange. Why would he leave his car at her place? She got back in and pulled into the garage. Seeing Reed's car in her drive had almost made her forget about Tiger, but when she got out of the car and no kitten came running, a dull ache settled in her throat.

She opened the side door from the garage and stopped short. Reed sat on the lone chair on the patio. Tiger lounged contentedly in his lap.

"What in the world…?" A bubble of joy rose inside her.

When the cat saw her, his ears pricked and he gave a short, squeaky meow.

"Hi." Reed grinned like the proverbial Cheshire cat and ran a tanned hand down Tiger's back. The kitten arched his spine to meet the caress, his purr so loud Olivia half feared Mr. Burnside would hear him and come to take him away again.

"What is going on?"

He shrugged. "Tiger just found his way back home."

"But…how? I don't understand." An incredible lightness came over her, and she felt a slow grin spread over her face.

"Did you know the Humane Society has cats?"

Olivia crossed her arms, deciding to play along, and loving it. "You're kidding? They have animals there?"

Reed nodded, acting very proud of himself. "But only on Thursdays. They had dogs, too, but I thought, nah, this little guy looks just about perfect for Olivia Cline."

Buoyant, Olivia hurried over and reached to take the cat from him. Reed lifted Tiger up and placed him in her arms.

"Had to pay twenty-five dollars to get the stupid thing back," Reed said, letting the act slip. Even as he called Tiger "stupid" he gave him a good scratching behind the ears. "But that included shots and…well, you know… So there won't be a bunch of little Tigers running around your neighborhood. You might want to be careful not to squeeze him too tight for a few days."

She laughed and held Tiger closer anyway. "Hey, buddy." The cat purred louder, if it were possible, and flicked his sandpaper tongue under her chin. "Did you miss me, little guy?" She talked baby talk to him and willed herself not to cry again. Reed had to be sick to death of her tears.

After a minute, Tiger wriggled out of her arms and jumped onto the patio, then sauntered over to his food bowls as if he'd never been gone. Olivia watched him for a minute before noticing the supply of food and kitty litter stacked by the back door. Two huge bags of cat food and two large plastic containers of kitty litter.

She studied Reed. "What's all this?"

Reed's mouth quirked in feigned innocence. "Oh. That. The Humane Society was giving that away today. Free food and kitty litter with every cat."

Olivia raised a brow. "But only on Thursdays, right?"

The smile he gave her then melted whatever semblance of resolve she had left. "Oh, also…I hate to separate you two so soon again, but I'll be picking Tiger up early in the morning. He has an appointment at the vet…just to have him checked over."

"Oh, but, Reed…" Her joy deflated a little. "I can't afford to take him to the vet."

"Nothing to afford," he said, shaking his head. "It's all taken care of. I'll drop him off in the morning and you can pick him up after work. They said he'd be done by then, unless you want to have him declawed, too. But…I bought a scratching post." He motioned in the direction of the driveway. "It's still in my car."

"But… You can't—"

"Olivia, please." He held up a hand. "The bill's already been paid. I *want* to do this. You obviously love this cat and if the only thing standing between him and the pound is a few dollars' worth of vet bills, then please let me take care of it. Call it an employee benefit."

She gave him a wide grin in spite of herself.

"Besides," he said, "if the work you did today is any example of what you're like sans kitten, then it's to my advantage that you have Tiger back."

"Hey!" She swatted at him, laughing. "I wasn't that bad, was I?" She knew the answer before his frown confirmed it. "Oh, but I'm so happy to have him back!" She scooped Tiger up again and snuggled him to her neck, joy flooding through her.

Reed unfolded himself lazily from the chair. "Well, I'll leave you two to get reacquainted." He scooted the chair back in place and started around the house toward his car.

Olivia set the cat down and caught up with him, laying a hand on his arm. "Thank you so much, Reed." Impulsively, she gave him a quick hug. "That's the sweetest thing anyone has ever done for me."

He returned her hug, patting her back lightly. But then he backed away, dipping his head and mumbling something about getting the scratching post out of his car.

She looked away and folded her arms. She probably shouldn't have hugged him—especially after his confession the other day. But it had been an honest reaction to his gift of redeeming the kitten and nothing could quell her joy over having Tiger back.

She followed Reed around the side of the house. "Here, I'll come with you and carry the scratching post." Thinking about what had just happened, Olivia couldn't suppress the peal of laughter that bubbled up. She clapped her hands together like a little girl on Christmas morning, and practically skipped the short distance to where the Escape was parked.

Reed smiled and shook his head as if to say "you crazy woman." But she didn't care. She was elated over Tiger's return—and if she were honest, about seeing Reed here—and she wasn't going to spoil the evening worrying about what he thought of her.

He opened the back hatch of the Escape and lifted out a tall, carpet-covered scratching post with a platform on top.

"Oh, he'll love napping up there. Here…I can carry it," Olivia said, trying to take the unwieldy post from him.

Reed ignored her protests. "I've got it," he said. "It's heavy. Besides, I need to carry that kitty litter in for you. That stuff weighs a ton."

She hurried ahead to unlock the back door for him, and made a quick decision to place the scratching post by the dining-room window. "He'll love watching out the window."

Reed made sure the post was steady on the hardwood floor, then went back for the other things.

He reappeared a minute later, lugging a heavy pail in each hand. "Where do you want these?"

"Oh…probably in the laundry room. Here…" She led him to the tiny room on the other side of the kitchen.

"Nice place," he said behind her. "You get good light in here even this late."

"It is nice, isn't it? It was a little scary buying it sight unseen."

"You did that?"

"Well, Derek had seen it before we made an offer, but I didn't see it until—" She backtracked, brushing away the memory of that first night she'd seen the house. And the reminder that she may soon be trying to sell this house. "Well, anyway, I do like it…"

She motioned for him to set the containers down beside the washing machine.

"Here," she said, leading the way through the hall and out to the living room. "You don't have to go all the way around. The front door is closer."

Reed wandered slowly through the room, looking around as he went. "I like what you've done in here. I forgot you'd said you were a decorator. That's very obvious seeing this place."

"It's funny you should say that. Until last night, I really hadn't done much at all. But I figured if I'm going to sell the place, I ought to make it look presentable."

He seemed taken aback. "Are you? Going to put it on the market, I mean?"

"Well, not right away, I guess, but I really don't see how I can afford to keep it. You can't give me *that* big of a raise. Not and still eat." She laughed nervously.

"It would be too bad to have to move from here."

She shrugged, uncomfortable with where the conversation was taking them.

Reed seemed to sense that she wanted to change the subject. He wandered into the living room, looking at the framed prints she'd hung on the walls just last night. As he worked his way around the room to the foyer, he came to her cow painting. She cringed inside, hoping he would just keep walking.

She opened her mouth to thank him again for bringing Tiger back, but not in time.

"Hey, this is an original." Reed leaned in to examine the brush strokes on her painting.

"Yes," she said, suddenly acutely aware of how amateur her work was compared to Reed Vincent's. She wished the canvas would disappear, and her along with it.

"This is nice," he said. He turned to look at her. "Do you know the artist?"

She glanced away and placed her tongue firmly in her cheek. "I…know her. Not well." That at least was true, and becoming truer all the time, apparently.

"I like it," he said, not getting her little joke. "Shows a lot of promise."

She studied his face. Was he just playing along, or did he really not realize that she was the artist?

He stepped back and to the left, perusing the painting from another angle. "Hmm…"

"Do you really like it?" she risked.

"I do. Something about the light really appeals to me. And the colors the artist chose. Not a lot of contrast, yet it works beautifully. Adds to the serene mood of it."

She dipped her head, feeling herself flush. "Well…thank you," she said quietly.

He turned and studied her with narrowed eyes. "It's yours? Seriously?"

"Seriously. Were *you* serious…about liking it?"

"I was. Really, Olivia. I'm impressed. I don't remember you ever telling me you were such an accomplished artist."

"Well, I said I paint a little."

"There's a difference," he said. "House painters paint. This is art."

She bit her lip, unable to resist the urge to fish just a little. "I just dabble. I haven't painted seriously for years. It's so strange that you like it, though. Derek never cared much for this—or for any of my work, actually."

"No?"

She shook her head. "He was a little more of a realist. As far as art went, anyway. He called this 'splotchy.'"

"Splotchy, huh?" Reed kept his eyes on the canvas, as though he were taking notes. "Well, this is a very nice bunch of splotches."

Olivia beamed inside and out. This man really, really knew how to make a girl's day.

Chapter Twenty-Four

Reed drove home with a wide smile on his face and a deep feeling of relief. He'd second-guessed himself all the way to Olivia's from the Humane Society, worrying that Olivia may have already had a change of heart and decided it was all for the best that the cat was gone.

He'd had visions of her sending him straight home, cat in tow. And being angry because he'd made her grieve all over again. And then what would he have done? He didn't even like cats. Although he had to admit that Olivia's kitten was a rather nice exception. To be fair, Tiger was the first cat he'd really been around for any length of time. He'd always avoided felines whenever possible. He wasn't sure why, except maybe that his father had had the same attitude about cats.

He replayed his afternoon at the Humane Society and mentally rolled his eyes. He must have it bad for Olivia Cline if he was willing to go to all that trouble for a stupid cat. It had been worth it, though, just to see the glow on her pretty face. He'd known the minute he saw her with Tiger in her arms that he'd done the right thing. And the hug she'd given him was a step in the right direction for sure.

When he pulled in his driveway a few minutes later, Maggie was sitting on his front steps smoking. When she saw him, she ground her cigarette under her heel before jumping up to follow his car into the detached garage.

He shut off the engine and opened the door. "Hey, Maggie. What's up?"

"Not a whole lot. Just haven't seen you for a while. Thought I'd come over and see if you'd starved to death yet."

He patted his belly. "I'm doing fine, thanks. Not that I'd turn down a neighborly offer of baked goods should one come my way."

She hooked a thumb over her shoulder. "I put a plate of brownies on the counter by your fridge."

"Oh, bless you."

She graced him with a smile.

He got out of the car and pulled the garage door down, motioning for Maggie to follow him back to the front stoop where she'd been sitting. He plopped down on the top step and she sat below him, leaning against the iron railing.

He spotted the cigarette butt she'd crushed earlier. "I see you're still smoking those coffin nails."

She shrugged. "A fella's gotta die from something."

He'd been bugging Maggie to quit ever since he moved in next door. As he'd grown to know and love her, he'd stepped up his campaign, but his pleas seemed to fall on deaf ears. "It's nice out here." He changed the subject. "Finally cooled off a little."

"Finally. I wish Missouri springs lasted longer than a week. Seems like we always jump from April straight to July. The older I get the more I dread the summer."

He shook his head. "I'm not crazy about the heat, either. Thank the Lord for my air-conditioned studio."

"Speaking of which," Maggie said, "how's your new assistant working out?"

Reed knew a leading question when he heard one, but he played dumb. "Olivia's great. I hardly had to train her. I just discovered tonight that she's a pretty good artist herself."

"Tonight? What, did she have a show or something?"

Oh, boy. He'd walked blindly into that one. Oh, well. He'd never had any secrets from Maggie. "No, I had to take something over to her house. Just happened to see some of her paintings. She's good. But I kind of hate to encourage her. I'd hate to lose her."

"Not to mention she could be your competition."

He winced. "I hadn't thought of that. Really, though, I don't know how I'd keep up around here without her. I'm sure glad you had your daughter put that notice on the church bulletin board."

"Yeah, well, how come I haven't gotten to meet her yet? Seems like you'd want to introduce us, seeing how she's so wonderful and all?" Maggie winked.

He shrugged one shoulder, goading her. "You'll have to come over some time when you see her car in the drive. I'm sure she likes brownies, too."

"Well, maybe I'll just go get that plate I brought you and bring them back over tomorrow when she's here."

"Oh, that would be subtle."

She beamed. "Since when was I ever known for my subtlety?"

"Oh, yeah. I forgot who I'm dealing with here."

She tilted her head and examined him with a playful glint in her eyes. "Okay, since I've already got a reputation, let me just come out and ask—is there more between you two than a working relationship?"

He tried to look innocent. "Me and Olivia? Now why would you ask that?"

"Two reasons," she said, counting them off on heavily ringed fingers. "One, I never see you anymore. Seems like you used to get a little lonely once in a while and at least come over and tell ol' Maggie hello, shoot the breeze. Haven't done that for a while. Two…" She leaned in as if she had a secret to share. "Don't know if you're aware of this, Mr. Vincent, but you get this peculiar gleam in your eyes every time you mention her name."

He felt his cheeks heat up. Man! Was he that transparent? He ran a hand through his hair and looked at the sidewalk, but he couldn't stop the smile that tugged at his mouth.

"That's what I thought," Maggie said. She punched him in the bicep. "Well, come on. Let's hear all about it."

Reed turned serious. "There's nothing to tell, Maggie. Olivia lost her husband a few months ago. She's still grieving."

"Lost him? You mean he died?"

He nodded.

"That's gotta be tough."

"It gets worse. She's pregnant."

Maggie's white eyebrows rose an inch. "Really? I've seen her from a distance. Didn't notice she was pregnant."

"She's just a few months along. Not really—you know…"

"Showing," she filled in. "So are you going to lose her when the baby comes? I mean, will she quit her job then?"

"I hope not. She'll need her job even worse after the baby."

She cocked her head. "So did I totally misread the gleam in your eyes?"

He hesitated, sighed heavily, then shot her a guilty grin. "Not totally."

"You like her."

"I do, Maggie, but she's not ready for a relationship." He quoted Alissa. "I've got to give her time. She needs to grieve."

"Well, I'll grant you that. But that baby will need a daddy, too. She might be ready sooner than you think."

"Maggie."

"I'm just saying." Maggie pulled herself up by the railing and stretched, rubbing the small of her back. "I better get going. My show starts in a few minutes. An episode I missed in the regular season. Can't miss it in reruns, too."

Reed watched her walk across the lawn. He sat on the steps until the sun dipped below the rooftops, replaying their conversation and wondering why her simple words gave him such hope.

Tiger raced through the living room on the slick hardwood floors, skidding to a halt in front of Olivia. In spite of Olivia's careful trimming, his claws had already feathered faint scratches on the shiny surface. But she didn't care. Tiger had brought so much sunshine into this house, into her life, she didn't think she'd bat an eye if he shredded the drapes and ruined the floors.

She took another bite of her Raisin Bran and set the bowl on the floor. Tiger pounced on it and lapped up the last drops of milk. He was growing out of kittenhood, and had that gangly, awkward "adolescent" look about him now. He ate like one, too. He'd already gone through half of one of the big bags of Cat Chow from Reed, yet he always seemed happy to clean up any scraps of food Olivia put out for him.

Every morning when she came to the kitchen for breakfast with the kitten pattering after her, Olivia couldn't help but think of Reed and the sweet thing he'd done for her. She still could hardly believe he'd gone to such lengths just to make her happy.

He'd come upon an article that said pregnant women were supposed to avoid cleaning the litter box for fear of being exposed to toxoplasmosis. He read the warning aloud to her and offered to come over every day and perform the unpleasant task of scooping out Tiger's litter box. She smiled over her coffee, remembering the serious expression he'd worn as he looked at her over the newspaper.

"Thanks for offering, Reed," she'd said, "but I'll be careful. Besides, Tiger rarely even uses the litter box. He's pretty much turned into an outdoor kitty."

"Just don't let him caterwaul under your neighbor's window."

A smile tugged at her lips. He'd become quite protective and possessive of Tiger. Her smile faded a little when she realized that his protectiveness extended to her, as well. Reed still had feelings for her, that was clear. She didn't want to take advantage of him, and yet her feelings for him were genuine, too. Maybe not as serious, but she thought the world of him and saw him as a dear friend. No, a bit more than that...

They'd become comfortable with each other, finally settling into a routine they both felt easy with. Reed had sent her to St. Louis solo one day last week, since she'd already met Gavin and knew the ropes there. She'd enjoyed the drive, and it was fun to be in the city once again, with access to something more cultural than Betty's Bead Boutique. But she'd had to admit that it had also felt good to get back home to the quiet of the Falls.

She enjoyed her work in the studio and no longer dreaded the days they went out on photo shoots or visited galleries. She'd grown to trust Reed not to make another pass at her. Not that he'd want to in her present condition.

She looked down at her belly. Her morning sickness had abated, but it'd been replaced by another disconcerting symptom: she was getting huge! According to the most recent sonogram, she was only about five months along, but she sure didn't remember any of her friends showing this much at five months. She couldn't get into half the things in her closet and even her loosest clothes were snug. She would have to do some maternity shopping soon. Not a prospect she relished.

Reed hadn't commented on her changing shape, other than becoming even more solicitous—not letting her carry anything that weighed more than two pounds, helping her with her chair, and pestering her if he thought she wasn't eating enough for lunch. She knew he noticed everything. She felt his eyes on her while she worked. He was, after all, an artist, gifted with an ultra-observant nature.

She picked up the licked-clean cereal bowl Tiger had abandoned and went to finish getting ready for work. Reed had asked her to put together an order of art supplies this morning and she didn't want to be late.

Chapter Twenty-Five

Monday mornings had become Reed's favorite day of the week. He heard the front door open and listened to the now-familiar music of Olivia's footsteps in the hall, then moving through the kitchen, her cheery "good morning" the prelude that signaled the beginning of his day. He had come to dread the weekends because she wasn't in them.

He hoped to change that for next weekend anyway. He'd seen the advertisements for Hanover Falls's annual Summerfest in the *Hanover Falls Record* last week and he'd decided to risk asking Olivia to go with him.

She poked her head in the studio. "Good morning."

That music again.

"Hi," Reed said. "You're bright and early this morning."

"I thought you wanted to get that order in before noon."

"Well, I do, but I don't think it'll take all morning."

She shrugged. "Oh, well. I'm here. Let me get the coffee going first." She started back for the kitchen.

"Sure," he said. "How are you feeling?"

She popped back in the doorway, this time coming down two steps. "I'm fine. Why do you ask?"

He shrugged, afraid he'd been too obvious. "Just wondered. I haven't asked lately."

She looked at him for a minute, as if trying to decide how to answer. "I'm fine. Feeling better than I have in a while, actually. Thanks for asking."

"Good. I'm glad."

A few minutes later, the smell of fresh coffee wafted into the studio. His mouth watered in anticipation. Olivia set a mug down for him.

"Coffee on your right."

"Got it. Thanks." Reed took a sip of the hot brew. "Hang on a couple minutes and we'll go through those catalogs."

"No rush," she said. "I need to clean up my framing mess from Friday first, anyway."

It struck him that they were acting like an old married couple, each knowing the other's habits and quirks, communicating almost without words sometimes.

He liked it. Liked having her in the studio with him, filling it with her feminine presence and the subtle fragrance of her perfume. He liked having someone to laugh at his jokes. He liked the comfort of having someone grow to know him well.

"Reed?"

Olivia's voice disturbed his reverie. "Sorry…what was that?"

"I wondered if you wanted something to eat before we get started."

He waved her off. "No, I'm fine, thanks."

"Okay… I've got the catalogs out whenever you're ready."

He moved the easel back and slid off the stool. He hadn't accomplished much this morning. Might as well get the ordering over with.

"I'm going to get a refill before we get started. You want some?"

She held out her cup. "Sounds good. Thanks."

He poured coffee for both of them and set the steaming mugs on the table where Olivia had spread out an array of artists' supply catalogs.

"Okay," he said, pulling a chair up to the table and straddling it backward. He leaned over the back with a sigh. "Let's get this over with."

She gave a huff of mock exasperation. "How can you say that?

This is shopping, Reed. *Shopping*." She exaggerated the pronunciation. "This is supposed to be fun."

He groaned for her benefit, because he was definitely not dreading the chance to sit next to her.

"Come on." She gave him a playful nudge. "You get to pick out new colors and fancy brushes."

"Okay, okay. Let's do it."

She gave him two solicitous pats on the back. "That's the spirit."

He rolled his eyes at her, but she ignored him and turned all business, sliding a sheet of notepaper in front of him.

"These are the colors you're almost out of, and this column is some that I didn't see in the cabinet, but I know you've used them before. They must not have ever been replaced."

The list swam in front of him, a jumble of squiggles. His eyes were giving him fits today. He squinted, took off his glasses and cleaned them on his shirttail. Not much better. He leaned over the chair and switched on the gooseneck lamp. Still no good. He picked up the paper and moved it back and forth in front of his eyes, trying to find the distance that would allow him to focus.

"Hey! My handwriting isn't *that* bad." Olivia feigned a pout.

"It's not that. My eyes aren't cooperating today." He handed her the list. "You're going to have to read that to me."

She was quiet for a minute, her expression suddenly serious. "I'm sorry. I didn't realize…" Her voice trailed off.

"Don't worry about it. I have bad days sometimes." He looked at the floor, trying to decide how much to say. He had always tried to downplay the problems with his vision. Even back when the doctors had told him he might be going blind, he hadn't wanted anyone feeling sorry for him. But he thought Olivia would understand. And didn't she deserve to know why he sometimes had to take it slow? "I'm doing a lot better since my surgery," he started. "But it's only been five months. The doctor said it may be a lot longer before I really know where I am. With my eyes, I mean."

Her brow wrinkled in concern. "I'm sorry," she said again. "I totally forget sometimes that you even have a problem. With your eyes, I mean."

He smiled at her obviously unintentional parroting of his words. "You're lucky I do have a problem," he said, grinning, attempting to lighten the mood.

"Huh?"

"If you recall, that's why I hired you in the first place."

"Oh. Yeah. That." She followed his lead and they were instantly back to the light banter they'd finally come to do so well.

They finished the list and Olivia filled out the order forms for two different catalogs. Reed watched her surreptitiously as they worked. Being so close to her, smelling the clean scent of her hair and skin, it was all he could do to keep his thoughts—and actions—from going where he'd promised her they wouldn't.

He stood, lifting his chair with him as he rose. If he didn't get out of arm's reach of her right now, he'd be sorry. "Can you handle it from here?"

She glanced over her shoulder and gave him a funny look, as if she sensed his mood. But she nodded. "I'm on it. I just need your signature for the credit card, and you need to initial here." She leaned to one side so he could sign the forms.

He scratched his name and initials on the appropriate lines, and made a mental note to scratch his plans to ask Olivia to Summerfest. He picked up both their coffee cups, using them as an excuse to escape to the kitchen.

Olivia glanced at the clock. If she hurried, she could get the orders out in Reed's mailbox and save herself a trip downtown to the post office. She folded the first order form and slid it into the envelope. She sealed the flap and started to do the same with the second order. But something made her stop. An odd sense that something was amiss.

What was she forgetting? She pulled the form out and studied it again. She'd correctly totaled the quantities and amounts and included sales tax and shipping charges. Everything looked to be in order. Reed had signed and initialed in all the appropriate places. She stared at his signature. Beautiful handwriting. An artist's script. But the signature on his checks and credit card was different from the way he signed his paintings.

It was the box where he'd jotted his initials that kept snagging her attention. Had she ever heard his middle name? He didn't use a middle initial in his signature, nor could she remember seeing it on any of the dozens of forms she'd filled out for the galleries and art show entries. She wondered what that *E* stood for. Probably something that embarrassed him, since as far as she could remember, he'd never used the initial. She took a wild guess. Erasmus? Ezekiel maybe? Ebenezer. She giggled at the thought.

"What's so funny?" Reed appeared on the wide steps that led from the kitchen.

She flushed, caught in her silly mental game. But she decided to have fun with it. "I was just trying to guess your middle name."

He lifted a brow. "What'd you come up with?"

"I'm placing my bets on Ebenezer."

He made a face. "Oh, please. It's bad, but it's not that bad."

"What is it?"

"I'm not telling you now."

She shot him a coy grin. "Erasmus? Eugene?"

He shook his head. "Where are you coming up with these?"

She giggled. "Eustice?"

"Okay, okay. I give. You're making my real middle name sound downright good."

She smiled, waiting.

"It's Elliott," he said finally.

"Elliott? That's a *nice* name."

"Well, I'm glad you like it. You can have it if you want. I never use it."

"That's generous of you. I might just take you up on that offer. It beats *my* middle name."

"What's that?"

"Oh, no. That is classified, top secret information."

"No fair! I told you mine."

"I didn't exactly twist your arm."

"Hey, wait a minute." His eyebrows lifted. "I know where I can find out your big secret."

"Where?"

"As your employer, I just happen to be privy to certain documents…" He rubbed his hands together like the villain in a melodrama.

"Hey, now *that's* no fair. Isn't there some law about accessing that information for sinister purposes?"

"Sinister? I'll tell you what. I'll keep your secret if you'll keep mine." He held out his pinky in a truce.

She laughed and hooked her little finger with his. If anyone had told her a few weeks ago that she would be sitting here enjoying this lighthearted banter with Reed Vincent, she would have told them they were crazy. But it felt good. She was glad they'd been able to get past their uneasiness with each other and become real friends.

Sometimes in the evenings, when Tiger hopped up on her lap on the sofa, and she remembered Reed's sweet gesture, she was tempted to dream about him becoming more than a friend. But shards of guilt always sliced the thoughts away. Derek's death should be still fresh and raw. Why was she daydreaming about romance a mere five months after her husband had died? Not to mention the baby on the way.

"Penny for your thoughts?"

She started at Reed's voice. Good grief! Now she was daydreaming about him in his very presence. She waved him away, pretending to be adding up the columns on the order form.

She felt like a heel when he apologized and slunk off to his stool in front of the easel.

She was quiet the rest of the workday, and unlike usual, a little relieved when it was time to go home. She had to get her act together. She had a schoolgirl crush on Reed and if she didn't grow up and quit acting like an idiot, she was going to put herself right out of a job she needed desperately. Sometimes, when she thought about that day in the woods when Reed had said he wanted to kiss her, she wondered if she had encouraged him. She hadn't thought so at the time, but she was pretty sure a shrink might tell her differently.

She fixed a salad and took it out onto the patio, but the heat soon drove her back inside. She felt restless and out of sorts and she wasn't sure why. For some strange reason, she kept seeing Reed's signature as he'd signed it on the order form this morning. She traced his initials in her mind's eye over and over, thinking about their conversation, smiling to herself at the thought of their good-humored banter. Reed Elliott Vincent. *REV.* Why did those three scripted letters haunt her? Something about the way he'd written them. That artistic flourish that gave them almost the look of an advertising logo. One she'd seen somewhere before.

That was it. She'd seen his signature before—that distinctive combination of letters, written just that way. Maybe he did sign some of his earlier work, or his smaller pieces with his initials. But why did it seem so significant?

She gave a growl of frustration that caused Tiger to look up from his perch on the arm of the sofa. "Hey, kitty. Sorry. Did I scare you?"

He gave a tiny meow in response, and at that moment, she felt a rolling, watery sensation inside her. It took her breath away. *Her baby.* She'd felt some fluttery sensations over the last few weeks, but there was no mistaking the baby's movements now.

She placed her hand over her stomach and held her breath, willing the baby to kick again. What an amazing thing! Derek would have been so excited. A wave of something like home-sickness swept over her, and she realized how desperately she wished for someone to share this moment with.

Just as quickly, a blanket of warmth fell over her as she realized she wasn't alone. Not really. Though she had put God at arm's length when Derek died, and wandered even further when she'd discovered she was pregnant, God had never left her for even a moment. He'd provided a house, a job, a church, her friendships with Michael and Claire Meredith and Reed. Even grumpy Mr. Burnside.

Tiger hopped up on the sofa and paced back and forth over her lap as if to say, "Hey, what am I? Chopped liver?" Olivia smiled at the thought, and stroked his silky fur. "Oh, dear God, You've been here all along. I just didn't see it. I don't understand

why things have happened the way they have. I'll never understand why You took Derek just when we were beginning to be
happy together. But this baby, this new little life I'm carrying is
such a miracle. I'm sorry it took me so long to acknowledge it.
Forgive me." Hot tears burned her throat and she swallowed
them back.

She thought about calling Reed to tell him about the baby
moving. But somehow it didn't seem right. It seemed too intimate, too close to the very things that had made her uncomfortable with him in the beginning. Maybe someday she could share
more personal things with him, but for now, it was too soon. She
didn't want to jeopardize the friendship they'd built.

Claire Meredith's face came to her mind and it was as if the
Lord told her, "Call Claire."

Claire would be happy for her, rejoice with her. She knew
exactly what Olivia was going through. Maybe she could even
answer some of the questions that had been brooding as Olivia's
pregnancy progressed.

And if Claire happened to give her a hug and let her cry on
her shoulder, it wouldn't turn into an international incident the
way it might with Reed.

Yes, talking to Claire would be much safer for her heart than
if she shared her feelings with Reed.

Chapter Twenty-Six

Reed's Escape sat running in his driveway when Olivia got to work the following Monday morning. They were delivering several canvases to a gallery in Springfield and if time and weather permitted, he wanted to stop and take some photographs of a garden a friend had told him about.

She had looked forward to the trip all weekend long, but now that the day was here, she wasn't so sure. She and Reed had been getting along so well lately. She hated to put their feelings to the test and risk ruining the comfortable thing they had going.

She couldn't help but remember that first drive together to St. Louis when she'd been forced to reveal to Reed that she was pregnant. They'd come a long way since then.

He came out of the house, camera case in hand, waving when he saw her.

She came around to his passenger door and threw her purse onto the seat.

"Do you need anything out of the office?" he asked.

"You didn't make coffee, by any chance, did you?"

"I just happen to know where there's a Starbucks on the way. You'll be fully caffeinated by—" he turned over his wrist "—I'd say no later than 9:00 a.m. Can you make it that long?"

"I think I can handle it. But remember, I'm a decaf gal now."

"Oh, that's right. I forgot." He glanced toward her midsection, as if he'd just remembered the reason she was watching her caffeine intake.

She hurried to change the subject. "How long does it take to get there?"

"Why? Are you calculating bathroom stops?"

So much for changing the subject. "No." She rolled her eyes, but couldn't help grinning. "If you must know, I was thinking more about how soon we could eat."

He laughed. "Last time I drove it, it only took about an hour and a half, but Maggie said when she was down there last week there was all kinds of construction on I-44. So I'm not counting on being there much before eleven o'clock. We can stop for a snack if you get desperate. Or grab a muffin at Starbucks."

"Thanks. I feel better now." She flashed a grin.

The construction was worse even than Maggie had warned, but they sipped their coffees and Olivia felt more comfortable with Reed than ever.

It was almost noon when they finally hit Springfield. They hadn't made any stops since Starbucks, where they'd only stayed long enough to order coffee and give Olivia a chance to stretch her legs.

Reed glanced pointedly at the digital clock on the dashboard. "Can you wait until after I drop my stuff off to eat lunch?"

"Sure." She patted her purse. "I think I have some crackers in here if I get desperate."

"Good thinking. If it goes too long, I may be asking you to share."

She cradled her purse possessively. "You'll have to fight me for them."

He laughed as he pulled into the gallery's parking lot. Reed parked the car and came around to open the door for Olivia. "You're going to love this place," he said.

"Oh? Why's that?"

"You'll see." He looked like a little boy with a frog in his pocket.

He hefted the bundle of paintings from the back of the Escape and onto one shoulder. Olivia followed him up a narrow stairwell. The gallery was above an old storefront and immediately she knew why Reed had been excited to show her. The space looked as if it might have been a dance studio once upon a time. The floors were shiny hardwood with a patina that had probably seen a century. The entire north wall boasted fanlight windows that painted saffron patches on the floor and illumined the room with a perfect light for viewing the rows of paintings hung at wide intervals on the brick walls. Something about galleries like this made Olivia's blood race and every cell in her body want to explode with creativity.

She twirled on one heel in the middle of the main gallery. "This is fabulous!"

Reed flashed an I-told-you-so smile. "Isn't it great? Wait till you see upstairs." He slid the paintings off his shoulder and leaned them against a display cabinet.

"I thought we were upstairs."

"There's a cupola gallery." He pointed to a low, narrow doorway at the end of the spacious room. "I want you to meet Lavonna, but then you can browse while I finish up here."

She nodded, eager to begin her tour of the place.

Another door in the back opened and a gray-haired woman who must have been in her eighties bustled out to greet them.

"Olivia, this is Lavonna Burgess." He turned to the woman. "This is my new assistant, Olivia Cline."

"An assistant now? You're moving up in the world."

He shrugged one shoulder and shook his head. "I don't know about that. But I can't complain. Business is pretty good."

"Don't I know it. I hope you brought me plenty of work."

Seeming embarrassed, Reed turned to Olivia and changed the subject. "Lavonna opened this gallery...well, before I was born, I think."

The woman laughed, a lilting melody that made Olivia like her immediately.

The older woman looked over her half-glasses. "I don't think we've been here quite that long, unless you're an even younger whippersnapper than I thought. Nice to meet you, Olivia." She looked pointedly at the front of Olivia's loose blouse. "When is the blessed event?"

It was the first time a stranger had openly acknowledged her pregnancy and it took her aback a little. "I…I'm due at the end of November."

"Ah, a Thanksgiving baby. Truly something to be thankful for. Is this your first?"

"Yes," Olivia said.

"Your husband must be so excited."

Reed put a hand lightly on Olivia's back. "Olivia lost her husband a few months ago. An accident…"

The woman's hand flew to her mouth. "Oh, I'm so sorry. What an awful thing."

She nodded, not knowing what to say.

Reed jumped in. "We'd better get these paintings hung so we can get Olivia to lunch. She's eating for two these days."

She could have kissed him. Not only had he defused the awkward moment, but he'd done it with utter grace. And the promise of lunch.

"Oh, my, yes… By all means. You go ahead," Mrs. Burgess cooed.

Reed reached for one of his paintings. "Olivia, why don't you tour the gallery while we finish up?"

She admired the impressive selection of original art, and listened as Reed and Mrs. Burgess talked while they hung the two canvases Reed had brought. She was touched by how tender he was with the grandmotherly proprietor. When she went up to the cupola gallery, Reed was offering to help Mrs. Burgess hang several pieces that another artist had dropped off earlier in the day.

They were just finishing when Olivia came back down to the main gallery. Mrs. Burgess dusted off her hands. "I appreciate your help, Reed," she said, as the three of them surveyed his handiwork. "You be good to this young man," the old woman told her, with a spark in her eye. "He's my favorite."

"He is pretty talented, isn't he?" Olivia winked at Reed, who stood basking in their compliments.

"Oh, he's a good artist, but I'm not talking about his art. I'm talking about the man. He's a fine example of the species. And I'm here to tell you there aren't many of them left."

Reed colored and brushed the comment away. "Okay, ladies, it's getting a little thick in here. If I didn't know better, I'd think you were conspiring to get me to take you both to lunch."

Mrs. Burgess clicked her tongue. "Oh, no, I have to hold down the fort here, but you two go ahead."

Olivia squirmed. She was beginning to fear they were victims of a matchmaking scheme, but Reed seemed not to notice. "I'll tell you what," Mrs. Burgess said, moving toward the cash register, "you let me buy lunch for the two of you."

Reed held up a hand. "No, no… You don't need to do that."

"Well, I know I don't *need* to, but what if I just wanted to?"

Reed winked at Olivia. "Then I guess we'd have no choice."

Mrs. Burgess pushed some keys on the old-fashioned cash register. The drawer slid open and she pulled out two bills and handed them to Reed. "You know the bistro just up the street?" She pointed out the bank of windows that overlooked the street.

Reed nodded.

"They have the best Reuben in town. It might be too spicy… for the baby." She gave Olivia a knowing look. "But you'll love the ambience. Very romantic."

Reed seemed to ignore her innuendo and for a fleeting moment, Olivia wondered if he had put Mrs. Burgess up to this. But she quickly dismissed the thought. There was no reason for him to do so, knowing they'd have no choice but to have lunch together.

At the thought of lunch, her stomach growled. The crackers in her purse were probably packets of crumbs by now, but she was going to pull them out anyway if she didn't get something to eat soon.

They thanked Mrs. Burgess for her treat and Reed led the way down the steep stairs to the street. "We can just walk from here," he said. "It's only a couple of blocks." He stooped to peer into her face. "Are you hanging in there?"

"I'm hungry," she admitted.

"Okay. It won't be long. We'll have them bring soup or a salad or something right away."

"Thanks."

The bistro was as charming as the gallery, and their solicitous server got a basket of rolls and fresh green salads to their cozy booth within minutes. Reed said grace over the meal and Olivia dived in. The food was delicious and she ate as though she'd been starved for a week.

When she'd finally warded off the worst of the hunger pangs, she looked up to find Reed watching her with a look of satisfaction on his face and a glint of humor in his eyes.

She gave an embarrassed shrug. "I was hungry."

He burst out laughing. "I noticed. My goodness, for a minute there I thought you were going to start eating the flowers." With an ornery spark in his blue eyes, he picked up the vase of alstroemeria and moved it to the end of the table, out of her reach.

She rolled her eyes.

"Just kidding." He slid the flowers back to the center of the table. "I like a woman who doesn't pick at her food."

"Well, hey, I *do* have an excuse." She usually avoided mentioning her pregnancy or using it as an excuse, but a woman did have her pride.

"I know, I know." Reed smiled, but then his expression turned serious. He stretched out his hand and for a minute she was afraid he was going to place it over hers on the table. But he only propped his elbow on the edge of the table and rested his chin on his palm, watching her. "I've enjoyed the day, Liv… Being with you."

"Me, too." The moment grew awkward and she looked down, arranging and rearranging the linen napkin on her lap.

The server brought their entrées and Reed started talking about his dream of adding a gallery to his studio. Things grew more comfortable after that and they recaptured the easiness between them.

Though they didn't talk about it, as the day went on, Olivia felt something subtly shift in their relationship.

Lying in bed that night, smiling to herself, reliving their time together, Olivia knew they had crossed some sort of barrier. She wasn't sure what to make of it. She only knew that it thrilled her and terrified her at the same time.

* * *

Reed was in what he thought of as "the zone," that wonderful place where the paint seemed to take on a life of its own beneath his brush and the patches of color that resulted were exactly as he'd envisioned them in his mind. It didn't happen often enough, but when it did, he felt as if he were doing what he'd been created to do.

He dipped the brush again into the thick paint and dabbed another perfect splotch of cerulean-blue onto the canvas.

From the corner of his vision, he was vaguely aware of Olivia working at his desk, getting his sales tax statement ready to send to the accountant. She hadn't exactly balked at the idea of adding bookkeeping to her duties, but he could tell she was a little uncomfortable with that aspect of the job. Still, it was another way to free up more time for him to paint, and one more way he could justify the raise he'd given her. And it kept her working by his side a little longer.

Even when each of them went about their tasks in silence, hers was a welcome presence in his studio. Too often now, he found himself wishing she didn't have to leave at the end of each day. He'd always valued his solitude, and the change she'd wrought in him amazed him. He couldn't remember ever wishing Kristina could stay longer. As much as he'd thought he loved her, sometimes he'd been almost eager for time away from her constant chatter.

He dipped his brush again into the vivid blue paint, enjoying the feeling of slipping into the fantasy. Olivia as his wife…living here with him, sharing his life.

The harsh scraping sound of Olivia's chair across the room broke the spell and made him look away from the easel.

His pulse lurched. Olivia was standing hunched over, holding her stomach. The half of her face he could see was a mask of pain.

"Olivia?"

She looked up, and he saw panic in her eyes. It worried him most that she didn't even try to cover up her obvious agony. That definitely wasn't like her.

He leaped from the stool and crossed the room in half a dozen long strides.

"What's wrong?" He put an arm around her hunched shoulders and bent beside her, trying to read her eyes. "What is it, Liv?"

"I...I'm not sure," she said between shallow breaths. "Something's wrong. I...I'm having cramps." Her words warbled weakly and trailed off. "I think...I might be bleeding."

Chapter Twenty-Seven

Reed didn't understand all the medical business of how these things worked, but he knew enough to know that bleeding was not good. "Is it the baby? Do you need to lie down? Should I call Maggie?" He cast about the four corners of the room as if the answer might be written on one of the walls.

Olivia's next sharp gasp of breath made the decision for him. "I'm calling an ambulance."

"No!" The smooth muscles of her jaw tensed, then slowly relaxed. She held up a hand. "I…I don't think I need an ambulance, but maybe I should go to the hospital. I'm kind of having cramps."

He bent close and studied her face. She was pale, her eyes glassy with fear, but she was still standing on her own, and speaking more calmly. "You're sure?"

She nodded. "Just let me sort out these receipts first." But her knees buckled as she turned back toward the table. She caught herself, grasping the back of the desk chair as if it were a lifeline.

"Leave the stupid receipts." His voice came out angrier than he meant it. What was she thinking? She needed medical attention now.

He turned her gently toward the kitchen. "You're going to the hospital this minute."

She didn't argue.

He took her arm and draped it around his neck, then put a steadying arm around her thickening waist. *Lord, please help me get her there in time. Please don't let anything happen to her.*

She clung to him as he ushered her out to the car. She managed to get into the seat, but he had to lift her feet and swing her around to sit properly in the passenger seat. A dark stain of blood on her jeans caused his breath to catch. He buckled her seat belt and raced around to take the wheel.

Olivia sat with her head in her hands as he wove through the noon-hour traffic, praying for God to part the sea of cars on the narrow two-lane street.

"You okay?"

She gave a barely perceptible nod. "Please hurry."

Once off the main road, he gunned it to sixty. After what seemed an eternity, he finally pulled into the emergency entrance to Hanover Falls Regional Medical Center. He parked under the overhang, killed the engine and ran to open Olivia's door. "How're you doing?"

This time she shook her head, her chin quivering violently. "Oh, Reed… I…I think I might be losing the baby. What am I going to do? What am I going to do?" Her voice escalated to hysteria.

"It'll be okay, Liv. We're going to get help. Everything is going to be okay." *Oh, dear God, help us! Let everything be okay with the baby. With Liv.* He helped her from the car, and with one arm around her, propelled her through the wide doors marked Emergency. Pungent, antiseptic odors assailed him, and for a minute he was afraid it would be *his* legs buckling. All the memories and fears from the time of his surgeries rushed back, sapping his strength.

He forced his thoughts in a different direction, but quickly discovered that Olivia's pain and the growing stain of blood terrified him far more than any memories of a surgery that had ended so well. *Please, God, let this end as well. Please God.*

Before they were through the second set of automatic doors, a woman in a colorful uniform came toward them. "What do we have here?"

"She's pregnant. About five months along, I think. She's bleeding and…having cramps." He looked to Olivia to confirm his layman's diagnosis, but she seemed oblivious, holding her stomach and moaning a little now. *Please God.*

The nurse eyed him. "You're the father?"

"No. No, I'm a friend."

A wheelchair materialized and before he could gather his wits, before he could whisper a word of encouragement or the truth of his feelings for her, they were wheeling Olivia through the wide swinging doors at the end of the corridor.

The fetal heart monitor beside her bed emitted a steady, comforting *scritch scritch scritch,* but Olivia couldn't unglue her eyes from the neon numbers skittering across the screen and the paper printout that collected in a heap on the nightstand, documenting her contractions and her baby's heartbeat.

Her baby was fine, the doctor said, but Olivia was having mild contractions and they hadn't been overly encouraging about whether they could keep her from going into labor.

She'd been admitted to the hospital within an hour of being brought to the emergency room. The nurses had told her how important it was that she keep as calm as possible, so now she was lying here, struggling not to worry about how she would pay the bills for the emergency room, how she would afford it if the doctor prescribed an extended stay in the hospital, and how she could ever raise a child on her own.

Reed had left a note at the front desk for her. One she suspected the nurse had "previewed" before allowing her to have it. It was written on a sheet of paper with bright purple advertising for some prescription drug, obviously borrowed from the nurses' station. But it was Reed's handwriting that made her smile. Made her feel a sense of warmth and comfort and belonging that she hadn't felt for a long time.

She read his now-familiar script for the dozenth time.

Liv,
    I'm praying for you. Please don't worry about anything.
I went over and fed Tiger a few minutes ago and he's fine.

Maggie is going to help me out at the office for a couple of days and I'm mowing your lawn tonight, so there is not one thing for you to worry about. You only have one job: take care of yourself and that baby. I'll stop by and check on you later tonight.
Reed

She reached up and touched her hair. It felt matted and stringy. She must look a mess. No doubt tears had streaked her makeup and given her raccoon eyes. She tried to catch her reflection in the television that was anchored near the ceiling in the corner of the room, but in the dark screen she could only see a ghostly outline of her rounded form under the sheets. She didn't care. She just wanted to see Reed.

What was it about that man that had the power to make everything seem safe again? That made everything seem hopeful once more?

As if he also had the power to grant her wish, Reed materialized in the doorway to her room. He smiled when he saw her and knocked softly, after the fact, waiting for her invitation.

She beckoned him into the room. He came to stand at the side of her bed and reached to pat her arm. "You look worlds better than you did last time I saw you."

"I've been afraid to ask for a mirror, but ick! If this—" she pushed her hair away from her face "—is better than I looked before, I've got a serious problem."

"You've got some color back in your cheeks," he explained, patting his own cheeks. "Everything's okay with the baby?"

His furrowed forehead made her look to the monitor again for reassurance. It spit out a steady ribbon of graph paper. "The baby's fine. But I'm still having some mild contractions. I guess they're still worried I'll go into premature labor."

He shook his head. "Don't do that."

She smiled. "That's the goal."

"I'm serious, Olivia. Don't worry about anything. Your house, Tiger, the studio…everything is taken care of. You don't have to worry about anything except taking care of yourself and your baby."

"Thank you, Reed."

"I…I hope you weren't working too hard…at the studio. I hope that wasn't the reason for—"

"Reed. No. Of course not. This isn't your fault! This probably would have happened whether I'd been sitting on the sofa at home or working for you. The doctor even said that. I was afraid I'd done something wrong, too, but he assured me I hadn't."

Reed looked at her, then took a step closer to the bed. "I'm so glad you're all right, Liv. Or that you will be. Both of you," he added, his gaze moving to rest on her swollen midsection.

From the tenderness in his eyes, Olivia almost believed that he wanted to soothe the child within her the same way he was comforting her now. That if they'd had the kind of relationship that would allow it, he would lay his hand on her abdomen right this moment… Much as she'd pictured Derek doing, if he were still here.

"I'm going to be okay, Reed." She smoothed a hand over the mound of her abdomen. "And so is this little one."

He nodded, his eyes meeting hers again. But the creases in his forehead told another story.

Reed stared at the empty canvas and listened to the giant clock tick off the seconds. The studio was quiet. Too quiet. It seemed dim in the room. Without Olivia, a light had gone from the space.

They'd kept her in the hospital for two days, until they were certain the contractions had abated. But now she'd been placed on strict bed rest for at least two weeks. He hadn't even dared to broach the subject of her coming back to work. As much as he missed her presence in his studio, in his house, he would quit painting and close up his studio before he'd be responsible for her contractions starting again, or worse, Olivia losing the baby.

He heard Maggie in the kitchen and tried to gather his wits. What needed to be done today? Olivia had taken over the menial tasks of his business so completely that he barely had to give her an assignment anymore. His neighbor was a blessing in Olivia's absence, and he enjoyed Maggie's company. But she didn't bring the same spark with which Olivia filled this place.

"Good morning." Maggie's cheery greeting echoed from the kitchen.

"Hey, Maggie. Is it getting hot out there?"

She tucked a long wisp of gray hair back into her bun. "It's miserable. Did I mention that I hate August?"

He chuckled. "I believe you did mention that once or twice."

Maggie brushed her hands together and perched her reading glasses on the end of her nose. "So what's on the docket today? You said you'd have a delivery…."

He squirmed, and busied himself with squeezing a blob of paint onto the glass palette. "I don't have anything ready yet."

"You don't?" She stood with hands on hips, obviously seeking an explanation.

He shrugged. "I went over and mowed Olivia's lawn last night. I was just too wiped out to get back in the studio after I got home." The truth was, after he finished the lawn he'd gone for sandwiches at Subway and brought them back to Olivia's house. They'd popped in a DVD—*The Sound of Music,* since doctor's orders were to not do anything that might bring on stress—and then he sat with her until almost ten-thirty so she wouldn't be tempted to sit by herself and worry. Plus, he hadn't wanted to leave. He'd enjoyed every minute of their time together.

But with Maggie glaring at him now, he felt like a fifth grader who'd tried to use the old the-dog-ate-my-homework excuse.

"Well, I'm not trying to be your mother or anything, but Gilbert or Gavel or whatever-his-name-is didn't sound like he was any too patient when he called the other day."

"Gavin, you mean?"

"The guy at the St. Louis gallery."

He sighed. "I'll call him this afternoon and let him know what's up."

Maggie put her hands on her hips and studied him. "Just what *is* up, Reed?"

"What do you mean?" His attempt at nonchalance failed miserably.

"It's not one iota of my business, but if I'm going to be covering for you while all your galleries wonder whether or not you're all washed up, I think I have a right to know what's going on."

"What are you trying to say, Maggie?" Sometimes this motherly routine of hers got old. He felt his defenses rising.

She twisted a thick silver ring on her index finger. "You're investing an awful lot of hours in a certain project that I'm not sure is going to pan out like you hope it is."

He glared at her. "And just how do you think I'm hoping for things to turn out?"

That seemed to take the wind out of her sails a little. The lines of her face softened and she reached out to put a hand on his arm. "Reed, I just don't want to see you get hurt. You haven't known her but a few months and it looks to me like she's by far getting the better end of the deal around here."

Reed didn't have to ask who "she" was. But what had happened to the Maggie who'd encouraged him only a few weeks ago that Olivia might be ready to fall in love sooner than he thought? Why had she suddenly changed her tune? "What are you implying?" he risked.

Maggie tugged at the short gray tufts sprouting from her head, giving her hair a spikier than usual appearance. "Reed, I know you love that woman, and I only want the best for you. You know that. But I wonder if she's ready to return your love. It's not like—"

"Excuse me?" He narrowed his eyes at her. "Aren't you the one who said—?"

"I know what I said." She held up a hand. "I'm just not sure who's getting the better deal out of all this, that's all."

"Why does this have to be a *deal?* I know you don't think love is something to be bargained for. C'mon, Maggie." She was starting to sound like his sister.

"I just don't want to see you get hurt, Reed. You deserve better than a woman who is still grieving, a woman with nothing, a woman who is having another man's baby."

He cringed inwardly to hear Olivia described that way.

"Maggie, I'm a big boy. I know what I'm doing, okay? Besides, you don't know Olivia. I'm not going to get hurt." He was starting to sound like a broken record. Hadn't he given his sister the same speech last time they'd talked?

He put down his paintbrush and slid off the stool. He went to Maggie, putting his hands on her shoulders. "Tell you what. As soon as Olivia gets off bed rest, you're coming over to meet her. Once you get to know her, you'll see how dumb it was for us to even have this conversation."

Maggie laughed and shook her head. "Great. Now I'm dumb."

"No, no… Not you. The conversation."

"Whatever."

"Said the surly teenager," he deadpanned.

Maggie laughed and Reed joined in, grateful that with their laughter the tension seeped from the room.

"It'll take a couple days for the paint to dry, but I promise I'll have something ready for Gavin by Monday morning."

Maggie went to the worktable—the table he'd come to think of as Olivia's—and went to work assembling a new batch of stretcher boards. Between what Olivia had accumulated before she left and what Maggie built today, he would have enough to last for two years. Maybe three, if he didn't get in gear and start painting faster.

The thought spurred him into action and he picked up his brush again, determined to finish a piece before he went to see Olivia tonight.

Chapter Twenty-Eight

The drone of the television had become the background music of her life. Olivia sighed and groped the sofa cushions, searching for the remote. After a full week of watching nothing but the five local channels Hanover Falls had to offer, she yearned for a patch of silence—and at the same time she was starving for company.

She'd always enjoyed any moment of solitude she could find in her life. But before Derek's death, her alone times had been minutes snatched here and there while juggling a demanding career and a difficult marriage. Derek had often complained that she scheduled more time for being alone than she did for being with him.

It was probably true. It made her sad now to admit it. More and more, she was realizing how selfish she'd been in their marriage. Because Derek had been the one committing the "ultimate" sin, she'd always slapped the selfish label on him. Now she had awakened to the truth of the matter. It wasn't an easy burden to carry, especially since there was no way she could ever make amends. *Oh, Derek, I'm so sorry. God, forgive me.*

She aimed the remote at the TV and clicked it off. In the sudden silence, her guilt was compounded when she realized how deeply she longed for Reed's presence right now. He'd come over every evening since the doctor ordered her to bed, bringing her something to eat, feeding and watering Tiger, and mowing the lawn for her. Twice, he'd insisted on staying while the sprinklers ran so she wouldn't have to get up to turn them off. She suspected that was merely an excuse for him to spend more time with her. She didn't mind. She was as hungry for his company as he seemed to be for hers.

She glanced toward the end table to the sketchpad and a set of watercolor paints Reed had brought her yesterday. She hadn't mustered the energy to use them yet, but the gift touched her deeply. Reed was constantly affirming her in one way or another. And every moment of joy he gave her was paid for with another brick of guilt on the already-impressive stack she carried in her heart. Guilt because Reed was practically supporting her, and now she could never work enough hours to pay him back. Guilt because she was afraid she was tacitly promising him something she wasn't sure she could deliver emotionally.

Worst of all, guilt because she had feelings for Reed that she'd never had for her own husband.

She laid a hand flat on her belly and waited for the peace that now seemed to follow the simple action of touching the place where her body cradled her child. It was one very good thing that had come out of this scare with the baby.

She was ashamed to remember how desperately she had *not* wanted this child in the beginning. How callous she'd felt toward Derek's baby. At first, her pregnancy had been nothing more to her than an inconvenience, a setback. But lying in the hospital, coming to terms with the fact that she might miscarry, something changed. She began to realize that she was terrified of losing the baby.

And it surprised her to discover that she already loved him… Or her. For some reason, she always thought of the baby as a boy. Maybe because she knew Derek had secretly longed for a son. Someone to carry on his name. And someone to share his love of baseball and motorcycles and all the other things Derek's own father had been too busy to do with him. She wondered if it was worse for a child to grow up with a distant father, or without a father altogether. It made her sad that her baby would never know Derek. For the first time, she understood what a good daddy he might have been.

If God allowed her to carry this baby to term and raise Derek's child, she would be sure the child knew how much Derek had wanted and loved him—even without ever actually knowing about him. At the last sonogram, she'd decided not to find out if the baby was a boy or a girl. She wasn't sure why, but she didn't regret her decision. She didn't care if she was carrying a son or a daughter, healthy or handicapped. She loved this child. And she finally understood what a gift God had given her in this pregnancy.

She still didn't know how she would manage to work and take care of a baby, yet still pay the bills. But then, she hadn't known what she'd do for a job when she first moved to the Falls, and God had taken care of that, hadn't He? And given her dear friends in the process. Claire and her family, Reed…

She smiled, thinking of Reed. He had become a wonderful friend. Someone she could count on. He'd been so good to her through this whole scare with the baby, bringing her fast food and leftovers from his neighbor, Maggie. Heating up the casseroles that had started showing up from the church once Claire got out the word that Olivia was bedridden. Reed had taken care of a host of things for her—tasks she knew he didn't really have time for.

She just hoped he wasn't doing these things for the wrong reason. That they were only done out of friendship. Or even a sense of duty because she worked for him. Either of those would have been better than what she suspected was his true motivation.

Reed had been careful to keep the boundaries they'd talked about, and she'd tried to help him do so. But she sensed that he still had strong feelings for her.

She wondered if he guessed how deep her feelings for him had grown. She felt herself drifting into a daydream, a fantasy that had become unnervingly frequent—where she and Reed were together and happy, where she was free to love him. Free of guilt and free of the labels of widow and single mother…and gold digger.

Most of the time she fought against the fantasy, but tonight it was too tempting to pretend she had someone who treasured her, someone who wanted to take care of her every need. She closed her eyes and let the delusion carry her away.

"Olivia?" Claire's voice at the front door jarred her from the sweet thoughts. She looked up to see her friend standing on the other side of the screen.

She pushed herself up on the sofa cushions and ran a hand over her disheveled hair. "Come on in, Claire. It's open."

Claire swept into the room, a canvas tote bag on her shoulder and a cake pan in her arms. "Hi there. How's it going?"

"Oh, I'm fine. Getting a little tired of being so helpless, but I feel okay. I really think I could probably go back to work—"

"Don't you dare," Claire said, shaking a finger in Olivia's face.

"Don't worry. I'm being a good girl."

Claire slid the bag from her shoulder and set the pan on the end table. "From the Millinger family…at church. And I brought you some books. Thought you might be getting bored with television."

"Bless you. It is getting a little lonely here."

"Hasn't Reed been over today?"

"Not yet. I'm not sure he will. I can't expect him to come *every* night."

"Sure you can," Claire joked. "But seriously, he is such a sweetheart. Not that I know him that well, but from what I can see, you're lucky to have him."

Have him? Claire's terminology made her cringe inside. "He's just…being a nice boss."

Claire tilted her head and looked at her askance. "You're kidding, right?"

"What do you mean?"

"I think it's a little more than him being a nice boss, Olivia."

"Why do you say that?"

"Oh, come on. You'd have to be deaf, dumb and blind— emphasis on the dumb—to not see how Reed Vincent feels about you."

Olivia took in a deep breath and blew it out. "Oh, Claire, I don't know what to do about that."

"What do you mean?"

"I don't know… It just doesn't seem right. Look at me! I'm fat as a barn and—"

Claire sat on the arm of the sofa and leaned to pat Olivia's leg affectionately. "You're beautiful. Absolutely gorgeous."

Olivia wagged her head. "And…it's not only that. I…I think the world of Reed too, but…everything about it just seems wrong. It's too soon. Isn't it? Derek's only been gone for six months. Shouldn't I still be…?" Her voice broke and the old confusion tangled her in its web. "Can I ask you something, Claire?"

Concern creased her friend's brow. "Sure. Anything."

"Is it…? Do I have the right to feel something for Reed that I…never even felt for my husband?"

Claire's eyes widened and her brows lifted in question.

Olivia sighed and nodded. "It's true. Things weren't…they weren't like that with Derek and me."

"I didn't realize," Claire whispered.

"No. I wouldn't expect you to. But…we had problems. Big ones. But we were working them out," she added hastily. "This move… Hanover Falls was supposed to be a fresh start for us."

"Oh, Olivia. I'm so sorry. And you never got the chance…."

"No." She bent her head, feeling the weight of it all over again.

"Well, you're wise to be cautious where Reed is concerned. Give yourself time to grieve, time to come to terms with…everything that happened in your marriage. But Olivia, honey—" Claire smiled and gave Olivia's knee another motherly pat "—it's not a sin for you to be attracted to Reed Vincent. He's a sweetheart of a guy, and mighty easy on the eyes, I don't mind saying. You could do far worse than to fall in love with a man like that."

Olivia felt as if a window had been opened and fresh oxygen rushed in to replace the stale air she'd been breathing. She touched Claire's hand. "Thank you for that. You don't know how much I needed to hear it."

An impish grin painted Claire's face. "Oh, honey, yes, I do."

Chapter Twenty-Nine

"You crazy cat!" Reed lurched after Tiger as the cat leaped to the back of the couch. He missed and Tiger's tail swept a water bottle off the end table. The uncapped bottle tumbled, and Reed caught it a split second before it hit the floor. He juggled it from hand to hand, trying to steady it. But he squeezed too tight, sending a stream of water shooting out.

Olivia squealed and sputtered as icy water sprayed her in the face. Her screams sent Tiger darting down the hallway for safety as Reed tried desperately to gain control of the errant bottle.

By the time he finally succeeded, droplets of water dripped off Olivia's hair and down her face. The front of her shirt was soaked.

Reed tried to suppress the chuckle that rose in his throat at the sight of her droopy hair and the look of shock on her face, but he had no more control over his emotions than he'd had over the water bottle. Finally, he rolled with laughter, falling into a limp heap on the end of the couch where she reclined.

Her laughter echoed his until she finally held out her hands in supplication. "Hey, can you help me out here? I'm drenched." She tugged at her sopping shirt, trying in vain to fan it dry.

"Hang on, I'll get a rag."

Shaking water from his hands, Reed lumbered up from the couch and took the bottle into the kitchen. He found a dish towel in a drawer and took it back in to the living room where Olivia was attempting to finger comb her hair.

"Didn't I tell you cats were nothing but trouble?" he said, still chuckling.

"Hey, now, watch it. He can hear you."

On cue, Tiger peered around the corner from the hallway into the living room with a look of pure guilt on his feline features. Reed and Olivia exchanged glances and fell into another fit of laughter.

When they finally caught their breaths Reed snatched up the cat and deposited him on Olivia's lap. "I think you owe your mistress an apology, mister," Reed scolded.

Purring, the cat nuzzled her chin while she stroked him and rewarded him with cooing and kisses.

"Oh, that's real nice." Reed plopped back on the end of the couch and feigned a mope. "He drenches you. I risk life and limb to save the day, and *he's* the one getting hugs and kisses." He winced inwardly at the unintended implication of his words. But maybe it wasn't unintentional. For weeks now, he had been a perfect gentleman with Olivia, not pressuring her for more than friendship. But he'd be lying through his teeth if he pretended he was content with the situation. He was impatient as all get-out, and he didn't think he could ever be happy with only being friends. *I love her.* He started at the thought, wondering for a moment if he'd said it out loud. He'd never let himself bring the thought to completion before, but here it was now, plain and simple. He loved Olivia Cline.

Olivia lifted Tiger and set him on the carpet beside the couch. "Aww…" She tilted her head and gave him a coy smile. "Is somebody feeling a little jealous?"

She was teasing, but she'd nailed his feelings on the head. "Okay. I feel like an idiot being jealous of a cat, but yes. I am jealous."

A look that was part fear, part something he couldn't interpret, came to her eyes. "Reed…"

He held out a hand. "I'm not going to lie to you, Olivia. I've been patient for a long time. I'm doing my best, but it's getting old." Okay. He'd said it, walked right into it with his eyes—and his heart—wide-open.

"Oh, Reed. I don't know what to say. I've loved having you here with me, keeping me company. I've appreciated everything you've done for me more than you can know. I... You're the best friend I could ever ask for and—"

He felt his jaw tense. "Best friend...? I don't want to be just your friend, Olivia."

She closed her eyes, as if she were staving off some sort of pain. When she finally looked at him again, there was a new determination in her expression.

His heart dropped like a stone. But then her words took him by surprise. "Reed. Oh, Reed." Her voice dropped to a whisper, but her eyes held his. "I have never felt about any man the way I feel about you. Not...not even my own husband."

Her voice caught, and she surprised him by reaching over the blanket covering her legs to take his hand. The effect was electrifying. The heat of their fingers, touching, entwining, seared him. Not taking his eyes off hers, he lifted her hands to his face and kissed her fingertips. He saw in her eyes, felt in her touch, that she was feeling the same sensations. Desire filled him until he didn't think he could bear it another moment.

Unknitting his fingers from hers, he leaned across the couch and took her face in his hands. He traced the outline of her lips with his thumb and then he leaned in and kissed her with a tenderness that came with difficulty. What he wanted to do was take her in his arms and crush her to him.

At first she matched his kiss, but then she gently pushed him away, yet still gripping the front of his shirt.

Her hands trembled. "It's too soon, Reed. I...I can't. Give me time. Please. Be patient with me."

It took every ounce of his strength to disengage himself from her gentle touch, but he took her small hand between both of his and moved it from his face, and with a reluctant pat, placed it back in her lap. "I understand, Olivia, and I'll respect that. But...I'm not sorry."

A puckish grin spread over her face. "Me, neither," she whispered.

* * *

From her perch on the sofa, Olivia looked around the living room. As much as she'd loved the changes she'd made to this house a few weeks ago, after three weeks of staring at the same view, she was sick to death of this room. The very upholstery on the sofa was starting to drive her batty.

Tonight, however, the luscious smell of popcorn improved her outlook considerably. Olivia inhaled deeply and adjusted the pillows at her back.

"Here we go…" Reed stepped from the kitchen juggling a giant bowl overflowing with fluffy white kernels, and two cans of Dr Pepper. He leaned to transfer the icy-cold cans to the coffee table, and she reached to take the bowl from the crook of his elbow.

"Mmm, this looks great," she said, scooping up a fistful of popcorn.

"So what do you want to watch tonight?" He picked up three DVDs from the floor beside the sofa. "I've got *The Sound of Music*—again. Or *Peter Pan* or—"

"Would you mind if we didn't watch a movie tonight?"

He looked up in surprise. "Is something wrong?"

"Oh, no. It's just…well, how many times can a woman watch *Peter Pan* without going absolutely stark raving out of her gourd?" She feigned yanking her hair out by the roots.

Reed laughed. "We have kind of overdosed on that one, haven't we?" He held up a hand defensively. "Hey, I'm just trying to follow doctor's orders. Nothing upsetting for the little lady." He gave her knee a proprietary pat.

"And I appreciate it. Really I do." She patted him back, letting her hand linger on his. They were hungry for excuses to touch each other these days. Reed hadn't tried to kiss her again. But oh, that one kiss had opened the door to a new, more intimate friendship between them.

If she had loved Derek at all, then what she felt for Reed Vincent was something she couldn't even define. The feelings he evoked in her made her heart soar. And made it ache at the same time with a longing she'd never known. She checked herself at yet another comparison of Reed to Derek, but it was sometimes hard not to compare the two men. She had to keep reminding herself of the man Derek had become in the final months before his death. Why couldn't she remember the gentler, penitent version of her husband as well as she remembered the man who had called her each evening to lie about his whereabouts?

Life was so unfair. Why had it been so easy to fall into marriage with Derek, and so difficult once the vows had been spoken? And now, with Reed, it seemed the opposite. It seemed that a host of insurmountable obstacles kept them from being together. She dared not even imagine what rumors were flying around town. The town's most eligible bachelor taking up with a needy widow who was about to deliver a baby. It was the stuff of supermarket tabloids in a town the size of Hanover Falls.

Reed had told her about his next-door neighbor's reservations. He'd said it almost as a joke, but because Olivia knew how much Reed valued Maggie's opinion, it stung her.

In the past weeks, Reed had shared so much with her about his life. They'd carefully steered clear of talking about "them," but in the few weeks she'd been bedfast, they had shared some of their deepest secrets with each other. And still, she couldn't seem to get enough of him. She wanted to know more about what made this wonderful man tick.

If she were honest with herself, she was terrified that she would eventually go deep enough to discover that, like Derek, Reed was horribly flawed. That loving him would lead to nothing but grief. That had been her experience with love.

Instead, it seemed the better she knew Reed, the more she respected the man he was. He wasn't perfect. But his own awareness of his flaws and his desire to be worthy of her respect made her trust him in a way she'd never trusted another man—another human being—before.

Reed's heart had been broken by a woman he'd once loved, and he had trouble trusting women for different reasons than she distrusted men. Kristina, his old girlfriend, had walked out of Reed's life at a time when it looked as though he might lose his eyesight. Reed so seldom spoke of the frightening disease that almost cost him his sight that Olivia had trouble realizing how awful it must have been for him. But apparently Kristina had decided she didn't love Reed enough to stick with him "in sickness and in health." Though he shrugged it off, it was obvious that he had been devastated by her rejection.

It had brought her to tears to realize that Reed's devotion to her even in her "condition" was probably the result of his own rejection under similar circumstances. Reed had allowed that sorrow to make him a better person. Had *she* become more compassionate because of what she'd been through with Derek? Or had she only become bitter? It was a question that weighed heavily on her.

"Hey, you." Reed's voice shook her from a reverie that had grown melancholy. "Where are you?" he asked, putting a finger under her chin and tipping her face to meet his gaze.

She shook off the heavy thoughts. "Sorry. I was far, far away for a minute there."

"Want to talk about it?"

"I'd rather watch *Peter Pan*."

"That bad, huh?"

"Just not a place I want to stay right now."

"Sometimes it helps to talk about it, Liv."

She shook her head. "Not tonight. Maybe someday."

"Okay." He gave a Tinkerbell grin. "Tonight we'll only think happy thoughts."

Chapter Thirty

Olivia flipped the car radio to a country station and adjusted her rearview mirror. She caught a flash of her reflection and even though her eyes and forehead were all that were visible, the crinkles in the reflection told her she was smiling to herself. Again. There were no words to describe how wonderful it was to be out of the house. Off that hideous sofa. But her smile was for more than that. Far more than that.

These days, the mere thought of Reed Vincent had the power to bring a smile to her lips. Something precious had grown between them these past weeks while she'd been restricted to bed rest. She lifted a hand to her throat, expecting to touch the silver locket Derek had given her. But she'd forgotten to put it on when she'd dressed this morning.

She had begun to admit to herself—though she dared not voice it to anyone else—that she was in love with Reed. And she suspected that he felt the same about her.

It was a knowledge she treasured in her heart. But for now, her energies had to stay focused on this baby. As much as Reed had made the downtime a joy, it had been difficult in many ways, too. She'd had far too many hours to think. And far too frightening thoughts to think.

She would soon be a single mom to a tiny infant. She needed to get the house on the market. But even if the doctor took her off bed rest today, as he'd hinted, she couldn't think of trying to make a move at this point in her pregnancy.

She pulled into the clinic parking lot, her mind reeling. With all her worrying, she'd probably spiked her blood pressure to the point where Dr. Bennington would send her straight back to bed. After she chewed her out for driving herself to the appointment.

She took a deep breath and willed her heartbeat to slow. After a minute, she turned off the ignition and mentally prepared for the doctor's verdict.

Dr. Bennington closed Olivia's chart and smiled. "I think you can resume normal activity…within reason," she said. "You haven't had any bleeding or cramping for over two weeks now and the baby's vital signs—and yours—are all good."

Olivia let out the breath she'd been holding. This must be how a prisoner felt when the parole board signed release papers. She'd been on bed rest for just over four weeks, but it had felt like aeons. She remembered when Jayne, in the sixth month of her first pregnancy, had been ordered to bed for the duration. She'd had little sympathy for her friend at the time. In fact she'd felt a little envious. Now she understood how difficult that must have been for Jayne. With her freedom returned to her, Olivia felt like running a marathon.

As if Dr. Bennington had read her mind, she narrowed her eyes and shook a finger at Olivia. "Just because I'm taking you off bed rest doesn't mean you can go crazy. You say your work isn't too strenuous, so I'm going to let you go back, but I want you to put your feet up whenever you can and let somebody else do the bulk of the housework. No heavy lifting, no jogging or other strenuous exercise. And if you start cramping or bleeding again, call me right away."

"I will."

The thought sobered her, and later, as she drove away from the clinic, she mentally adjusted her plans for the afternoon. Still, she couldn't wait to tell Reed that she would be back to work tomorrow.

* * *

Reed whistled an off-key tune under his breath as he un-clamped a painting from the easel. It was a good one. He'd have to get it sent out the minute the paint was dry. The gallery in St. Louis had sold three of his nautical pieces to a new office park and he was having trouble keeping them supplied.

But his happy whistling had far more to do with the lovely woman seated at the worktable in his studio than it did the lovely painting he'd just completed. Olivia was back at work, doing well, and he felt as if a light had come back on in his studio.

Funny, he'd had similar thoughts all those weeks ago when the gift of his sight had been returned. Now that seemed to pale in comparison. He loved her so much. He'd given up even trying to pretend to himself that he didn't. He hadn't spoken the words to her yet. She said it was too soon, and he meant to honor her opinion. But sometimes he was afraid his love for her would spill over into words.

He watched her as they worked. If she knew how constant his thoughts toward her were, she would probably quit tomorrow.

Over the weeks that she'd been at home on bed rest, he had learned to know her so well. And he liked what he saw. Olivia had deep hurts from her marriage, but she was a caring, giving woman. He wasn't sure she had come to terms yet with the pain her husband had caused her, let alone come to an acceptance of his death. She especially struggled to understand why her husband had died just when things were looking more hopeful for them. He didn't understand it any better than she did.

And he felt guilty feeling grateful that Olivia was free.

But was she really free? Until she could let go of the grief and anger, she would not be free to love him. He had to keep remind-ing himself that it had only been seven months. Olivia was right. It was too soon. Far too soon. He'd read somewhere just the other day that the grieving process after losing a spouse could take two years or more. He honestly didn't know if he could wait that long. He also knew plenty of people who'd remarried, happily, within a year of losing their spouse. He clung to those examples. *Oh, Lord, You know I'm not a patient man.*

"Hey, is that finished?" Olivia's voice broke through his thoughts. In answer, he held up the painting for her approval.

"I like it. Very nice. Except I'll be glad when you go back to the landscapes. Those are my favorite."

He shrugged. "Gotta give 'em what they want."

"Does that ever bother you?"

"What?"

"That you're getting so popular that now you can't paint what you really want to."

"Um, excuse me…" Amusement gathered in his eyes. "Aren't you the one who wants me to go back to painting landscapes?"

She blushed and hid a sheepish grin behind one hand. "Oh. Yeah."

"I'm enjoying doing the nautical stuff. I'm just happy to be selling my paintings at all."

"Good point." She turned back to the frames she was assembling.

"I'm getting hungry. Do you want to go for an early lunch?"

She looked up at the clock. "At ten-thirty?"

He followed her gaze. "Is that all it is?"

She laughed. "We could do coffee and doughnuts."

"Oh, good idea. Do you feel like going out, or would you rather I go get something and bring it back here?"

"As long as I stay on the clock, I'm game to leave."

"You're on."

She started to say something, then hesitated. Finally, she met his eyes, then dipped her head behind the visor of her hand. "That was a stupid thing to say."

"What do you mean?"

She looked up again. "You don't know how grateful I am for this job, Reed. I shouldn't even joke about being on the clock. I owe you so many hours right now I'll never make it up to you."

He went around the desk and put his hands on her shoulders. "Look at me."

She gazed up at him through wavy bangs that had grown too long, framing her face like a cherub's.

"Olivia Cline. Let's get something straight right now, okay?"

She nodded like a petulant child.

He made his voice firm. "I am grateful for everything you have done for me. Right now things might be a little stacked in your favor. In a few months, it might be me who needs some extra help…or someone else. For now, would you please just let me be there for you? After the baby comes, when you're settled in to that whole routine, then you can return the favor."

She opened her mouth, but he silenced her with an upraised hand.

"If not to me, then you can pay it forward to someone else."

She blew out a breath, as if he'd taken away her rebuttal.

"My point is," he said, "I want you to quit feeling guilty or beholden to me or whatever it is that puts that pathetic look in your eyes. Do you hear me?"

She nodded, her expression solemn.

"You're sure?"

"I hear you," she said. "Reed…"

He dropped his hands from her shoulders, letting his fingers trail down her arms, lingering to stroke her dainty wrists. "What?"

"Thank you. I don't know what I would have done without you. Not just this past month when I had to be off my feet, but ever since I met you. I'll never be able to pay you back, but I want—"

He clicked his tongue in exasperation and pinned her with a stern look. "Were you listening to a word I said?"

Again, that sheepish smile. "I heard you. Were you listening to a word *I* said?"

"I heard you. You're grateful. And I'm grateful. We're a pretty grateful pair. So that's the end of that. Okay?"

"Okay," she whispered.

"Now—" He brushed his hands in a down-to-business gesture. "Did somebody say something about doughnuts?"

Her laughter was musical.

Chapter Thirty-One

The roar of the vacuum sweeper was music to Olivia's ears. She was probably pushing her limits, but while she had the energy, she wanted to get some cleaning done.

It was so good to be up and off that sofa. Never again would she wish for mandatory bed rest. A month-long nap was not all it was cracked up to be.

The baby rolled lazily in her womb as she moved the sweeper in long, slow strokes across the carpet. She'd lost whatever momentum she'd had on decorating the house, but it was an improvement just to get it cleaned and straightened after her hiatus on the sofa. She glared at the offending piece of furniture. The minute she had a few extra dollars, that sofa was getting slipcovered.

She finished the carpets and dusted the living room before starting in on the desk in the dining room. The smooth oak surface was buried in a landslide of junk mail and bills, and dotted with the remains of half a dozen floral arrangements she'd received while she was bedridden—most of them from Reed.

She emptied the vases and baskets into a large trash bag, culled the urgent-looking envelopes from the junk mail and tossed the remaining heap into the bag, as well. She hadn't felt so energetic in ages. Wanting to take advantage of this burst of energy, she scooped the remaining contents of the desk into the apron of her maternity shirt and dumped everything onto the dining-room table for sorting.

She pulled out a chair and began the slow process of sorting the papers into various stacks—bills in one pile, coupons in another, catalogs and flyers to the trash. As she systematically worked her way through the pile, her eyes fell on a white business envelope.

She read the return address twice before she remembered what was inside. Mid-America Transplant Services. The thank-you note from one of the transplant recipients of Derek's organs. It was the only thank-you she'd ever received from the agency. She'd tucked it away in a pile of documents, not wanting to deal with it at the time. Now she thought of the story in the Bible where Jesus had healed ten lepers, but only one of them had come back to say thank-you. Again, she wondered about the person who had written the letter.

She slipped the single page from the envelope and unfolded the paper, letting her eyes roam over the words. Something told her to wait. She didn't need a reminder of that tragic time right now. She'd been doing so well, and getting agitated wouldn't be good for the baby's health.

But something drew her. She read through the letter, finding more comfort in the words this time than when she'd first received it. She saw more clearly from where she stood now, how God had brought something good out of Derek's death. The handwriting seemed almost familiar as she read to the end of the letter and wondered again about the person who had written it.

She looked at the signature. REV. She shook her head, trying to clear a sudden fogginess that had come over her. She knew that signature. Knew it well.

Her heart began to pound as the haze cleared.

Reed Elliott Vincent.

Those were Reed's initials. The signature belonged to him. She'd seen it a dozen times now, working in his studio as he'd signed order forms and delivery receipts.

But that couldn't be right. What did Reed have to do with this? It had to be a coincidence. She turned the letter over, seeking some clue that would explain it. She picked up the envelope and examined it. It bore a St. Louis postmark, but that was where the transplant services office was located. The letter writer could have come from anywhere.

She stared at the initials again. She hadn't even known Reed at the time of Derek's death. It had to be a weird coincidence.

Like a bolt of lightning, a snippet of a conversation she'd had with Reed came back to her. *I have to save my eyes for the more tedious work.... I had surgery a few weeks ago....*

Her hand flew to her mouth. Surely Reed wasn't...? "No, God," she whispered. "Please no. This can't be right. It can't be true." Like pieces of a bizarre puzzle, details started to snap into place.

And suddenly, the puzzle was complete and she knew beyond a shadow of a doubt that it *was* true. The letter in her hand had come from Reed Vincent. Looking at it again, in spite of the way the creased page shivered between her trembling fingers, she saw it clearly. Reed's handwriting had become as familiar to her as her own. Why hadn't she seen it before, the first time she'd read the letter?

But the letter had arrived in the mail weeks ago, before she'd grown to know Reed so well. Before she would have recognized his handwriting or his signature, or the gentle way he phrased his words.

She read the letter again, and she could hear the words in Reed's low voice. Could see the compassion on his face as he penned them.

An alarming new thought struck her. Had he *known?* Had Reed been deceiving her all this time, playing some kind of cruel trick on her? Making a fool of her?

Her brain whirled, trying to put the dates in some kind of order that made sense. The postmark was dated May 12. That was almost a month after she'd started working for Reed. Had he *known* he was writing to *her* when he penned those words?

She read them again. Nothing in the language hinted that he had targeted her, but maybe that had been purposeful. Maybe he'd worked hard to disguise his identity. After all, he had mailed it through the agency. But if he knew, why didn't he just tell her?

Her thoughts were a tangled mass. She dropped her head to her hands and rubbed her temples.

What did this all mean? The surgery Reed had referred to was a corneal transplant. That meant—

An icy finger of alarm traced her spine. Reed had received corneal tissue from Derek. From her husband's eyes. When she looked at Reed, when she looked into his eyes, it was really Derek's eyes she was seeing. She shuddered. The rational part of her mind understood that the transplant had only involved a thin membrane of tissue. But her heart...

Her mind raced. Reed had blue eyes and Derek's were—*had been*—hazel, with flecks of green. Not the same eyes at all.

Still, it was too unnerving, eerie even, to think that Reed looked at her through the same physical window through which her husband had viewed the world.

How could she ever look into Reed's eyes again without thinking about the chilling link that connected the two men she loved?

Chapter Thirty-Two

The air conditioner kicked off, leaving the *tick tock tick* of the big clock filtering through the studio. Reed looked away from his painting long enough to note the time. Strange. It was almost nine o'clock and Olivia hadn't shown up for work yet.

Maybe she had a doctor's appointment, but he didn't remember her telling him about one. It wasn't like her to be late.

He went back to work, basking in the satisfaction of a painting almost finished—one that had turned out particularly well, he thought. With Olivia back to work, he'd finally eased into a good production pace and was doing a better job of keeping up with the demand of the galleries.

He heard the key in the front door. Good. She was here. He hadn't realized that he was worried until he felt the muscles in his shoulders and neck relax.

"Good morning," he hollered when he heard her footsteps in the kitchen.

He daubed his brush back into the paint, but glanced up briefly as she came into the studio. "Did you have a doctor's appointment that I forgot about?"

Olivia didn't reply, but came to stand beside his stool at the easel. She held out a white envelope.

Balancing his paint palette on his forearm, he leaned to look at the letter, but his eyes couldn't focus on the small print. "What's this?"

"You tell me." She thrust the envelope under his nose.

The trembling in her voice made him start and really look at her. Her face was ashen, her lips set in a thin line. "Olivia? What's wrong? What is it?" He balanced the brush on the palette and slid them onto the counter beside the easel.

He took the envelope from her and adjusted his glasses. He read the return address. An alarm went off somewhere in the back of his mind. He looked at her for permission to open the letter.

She stood mute, but her chin started to quiver.

What was going on? He unfolded the page, and brought it close enough to decipher the words. His heartbeat staggered when he recognized his own handwriting. Quickly, he scanned the page.

It was his letter! The one he'd written to the family of the organ donor—the man who'd donated the corneas for his transplant. He turned to Olivia, pleading with his eyes for explanation.

"You wrote this." The words came out on a ragged breath. A statement.

"H-how did you get this?"

"Do you really not know?" Anger tinged each clipped syllable.

"I…" He held out his arms in bewilderment, the letter fluttering in his right hand. "No. I don't know."

"Did you have a corneal transplant in March?" Her words were measured, monotone.

He nodded slowly. "Yes. But…why do you have my letter? I don't understand."

"Don't you? You really don't know, Reed?" Now her tone rose to a wail.

"Know what? What is going on?" His mind reeled. How had Olivia gotten hold of that letter? And why was she so upset? What did any of this have to do with her?

She snatched the letter from his hands. It ripped and he was left holding a corner of the paper. "This is Derek!" With the letter crumpled in her fist, she jabbed at the air, her voice rising out of control. "Do you really not get it, Reed? This was my husband! He was killed March 14. When was your surgery?"

He heard a sharp intake of breath mingled with a low moan. It took him a few seconds to realize the sound had come from his own throat. "What do you mean? Olivia, what are you talking about?" But even while his questions still hung in the air, everything she'd said crystallized and he knew the awful truth: Derek Cline was the donor whose corneas he had received. Olivia was the "family" to whom he'd written that letter. Never in his most absurd dreams could he have conjured up this scenario!

Yet, it all came together now in one terrible moment of clarity. Derek had been killed in that explosion out at Parker & Associates. Olivia had told him that, and he vaguely remembered hearing about the accident when it happened. But he'd never really followed the story because only a few days after it happened, he'd been called in for the transplant surgery. He'd never imagined the two events could be connected. Never had any reason to.

Olivia backed away from him and slumped onto the wide steps that led up to the kitchen. She dropped her head to her hands, weeping without making a sound.

Numb, he went to her. Dropped down beside her, put an arm around her shoulders.

But she shrugged him off, as though his touch were repulsive to her.

He slid from the steps to his knees, knelt in front of her, trying to get her to look at him. "Olivia. Listen to me. I didn't know. I had no idea."

She remained head down, hands covering her face.

He laid a hand on her shoulder, trying to comfort. But she flinched as though he'd struck her.

He swallowed his pain and spoke softly. "Did you think I knew? That I deceived you? Olivia, I didn't know. I swear to you. I had no idea. But…even if it's true, this doesn't change anything. I love you, Olivia." His breathing came hard, his heart hammering in his chest. He hadn't meant to confess his love today. Certainly not under these circumstances.

She wrapped her arms around herself and rocked back and forth on the steps as if she were in physical agony.

He scooted on his knees closer to her and wrapped her in his embrace, whispered into her hair. "I love you, Liv. Nothing will ever change that."

"No, Reed. No." She wagged her head against him, but seemed powerless to fight him anymore. "It's wrong," she said. "I should have known. It…it was too soon. I…I barely know you, Reed. This just proves it."

"Proves what? What are you talking about?"

She jerked her head up and stared into his eyes. Then, as though his gaze had scalded her, she looked away.

He understood then, with sickening clarity, why this seemed so impossible to her. When she looked into his eyes, she saw Derek Cline staring back at her—the man with whom she'd shared her life, her love. The man who had fathered the child she was carrying. When she looked at him—at Reed Vincent—how could she help but see anything except a man who had everything—his sight, his livelihood, his very life—because of her husband's death?

Now he understood. And he knew it was too great a price. He could not ask that of her. He let his arms drop, knowing what he had to do. He straightened, then struggled to his feet.

She peered up at him now, huddled and small on the steps.

"I'm sorry, Olivia. I'm so sorry."

She only shook her head.

"Olivia, I—" He stopped short. They were both in shock. This wasn't something that could be resolved in five minutes with a few sincere apologies. But he couldn't leave things hanging—not this way.

"I meant what I said, Olivia."

She stared at him, cheeks flushed, eyes wild. "You don't know what you're saying."

"Yes. I do." He nodded violently, as if his physical effort could prove his words. "You—"

"Look at me, Reed!" She pushed up from the steps with her elbows, lumbering to stand in front of him. "Look at me! I'm pregnant with another man's child. He's only been dead seven months. What kind of woman falls in love when her husband—?" She cut off her sentence, her voice cracking. "This is all my fault. It… I never should have let it happen. Any of it…"

"It wasn't anybody's fault, Olivia. Things just happened. We didn't know! There's no fault in all this. Can't you see that?" He cupped her face in the palm of his hand. "You know, Liv, love isn't supposed to be such a struggle."

The panic came back to her eyes. "I have to go."

"I'll take you home. You're in no frame of mind to drive."

"No." She brushed him off, went to the worktable and started gathering her things. "I'm sorry. I…I just have to get out of here."

He watched her go, wondering if he'd ever see her again. And knowing that she might be better off if he didn't.

Chapter Thirty-Three

Reed put down the phone and raked a hand through his hair. He'd been trying to reach Olivia since noon. It was after five o'clock now and still she didn't answer. Was she ignoring his calls or had something happened to her? Maybe she'd never made it home. The thought sent a tremor of terror down his spine.

He should have insisted on taking her home. She'd been terribly upset when she left his house this morning. But he'd wanted to give her some space. She'd discovered some heavy truths to come to terms with. He was still reeling himself. But he was worried. Although she seemed to be doing well with her pregnancy since the doctor had released her from bed rest, maybe something had gone wrong. Maybe the shock had triggered labor and she was in trouble.

He paced through the house, trying her phone again every few minutes. Olivia didn't have anyone to check up on her. She'd made a few friends at her church, but no one who would make sure she was safely home each evening, no one to help her if she wasn't feeling well. That had become his job—his privilege—over the last few months as he'd grown to love Olivia. Without him, she was alone in the world.

The knowledge goaded him into action. He grabbed his car keys from the kitchen counter and hurried to the garage.

Five minutes later he turned the Escape onto Glenwillow

Road. September was nearly over and the days were growing shorter. Already the sky was gloomy with dusk. There were no lights on in Olivia's house, except for one that glowed dimly from the back of the house—probably the kitchen.

Reed got out of the car and rang the doorbell. No answer. His loud knocking got no response, either. He went around back and checked the door. It was locked, but Tiger came racing from the side of the house and meowed up at him.

"Hey, buddy. Where is she?" He scratched the cat under the chin, suddenly feeling silly talking to a dumb cat. It relieved his mind that Tiger was here—and made him realize that his biggest fear was that Olivia would pack up and go back to Chicago. But she wouldn't leave Tiger alone.

The cat followed him to the garage. He peered in the side window to see that her car was gone. That eased his mind further. Maybe she'd just gone for a drive to think things over. Or maybe she'd driven to her friend Claire's house.

Back in the car, he bent over the steering wheel. *Be with her, Lord. Keep her safe. Show me what You want me to do, Father. Get my attention if I need to look for her.* He sat there, doing everything he knew to open his ears to what God might be telling him. He heard no trumpets, saw no flashing lights, but gradually peace came.

He didn't know how things would ultimately end between Olivia and him, but for tonight, he felt constrained to leave her alone. God loved her more than he ever could. Tonight he needed to trust Olivia to His care.

He would face tomorrow when the sun came up.

The sky was inky black when Olivia finally turned her car toward home. She had left Reed's house in a fog, aiming her car in the direction of Parker & Associates, needing some connection to Derek. Something to sober her and help her understand everything that had happened. She'd sat in the parking lot for almost an hour, weeping and confused and not getting any of her myriad questions answered. Finally, she'd left the office complex and headed down a paved county road that led to who-knew-where. She'd passed through a series of tiny burgs. Finally, as the sun sank below the trees, she turned the car back and headed home, not knowing what else to do.

But now, as she approached the turnoff for Glenwillow Road, she simply couldn't face the empty house. She had to talk to someone. And it could not be the one person she'd grown to depend on to be her best friend.

But maybe Claire? She turned her car toward the Merediths' house. Ten minutes later, she pulled up in front of the cozy Cape Cod. The house was ablaze with lights in nearly every window. A tricycle was parked haphazardly on the uneven sidewalk in front and a huge gray tomcat sat curled on the porch. What a difference between this homey place and her empty house on Glenwillow Road.

Before she could lose her nerve, she hurried to the door and punched the doorbell.

The door opened and Claire's inquisitive face appeared behind the screen. "Olivia! Come in, come in. What are you doing in our neighborhood?" She took in Olivia's face. "What's wrong?"

Olivia stepped over the threshold into the scent of cinnamon and vanilla. "Do you…do you have time to talk…just for a minute?"

Concern creased Claire's forehead. "What's wrong?"

"Oh, Claire…" She looked around the room, worried that Michael and little Katherine might overhear.

"What is it, Olivia? Please, come sit down. Michael took Kat to her grandma's in Billings, but he'll be back in a little bit."

"I won't stay long…you guys probably had a nice quiet evening together planned."

Claire's expression told her she was right, but her words didn't give her away. "Don't be silly. Come on in." Claire closed the door behind them and led the way through the living room to the rumpled family room off the kitchen where they'd sat when Olivia visited before.

"Can I fix you some tea?"

"Oh, that would taste good. It's almost chilly out tonight." She pulled her baggy sweater around her belly.

Claire turned on the flame under a chipped teakettle and came to sit across the table from Olivia. "Tell me what's going on." She glanced at Olivia's round belly. "Everything's okay with the baby?"

She sighed, her breath coming ragged after a day of tears. "I'm going back to Chicago." The statement surprised her almost as much as it surprised Claire. She hadn't realized how strongly she'd entertained that possibility until the words were out of her mouth.

"Olivia…" Claire frowned. "Oh, but why?"

"Oh, Claire. I just found out something that…" She put a fist to her mouth to staunch her sobs.

"What is it? What happened?" She waited while Olivia collected herself.

"I got this—" She pulled the rumpled letter from the pocket of her sweater and handed it to Claire.

Claire read it and looked up, confusion on her face.

"Reed wrote this." She pointed to the signature. "REV is Reed Elliott Vincent."

Claire's jaw went slack. "You mean…? He got…?" She put a hand to her face.

Olivia nodded and let the shocking story spill out in a stream still tinged with disbelief.

When she finished, Claire shook her head slowly. "It's almost too incredible to believe. It makes me wonder if…it's more than just a coincidence."

"What do you mean?"

"I'm not sure, but…I don't pretend to have any special insight into how God works in our lives, but maybe…maybe God is in this whole thing. Maybe it's all part of His plan. For you…and for Reed."

"What plan could that possibly be, Claire? I…I've tried to get it to make sense and I just can't. Any more than Derek's death makes sense."

"Oh, please don't misunderstand. I'm not saying Derek's death was God's will. I just wonder if this is part of God working all things for good…even something as terrible as your husband's death."

"I still don't get it."

The teakettle's low whistle rose to a piercing wail and Claire excused herself and jumped up to turn off the burner. As she poured water over tea bags, she eyed Olivia. "You care a lot for Reed, don't you?"

Olivia felt the heat rise up her neck. She didn't know how to answer without giving her true feelings away.

Claire brought steaming cups to the table and set one on a saucer in front of Olivia. Olivia made a production of dunking her tea bag, stirring her tea, hoping Claire wouldn't notice her flushed cheeks. But she felt her friend's eyes on her.

"Olivia?" Incredulity stole into Claire's voice. "Do you… Are you in love with Reed?"

Am I? Do I even know what that means anymore? She shook her head. "What kind of woman would I be if I was? Oh, Claire. I've been so unfair to Derek. We had our problems, but we were working things out. I'm having so much trouble remembering that…remembering the good times. Because…well, frankly, there weren't very many. And it—" her voice caught "—it wasn't Derek's fault that he died before we could make new memories—good ones. But I don't know if I can live on what might have been."

Claire reached across the table and put a hand on Olivia's arm. "God doesn't expect you to. He's given you a hope and a future." She moved her hand to place it gently over Olivia's belly. "Just think about it! This child is the chance for you to make those new memories. To have something good out of—"

The muted mechanical grind of a garage door opening caused them both to look toward the back kitchen door.

"That's Michael," Claire said.

She said it with apology in her voice, but Olivia didn't miss the spark of love and anticipation that was there, too. It was time for her to go. They probably didn't get much time alone, just the two of them. She pushed her cup away from the edge of the table and started to rise, but Claire stopped her.

"Just wait. Stay a little longer. Talk to Michael for a minute."

The kitchen door opened and Michael Meredith ducked

through it. He waved when he saw Olivia. "I wondered whose car was in the drive. Hi, Olivia."

Michael went to plant a kiss on Claire's forehead. She touched his cheek. "Did you get the princess delivered to Grandma's?"

"Safe and sound. She and Mom were deep in cookie dough by the time I left."

Watching their affectionate exchange, Olivia felt awkward and in the way. She pushed back her chair. "I really need to go…"

Michael held up a hand. "Oh, no, please. Don't leave on my account." He went to stand behind Claire and massaged her shoulders. "How are you feeling, babe?"

"Shh… I'm fine." She slanted a glance at him and Olivia didn't miss the silent warning she tried to send with her eyes.

Olivia looked from one to the other. Had Claire been sick? It would be just like her to listen to Olivia's troubles without mentioning her own.

But Michael ignored his wife's warning. "Didn't you tell Olivia our news?"

"Michael…" Claire turned to Olivia with a sheepish smile. "We're pregnant," she said, the smile growing to a full-fledged beam. "I just found out Monday."

"Oh, Claire! That's wonderful."

For a moment, Olivia forgot her own troubles. She smiled across the table at the dear couple. No one was more deserving than they were. "I bet Katherine is beside herself."

"We haven't told her yet. We thought we'd wait for a few weeks."

Olivia eyed Claire. "Is everything okay?"

"Oh, yes. I'm doing fine. But nine months is a long time for a little girl to wait."

Olivia gave an inward sigh of relief. "Well, I'm just thrilled for you."

"We can compare baby notes," Claire said. Then, her smile faded, as if she'd just remembered why Olivia was there, and that she wouldn't be around to compare notes. "Can I tell Michael…?"

Olivia shrugged and nodded.

"Honey—" Claire looked up at Michael, put her hands over his on her shoulders "—Olivia got some…disturbing news today."

"Oh?" Michael's eyes filled with genuine concern. He pulled out a chair beside Claire and sat down. He looked from Olivia to Claire, then back.

Claire explained about the letter.

When she finished, Michael blew out a heavy breath and shook his head in disbelief. "That's got to be a tough one to handle."

Olivia shrugged and dipped her head, not knowing how to respond.

"Honey," Claire said, "you spent quite a bit of time with Derek, didn't you?"

"Well, I only knew him for a few weeks before he died, but yes. We shared pretty openly in our men's group and Derek wasn't shy." He gave Olivia a smile. "Your husband was a great guy."

"He *was* a good guy." Olivia gave him a grateful smile that turned quickly to a frown. "We had our problems…in our marriage. Pretty serious problems. But things had gotten better before…"

Michael nodded. "Derek told me a little about your struggles. He dealt with a lot of guilt over his…affair. But he was so eager for you to come to the Falls and live together here. He was nervous about the house—whether you'd like it or not. He bragged about how you'd fix it up when you got here. I didn't realize you did it professionally until Claire told me, but Derek said you were really gifted at that kind of thing."

Olivia sat, stunned by all this. "Derek said that? That I was gifted?"

"Oh, yeah. More than once. He thought you hung the moon." Michael smiled thoughtfully, then cocked his head and studied her. "I take it he never got around to telling you?"

She shook her head and swallowed back tears.

"He was learning, Olivia. Even in the short time he was in our men's group, we saw him grow in his faith. And he never missed a meeting. Church, too. If he wasn't going back to see you in Chicago for the weekend, he was in church on Sunday morning, sometimes Sunday night. He soaked it all in. He gave the rest of us a run for our money with his questions about the Bible and what it meant to live out one's faith."

"Oh, Olivia," Claire said softly. "It's so sad that you didn't get to know that stronger side of him."

Olivia took a sip of the now-tepid tea, trying to get rid of the giant lump in her throat. "I guess I'm thinking it's sad that he didn't get to know this other side of me, either. I…I wasn't perfect in our marriage, not by a long shot." She bit her lip. "And now, in a way, I've been as unfaithful to Derek as he was to me."

Michael and Claire exchanged glances. "What do you mean?" Claire asked.

Olivia bent her head. "What I've felt…for Reed. It's like I've been unfaithful to Derek. Comparing him to Reed…and not in a good way. I don't think I ever really grieved Derek. And already my affections have turned to someone else, and—"

"No." Claire's voice rose. "You've got it all wrong, Olivia. You can't be unfaithful to a dead man!" Her face blanched and she put a hand to her mouth. "I'm sorry. That didn't come out very tactfully. But…I just think you're making yourself—and Reed—out to be villains. It's no crime that you happen to care for each other. Sure, it's probably wise to give yourself some space—" she gestured toward the letter Olivia had laid on the table "—especially after that.

"Olivia—" Claire touched her hand "—you have a *lot* on your plate right now. But if you love Reed…my goodness, there's no shame in your feelings for him. You don't have to punish yourself." She turned to her husband. "Don't you agree, Michael?"

He looked thoughtful. "Derek's only been gone a few months, so you may be right about not giving yourself enough time to grieve. Only you can know that. But I certainly wouldn't compare it to being unfaithful. And I've known more than one person who was legitimately ready to find love again before that first year of mourning was up. I don't know who set that timeline anyway."

Olivia toyed with the handle of her empty teacup. Could Claire and Michael be right? But what about the bizarre bond that now linked Derek and Reed? She sighed. "Even if you're right, why would God have let Derek, of all people, end up being the donor for Reed? That just seems like a cruel joke."

"I don't see it that way," Michael said thoughtfully. "Obviously, the transplant was a blessing to Reed. You care for Reed. Is it possible that God orchestrated everything so that you would get to meet someone who directly benefited from the generosity that caused Derek to sign that donor card?" He shrugged. "I'm only speculating, but it seems possible. It seems like something God would do."

Olivia shook her head. "I don't know…I'm just so confused. About everything. I…I don't feel like I can think straight. Maybe time will heal these wounds. Maybe there will come a day when I can see this differently, but for now, I can't stay here. I can't. It's not fair—to Derek or to Reed." The baby turned flips inside her and she gave a little gasp. Knitting her fingers into a cradle under her belly, she bowed her head. "And it's not fair to Derek's child."

She scooted her chair back from the table. "I really do need to go."

"Can we pray with you first?" Claire asked.

"I'd like that."

To Olivia's surprise, Claire and Michael got up and came to put their hands on her shoulders.

Michael prayed, asking God to give Olivia wisdom and peace and direction. Listening to his sonorous voice, her thoughts calmed and she felt the first glimmer of hope since she'd discovered Reed's letter.

"We'll keep you in our prayers," Claire told her a few minutes later as she and Michael walked Olivia to her car.

"Thanks, you guys. And I'm so sorry to ruin your evening."

Michael shook his head. "Please. It was our privilege. If there's anything we can do to help, you let Claire know. We'll do whatever we can, Olivia."

Olivia drove home without an inkling of what tomorrow would hold. Would she be able to sell her house? Could she find a job in Chicago—especially now that she was seven months pregnant? Would she ever see Reed again?

And yet, over it all, she felt a tentative peace. She remembered a Scripture Claire had copied on a note card when Olivia was threatening to miscarry. "The eternal God is your refuge, and underneath are the everlasting arms."

She felt those everlasting arms carry her now into the unknown.

Chapter Thirty-Four

The doorbell pierced the silence of the studio. Reed slid his paint palette onto the counter and glanced at the clock. Nine-fifteen and Olivia hadn't come in to work yet, but he knew her special ring and that wasn't it.

Sighing, he plunked his paintbrush in a jar to soak and wiped his hands on a rag. He padded through the kitchen, praying he wouldn't be forced to give a studio tour or talk to a prospective client. He wasn't in the mood to see anyone.

His pulse quickened when he saw Olivia's car in the drive. He opened the door.

She stood on the porch, slump-shouldered and definitely not dressed for work, in black dress pants and a billowy blouse. Her eyes were red and swollen, her makeup streaked.

"You look terrible." He beckoned her inside.

She ignored his comment. "Reed, I'm sorry…I know this leaves you in the lurch, but—" she started crying "—I can't do this."

"Here…" He put a hand lightly on the small of her back and led her to an overstuffed chair in the living room. She slumped onto the cushions, still overcome by tears.

"It's okay," he said, sitting on the edge of the couch across from her. "Take your time." He waited for her to collect herself. She lifted the flared sleeve of her blouse and dabbed at her eyes.

"Here—" He jumped up and went into the bathroom and brought her back a wad of tissues.

"Thanks." She took them and blotted her cheeks, then blew her nose. She straightened and looked up at him, taking a deep breath. "Reed, I think the world of you. I really do. But I think…" She bit her lip.

It was all he could do not to take her in his arms and quiet her with his kisses so he didn't have to hear whatever she would say next. But he sat numb while she went on.

"I think I kind of got mixed up in my grief. I came here with all these hopes and dreams for Derek and me to…to finally have what we'd never had together. To finally be rid of all the baggage of our old marriage. And then he was gone and…well, I was still looking for that. I found it in you, but it was—it *is*—too soon." She swallowed hard and smiled an apology. "This whole thing with the transplant, realizing it was you who wrote that letter… Well, it served as a wake-up call for me. It made me realize I rushed into things with you. I was so lonely, and you…you've been such a good friend. But I can't stay with things…the way they are. I need some time. I need to sort things out. There're too many things I'm still working through. And it's not fair to make you wait while I get my head on straight and—"

"Olivia, I—"

"No, please, Reed." She held up a hand. "Let me finish. I've decided to put my house on the market. I'm moving back to Chicago."

The breath went out of him and he had to remind himself to take in the next gulp of air. "No, Olivia. Don't. You don't have to do that. I'm not going to bug you. I'll respect your—"

But she was already shaking her head vehemently. "I have to get away, Reed. I can't…I can't live my life wondering when I'll run into you next. When I'll see something that reminds me of you…"

He felt as if she'd struck him. She was eliminating the possibility of them having any contact at all. Saying that she couldn't stand even to look at him or think of him. "What will you do in Chicago?"

"I don't know, honestly. I just know I can't stay here."

"Olivia. Please…don't. I understand this is hard for you, but… Surely you don't have to leave town!"

She smiled a crooked smile. "Yes. I do." Her expression turned serious. "And I truly am sorry to leave without giving you more notice to—" she shook her head and her eyes misted again "—to find someone to take my place."

One solitary thought imprinted itself on his mind: *No one could ever take your place, Olivia. No one.*

By the following Friday, Olivia's life had undergone a metamorphosis as profound as the move to Hanover Falls had been. In a whirlwind week, she listed the house on Glenwillow Road, and arranged to stay with Jayne for a few days until an apartment in Chicago became available.

She'd had a final appointment with Dr. Bennington. The woman had expressed concern to hear Olivia was moving, but she set up an appointment for Olivia with a colleague in Chicago.

While Olivia had made phone calls and begun to pack up the house again, the maples outside her kitchen window had quietly changed into their autumn cloaks. It struck her that she'd seen three seasons now in Hanover Falls. But autumn would be her last. She would spend the cold winter back home in Chicago.

As if it had read her thoughts, the wind gusted around the corner of the house and whistled through the back door. Olivia emptied a row of kitchen drawers into a cardboard box. Fortunately, even after her decorating foray a few weeks ago, most of their things—*her* things—were still in boxes. She taped the box shut and wrote *Kitchen* in bold letters on two sides.

Money would be incredibly tight until this house sold. It depressed her to think how long it might be before that happened. But the Realtor said the housing market in the Falls had improved some over the last few months, and she was hopeful it wouldn't become an issue.

It didn't matter either way. She simply could not stay here.

She started in on a cupboard, wrapping the breakable items in newspaper. Tiger batted at a crumpled ball of newsprint, but he soon lost enthusiasm for the game and sat watching with narrowed eyes and tail twitching as Olivia taped another box shut.

Michael and Claire had agreed to take Tiger. She couldn't think too hard about leaving him behind without the tears starting. But the apartment didn't allow pets, and Tiger didn't have a "gravy train" in Chicago. Besides she could never again look at the cat, stroke his soft fur, without thinking of Reed. And wasn't that the whole purpose of this move? So she wouldn't think about him?

She tried to conjure up excitement about going back to Chicago, going *home*. But all she felt was fear. As much as she'd missed the challenges of her design job and the energy of the city, she was all too aware that she wasn't going back to the life she'd had before. She'd only seen the apartment in a pixelated photo on the Internet, but it was a far cry from this house. And she'd have to find a job. Probably not until after the baby came. She looked down at the chambray shirt—an old one of Derek's—stretched so tight over her middle that the buttons gaped. No one would hire her like this.

If there was anything good about all the changes to come— and the accompanying worry—it was that she had no time to think about what she was leaving. *Who* she was leaving.

She should have gone back to Chicago the day after Derek's memorial service. Then none of this would have ever happened. She would never have met Reed, never have had to say goodbye to Michael and Claire, never have had to leave her church or give away this little cat.

Slowly, the sadness in her heart gave way to anger and a bitter taste rose in her throat. She closed the flaps on another box and yanked the tape dispenser hard across the length of the top.

While the moving van idled on the street out front, Olivia walked through the house one last time. She had done this very thing so recently in the town house in Chicago. She couldn't help but compare her state of mind today to the mixture of trepidation and hope that had characterized her last move. Was it really only a little more than seven months ago? Who could have known the events that would transpire in that brief span of time?

I knew. From the time the foundations of the earth were laid, I knew every detail that would come to pass.

She started. The words hadn't come from an audible voice, but she was beginning to recognize that still, small voice through which God's Spirit spoke to her. It was the truth, of course. Yet she'd never considered it until this moment. God wasn't surprised by anything that had happened. Not by Derek's death, not by the revelation that Reed had been the recipient of Derek's corneas. And not when she'd conceived Derek's baby mere days before his death. All along, God had been aware of every minute detail.

"Ma'am?"

She turned to see the moving van's burly driver hulking in the doorway. He held out a sheet of paper. "We're ready to pull out. I need you to sign this before we take off."

The print on the page blurred. She made a show of scanning the legalese, but the words may as well have been in a foreign language. She finally signed her name on the line the driver indicated.

"Everything is labeled," she told him. "You have the number for the super? You'll probably beat me there."

He patted his breast pocket. "Don't worry about a thing, ma'am. It's all taken care of." His eyes panned the living room, where several pieces of framed art lined the floor, leaning against the empty walls. "You sure you don't want us to load the paintings? We've never damaged one yet. Besides, should you be lifting anything?" He looked pointedly at her rounded figure.

She forced a smile. "Thank you, but I'd rather bring them myself. They're not very heavy."

He shrugged in a way that said, "Have it your way, lady."

She didn't tell him that selling the paintings might provide her only means of paying his fee.

When the movers had gone, Olivia walked through the rooms once more. With her professional eyes, she could see that it was a nice place. Good bones. Tons of potential. But to her, it was only an empty, lifeless shell now. Tiger was gone—safely delivered to the Merediths', much to little Katherine's delight—and the house was empty of everything except the paintings and a pile of blankets she'd kept back to wrap them in.

She closed the door behind the movers and stretched, rubbing the small of her back. Her baby was due in six weeks. Sometimes that seemed forever. Other times—like when she considered what the delivery might be like, going through it alone—it seemed far too close at hand. She'd been careful to let the movers do the lifting, but her aching muscles let her know she'd overdone it the past few days.

All that remained now was to load the paintings in the car and get on the road. She would be glad to put some miles between her and this place.

Carefully, she swaddled each painting in a blanket and carried them out to the car two at a time. Walking back into the house for the last time, she saw her own painting leaning on the floor, the last one left to load. The gentle cows stared at her through the patina of oils. The piece still had a powerful effect on her, but now memories swept over her…the day Reed had come to her house and admired the painting, not knowing it was hers. He would never know how his simple compliments had soothed the wounds from Derek's thoughtless—

She stopped herself. When would she quit comparing Derek to Reed? That was why she was leaving. To rid herself of the memories that caused her to pit her defenseless husband against a man she'd rashly fallen for. She pinched the bridge of her nose, as if pain would banish the unwanted thoughts.

She picked up the last blanket, wanting to hide the memories beneath its folds. But suddenly she knew what she had to do. The painting had no monetary value. There was no reason to bring it with her. It would only recall things best left in the past.

She lifted the painting and fit its wire hanger back on the hook in the foyer. Maybe whoever bought the house would enjoy it. If not, they could dispose of it however they saw fit. She didn't need any reminders of what she was leaving behind.

Chapter Thirty-Five

A mist of snow swirled above the sidewalk like a vapor. Reed tucked the bulky package tighter under his arm and pulled his collar up against the cold as he trudged to the post office. He wondered what the weather was like in Chicago today. Was Olivia warm and safe? He'd heard from her friend Claire that Olivia had an apartment, but Claire didn't know what part of the city it was in, and she hadn't offered to share the address.

He'd mailed her final paycheck to her house in the Falls as she'd requested. He'd entertained thoughts of calling her on the guise of making sure the check had arrived safely, but he knew it had. It had come through with his last bank statement.

The post office lobby was decorated for Halloween. October would soon be over and winter was already making its presence known in the snow that had dusted the Falls last night.

Intense longing rose in him—to have the summer back, to have back the life that Olivia had been part of. Except for having Maggie help him on Saturdays, he hadn't hired someone new in the studio. He'd tried to fill the dead quiet of every breaking day with a new stereo system. But no matter what kind of music he played, the lyrics, the very notes themselves seemed only to remind him that Olivia was gone.

He knew it was irrational, but he couldn't seem to banish the guilt he felt because of all that had happened. If it weren't for him, she would have been happy in her new life in Hanover Falls. She'd have had a church where there were friends to love and care for her, and a town where her baby could grow up safe and strong.

Reed walked out of the post office and looked up into the darkening sky. The branches of the old Dutch elms that towered over the building stood in stark relief, every branch appearing crisp and acute in his vision. His eyesight had only gotten better as the months went by—a fact he was profoundly grateful for, yet one that continually reminded him of the reason Olivia was gone.

If only…

There were too many "if onlys" to count. If only he hadn't written that letter. They could have gone on, maybe never discovering the connection between him and Derek Cline. Or even if he hadn't signed the letter with his initials. Olivia might have someday shown it to him, but he wouldn't have had to admit that he'd written it. He could have gone to his grave with that secret and they would have all been better for it.

And why had God allowed Derek to be the donor for his surgery? Almost any donor could have been a match. It made no sense that it was Derek. In fact, sometimes Reed thought it too much of a coincidence *not* to have a God-designed reason. But if it were so, that reason remained a dark mystery to him.

His only prayer now was that God would allow him to forget Olivia. To accept that their friendship had been for a short time. That time had ended and it was time to move on.

He climbed into the Escape and started for home. He'd racked his brain to think of a way to help Olivia. He knew she would never accept financial help from him, but surely there was some way to make up to her for all the anguish he'd caused, even inadvertently.

On a whim, instead of turning left at Main Street, he took a right and headed to the other side of town. His vehicle turned onto Glenwillow Road as though it were on autopilot. Her house came into view just as the sun dipped below the rooftops in the quiet neighborhood. The windows of her house were dark, the grass unruly and scarred by the realty company's sign piercing the front yard.

He stared at the block letters announcing For Sale. Like lightning, an idea struck him and his excitement grew as the pieces of a puzzle began to snap into place. Maybe there was something he could do after all.

An icy wind lashed Olivia's hair about her face, turning each tendril into a whip that stung her skin and reminded her that she hadn't been to the salon in two months. Haircuts were a luxury she could ill afford these days.

Keeping her eyes on the sidewalk, she yanked at her coat, trying to pull it tight around her middle, but no amount of tugging could erase the fact that she was huge.

She rounded a corner and was hit with a blast of foul air. The sky was sooty and the skyscrapers smudged with the grainy stuff. The El thundered overhead as she crossed Lake Street. She clapped her coat collar to her ears and prayed her womb cushioned the baby from the earsplitting clatter.

How was it that these same streets used to make her feel alive and energetic? What had changed? Was it the fact that she would never be young and carefree again? Seemingly overnight, the city had become a lonely place, filled with hopelessness.

Soon she would be responsible for another life. And she felt she had nothing to offer.

She put her head down and trudged the remaining three blocks to the offices of Interior Ideas on North LaSalle. Elizabeth had offered her part-time work in the office helping with payroll and sometimes playing receptionist. The pay was pathetic and she didn't enjoy the work, but it was something…and maybe a foot back in the door to her old job. She stared at her protruding belly. She couldn't exactly be choosy at this point in her life.

She'd be glad to finally get into the apartment. She'd been at Jayne's for over a week now and things were growing a little tense. All her things were in storage at the apartment complex, and the super had promised the one-bedroom walk-up would be clean and freshly painted by Wednesday, but he'd promised the same thing last week, so she wasn't holding her breath.

The revolving door ushered her into the warmth of the lobby and a few minutes later the elevator opened on the reception area of Elizabeth's office suite.

"Good morning," Bridgett Silvan chirped from her place behind the desk. The pretty blonde was fresh out of college and eternally cheerful.

"Hi, Bridgett. Busy today?"

"Not too bad. I can probably handle it if you need to work on payroll. Oh, and Elizabeth wants to see you in her office."

"Now?"

Bridgett shrugged. "She said when you came in."

"Okay. Thanks." She started down the hall toward Elizabeth's office.

"Oh, wait, Olivia," Bridgett hollered after her. "I almost forgot. You had a call earlier. Some Realtor? I wrote it down somewhere."

Olivia came back to stand by the desk while the girl waded through a pile of memos. "Aha!" She came up with a pink memo and handed it to Olivia. The note was carefully filled out with the name and number for Judy Benton Realty. "You're supposed to call her back."

"Hmm." She'd given the Realtor the office number, just in case, after deciding she couldn't afford to renew her cell phone contract. But she hadn't expected to hear from her so soon. A reality check followed the surge of anticipation she felt. It was most likely nothing. Judy probably just needed to ask about some detail she'd forgotten to put on the disclosure sheet.

Still, Olivia couldn't help feeling hopeful. "Thanks, Bridgett." She took the memo from the receptionist and tucked it in her pocket. She'd call right after her meeting with Elizabeth.

When Olivia poked her head in the door, the designer glanced up from the specification sheet she was working on. Olivia had always appreciated Elizabeth's willingness—even after she'd made it big—to get right in with her team and get her hands dirty.

"Ah, there you are. Sit down."

Olivia took the elegantly skirted chair she offered, growing more curious about why Elizabeth wanted to see her.

"How are you feeling?"

"Fat." She laughed, rolling her eyes.

"You look lovely."

"Well, thank you. I'm fine. Just anxious for this to be over."

"And I assume you're planning to work after the baby comes? After maternity leave, of course."

"Oh, yes. I'll need to work."

Elizabeth propped her elbows on the edge of the desk and steepled her manicured fingers. "I'd like you to come back. As a designer."

Olivia's breath caught. "Really? I…I'd love that."

"I've been thinking of adding a designer for a while now, and I'd dearly love it if I didn't have to break in someone new."

"Thank you. That's wonderful news. But—" She framed her very pregnant middle with her hands.

"There is that," Elizabeth conceded, studying her. "Do you have a babysitter lined up? I understand you'll have the responsibilities of motherhood to deal with, and I'll allow you six weeks paid maternity leave, but I want to be sure I can expect full-time hours and the same quality of work you gave me before."

Olivia nodded eagerly. "Of course. And no…I haven't found anyone yet, but my friend Jayne gave me a few leads. I'll make some calls tonight."

"Good."

"Thank you so much, Elizabeth. This is an answer to prayer."

"Well—" The designer's eyes widened and she spread a graceful hand across her breast. "I don't know about that. But I'm glad to have you back."

Olivia practically floated back to the reception area. Bridgett was still handling the phones, which reminded her that she hadn't returned Judy's call. She took her phone card to a quiet desk and dialed the number.

The Realtor picked up on the third ring. "Judy? It's Olivia Cline…in Chicago…"

"Oh, Olivia. Good. I'm sorry to have bothered you at work, but I thought you'd like to know that I have a buyer for your house."

"You do?" Olivia straightened in her chair. Not merely an interested party, but a buyer? *Too good to be true, but please, Lord.* "That was quick. You mean an actual offer?"

"I do."

"But what's the catch?"

"No catch. He's offering your asking price."

"You're kidding? You didn't expect that, did you?"

"Well, not really, but you just never know in this business. All it takes is one buyer who wants what you're selling. And it looks like we found him."

"Oh, that's wonderful. Thank you for calling." She was having trouble believing it could be this simple. "What do I need to do now?"

"I'll get with the title office and start the paperwork. The guy is from here in town and he doesn't have a property to sell first. He's buying it as an investment…a rental," she explained. "We should be able to close around the end of the month. Let's see…"

Olivia heard papers rattling and the sound of a computer keyboard. She sat there, stunned. It had barely been a week!

"Okay," Judy said after a minute, "it looks like I have the documents I need. I'll get the inspection scheduled and you've already signed over power of attorney so I can sign for you. It should be an easy contract. I have the fax number you gave me if I need to have you look over anything before we close."

Olivia let out the breath she'd been holding and shot up a little prayer of thanks. "Oh, that's great."

"Oh, by the way, Olivia, did you realize you left a painting in the house?"

"Yes." She hesitated. "I don't want it."

"Are you sure? It's a very nice painting."

She smiled into the phone. "Well, thanks."

"You're the artist?"

Me and my big mouth. "Yes. I did it…a long time ago. But I really prefer for it to stay there with the house," she repeated.

"Okay… If you're sure. I'll be in touch if we run into a hitch."

"Thanks, Judy."

Olivia replaced the receiver and sat staring out the window. Two amazing answers to prayer in one afternoon! *Thank You, Lord.* She felt ashamed for ever doubting His care for her.

Her elation carried her through the afternoon, but as she walked to the train station to catch a ride with Jayne's husband, Brian, the reality of all that had happened began to sink in.

So that was that. In the space of an hour, her ties to Hanover Falls had been severed. She could turn the page on a very difficult chapter in her life. It was over now, and there were happier scenes ahead.

So why did she feel like crying?

Chapter Thirty-Six

Winter hit Chicago full force on the first day of November, turning the lake to ice and the streets to slush. Olivia looked out the only window in the apartment with a view and shivered as she watched people pass by on the sidewalk below. She'd been in the apartment a week now, and though it was convenient to the office and had allowed her to sell her car, it was a far cry from homey.

Most of her furniture was in storage and she'd done a bare minimum of decorating. Jayne had decided she was ready to get rid of all her baby things, and passed down a nice crib and changing table and an assortment of other baby gear that Olivia didn't even know existed. Even looking at the crib set up in the corner of her bedroom, she still had a hard time imagining that in a few short weeks, there would be another little person sharing this apartment with her.

She'd had her medical records transferred from Hanover Falls to Jayne's obstetrician, and her first appointment was tomorrow morning.

She would take the El to the doctor's office and catch a cab back to work after her appointment. She was anxious to hear what this doctor would say. In spite of the extra weight she was carrying around and all the energy she'd expended—both physical and mental—during the move, she'd felt surprisingly good the last few days.

Maybe it was just good to be back in the city. And away from the stresses she'd had in Missouri. She wondered if Reed had hired anyone to take her place yet. As quickly as the thought came, she pushed it from her mind. She'd come to the city to get away from all that. She forced her thoughts to the amazing events of the past week. It was surely no coincidence that she'd been offered her old job back and sold the house the same day. It felt like confirmation that she'd made the right decision.

Sighing, she pulled the blinds on the gloomy sky outside and flipped on the lights. There were still four large boxes stacked in the corner of the living room. Might as well tackle those. The movers had distributed the boxes as her labels instructed, but still, her back ached from lugging the cartons across the room and bending to unpack them.

She hoisted a box from the stack and slid it to the floor. A sharp pain arced across her lower back and she sucked in a sharp breath. She straightened and stretched slowly, testing, wondering if she'd pulled a muscle. Her back seemed fine now, but she went to rest for a minute on the sofa, the only piece of furniture that wasn't covered with boxes and moving paraphernalia.

She was just about to get up and get back to work when the pain came again, only this time not so sharp and it moved in a sort of wave from her back to her stomach. Odd.

She tried to ignore it, and went back to work, sitting cross-legged on the floor to unpack her collection of CDs. She'd never sorted through the discs after Derek's death, but she'd heard of a place that paid pretty well for used CDs and she decided to weed through the collection and sell some of the ones she never listened to.

The pain came again just minutes later. What was going on? It felt almost like a contraction…a stronger version of the contractions she'd had almost from the beginning of her pregnancy—Braxton Hicks, her doctor called them. Maybe it was normal for those to get stronger as pregnancy progressed. She should have read more on the subject over the months. If she was still feeling like this tomorrow, she'd search online for some answers.

But by ten o'clock she was concerned. The pains—if they could even be called that—had been coming at fairly regular intervals and were starting to feel more like what she imagined labor pains to be, yet not like the cramping she'd had before when the doctor in Hanover Falls had put her on bed rest.

She probably ought to call the doctor, but she hated to bother him after hours. She hadn't even seen this doctor yet. She got up and paced the living room, starting to feel a little stir-crazy.

What if she *was* in labor? How would she get to the hospital? Why hadn't she thought these things out before? But she thought she had plenty of time. She'd been so wrapped up in the move, her job, even setting up the crib and getting the few baby things she had organized.

She looked at the clock. It wasn't yet nine. Jayne would still be up. She would know. She let the phone ring a dozen times, but no answer.

She punched the phone off then on again and called Jayne's cell phone. But she was immediately routed to her voice mail.

She thought next of Claire Meredith. Unlike Olivia, Claire had begun devouring books on pregnancy and childbirth the minute she'd discovered she was pregnant again. She would know whether this was anything to be concerned about.

She punched in Claire's number. Merely dialing the area code for Hanover Falls brought memories careening back. But she didn't have time to dwell on them as simultaneously Michael Meredith answered the phone and another contraction swelled.

"Michael?" she breathed. "This is Olivia Cline. Is Claire there?"

"Hi, Olivia. How are you? Claire was just wondering about you this morning."

She took a slow breath, trying to make her voice sound normal. "I'm doing okay, thanks. How is Claire doing?"

"She's great. She thinks she's starting to…um…blossom a little already." He laughed. "Here, I'll let you talk to her."

She heard him tell Claire it was her on the phone, and Claire's happy squeal.

"Olivia! How are you?"

"I…I think I might be in labor, Claire."

"Really? Oh, I'm so excited for you."

Olivia could almost see Claire jumping up and down, her carrot-colored curls bouncing like springs.

"Where are you?"

"I'm at home. It's kind of early, though. My due date's not until the end of the month." She explained the contraction-like pains she was having.

"That sounds like labor to me," Claire said. "And lots of babies come a couple weeks early. Has your water broken?"

"I don't know…"

Claire laughed. "Oh, honey, you'd know!" Her voice turned serious. "But you probably ought to call your doctor. Especially if the contractions are that regular."

Olivia looked at her watch. "I haven't had one since Michael answered the phone, but it—" A powerful spasm moved through her. "Ohhh…"

"Olivia? What is it?"

She tried to catch her breath. "I just had another one. A pretty strong one."

"Olivia?" Alarm tinged Claire's voice. "We've only been on the phone three minutes. Those are coming pretty close together. Maybe you'd better hang up and call your doctor."

"Okay." Olivia didn't need convincing after that last one.

"I'm fine. Everything's great, but you don't have time to chit-chat. Call your doctor, okay?"

"Okay."

"You'll let me know what's going on, right?"

"I will. I promise."

"I'll be praying for you. Oh, Olivia, think of it! You're about to meet your baby!"

Those words brought tears…and then the trembling began. It was time. Ready or not, she was going to have a baby.

Chapter Thirty-Seven

"Oh, Olivia, he's beautiful. Absolutely beautiful." Claire looked down on the infant cradled in Olivia's arms.

Claire's face practically glowed and Olivia knew she was thinking ahead to the day when she'd hold her own baby in her arms. Claire's slim figure had already taken on new curves, and her face reflected a quiet joy.

The baby squirmed and stretched in Olivia's arms and she bent to kiss his forehead. She didn't think she'd ever get over the amazing experience of childbirth. Being wheeled into that room alone in fear and pain, and then, just twelve hours later, holding a new little life in her arms. And feeling a joy that had taken her completely by surprise.

"He is perfect, isn't he?" She looked up at Claire, feeling such a sisterhood with this woman she'd only known a short time. "I remember you told me—when I first found out I was pregnant—that someday when I held my baby in my arms, it would all make sense."

"Did I say that?"

She nodded. "I don't pretend to understand everything, but—" she cuddled the baby close "—at least a lot of things make sense that never did before." She teared up.

When she looked at Claire, she saw that her eyes were swimming, too. They looked away, then caught each other's eye again and both started to speak at the same time. As if it were choreo-graphed, they let loose sobs in unison, then broke into giggles, and soon they were laughing uncontrollably.

A nurse appeared in the doorway. "Is everything okay in here?"

"Never mind us," Claire said, when they'd gotten control of their emotions. "You just shouldn't allow two highly hormonal women in a room together."

The nurse rolled her eyes. "I'll remember that," she said drily.

That set them giggling again. It felt good to share laughter—and tears—with a friend on this occasion.

She wiped the tears away and shifted the baby to the other arm. "Thank you so much for coming, Claire."

"I wouldn't have missed it for the world." Claire reached to touch the hospital blanket covering the baby's feet. "Have you named him?"

Olivia ran a hand through his thick, dark head of hair and the sweet newborn scent of him rose up and filled her heart. "His name is Jonathan Derek." She had just decided on a name an hour ago and it was the first time she'd told anyone. It sounded just right. And it seemed fitting that it was Claire who heard it first.

"Jonathan Derek Cline. It's a wonderful name."

"I wanted him to have Derek's name. And Jonathan means 'God's gift.'"

"Oh, he *is* a gift from God, Olivia. He truly is."

Olivia rolled over in bed. The now-familiar sounds of the baby rooting around in his crib nudged her from sleep. Raising up on one elbow, she squinted at the clock. *Arrgh!* She flopped back on her pillow. Could people survive on four hours of sleep a night?

She held her breath, waiting for Jonathan to start wailing. She was exhausted. Jonathan seemed to want to nurse every two hours. And she was sure he was awake more than he slept. Apparently he hadn't read all the statistics about newborns sleeping twenty-some hours of each twenty-four.

The squall started in earnest and she flipped on the dim

bedside lamp and rolled out of bed. The November wind howled outside and the air in the room felt icy. She grabbed her robe from the end of the bed and shrugged into it.

She reached into the crib. The blankets were toasty and Jonathan's tiny hands and toes were warm. He quieted immediately when she lifted him from the crib, but fussed again when she didn't sit down with him soon enough to suit.

"Shh…shh…it's okay, Jon-Jon. Mama's here."

As soon as she sat down with him in the overstuffed chair beside her bed, he nuzzled in to nurse. In a week's time, they had become old pros at this. She waited for the calming sensation of her milk letting down, and soon the baby relaxed and gulped noisily. He looked up at her with bright eyes, as if to say "thanks for dinner, Mom." If she felt incompetent as a mother in a dozen different ways, in this she was a success. They were a team.

Within minutes Jonathan was asleep again, his head heavy and drowsy against her breast. She was wide-awake now, but knew she'd manage to get back to sleep—no doubt five minutes before the baby woke to nurse again. She pulled a quilt from the end of her bed and tucked it over her lap. The baby's warmth was pleasant, her own personal little furnace.

She watched him in the lamplight, his rosebud mouth still puckered and working in sleep, as though he'd forgotten dinner was over.

"Oh, Derek," she whispered. "I wish you could know him." Instantly, the tears came. "I'm sorry…so sorry you didn't get to meet your son. I'm sorry we didn't have time to make up for everything we lost."

The baby took a deep, shuddering breath and scrunched up his face, looking as if he was working up to a good cry. But then his brow relaxed and a fleeting smile flickered on his face. It was gone again almost before Olivia could take a mental snapshot. But it made her laugh. And gave her a tiny glimpse of the future. This little guy in her arms had already become her buddy. She hoped her son would always be her friend. She hadn't known many true friends in her lifetime.

Reed. His name was there before she could prevent it. Reed had been a true friend. She wondered what he was doing tonight. It made her sad to think of him. She'd wished a hundred times that she'd met him farther down the road of life. After she'd had time to heal. After she'd settled in to being Jonathan's mother. But then, Chicago was a long way from Hanover Falls. And some things simply weren't to be.

Maybe someday she could learn to look back on the joyful times with Reed—before they'd discovered the perplexing tie that connected Reed to Derek—and just be grateful that he'd been a dear friend.

It struck her that she had prayed a similar prayer concerning Derek. That, as Scripture said, she could forget what lay behind and strain forward to what lay ahead.

She wished she knew what that was. She and Jonathan had a cozy existence in this apartment now. But she didn't dare think ahead to the day when her maternity leave would be over and she would have to go back to work. And beyond that, when Jonathan began to crawl and then walk and run. There were so many dangers here for a little boy. And no yard to run in, no room to have a pet.

She thought of Tiger and wondered if the kitten was bringing little Katherine as much joy as he'd brought her. She could just see the two of them playing in the beautiful fenced-in yard on the Merediths' quiet street. Tiger probably wasn't much of a kitten anymore. What a sweet thing Reed had done when he'd redeemed that little cat from the pound.

Reed. Oh, so many memories. She reeled at the thoughts. And she was so tired. So very tired.

The memory of Reed sitting there on her back porch in the Falls, Tiger nestled in his arms, was her last thought as she surrendered to blissful sleep.

Chapter Thirty-Eight

"Reed, where do you keep the coffee filters?"

Alissa's voice drifted down to the studio and Reed huffed out a sigh and tromped to the kitchen where his sister was opening cupboard doors one by one.

"Why are you making coffee at nine o'clock at night?"

"I'm not. I'm making coffee for in the morning…setting the timer. I bet you didn't even know this fancy machine had a timer, did you? Now where are those filters?" She reached for another cupboard door.

"Alissa, you goose." He stood with hands on hips. "Think about it. Where would be the *logical* place to keep coffee filters?"

"Well," she shot back, "since I just found the dish soap in the refrigerator, I have no clue what *you* might consider a logical place for coffee filters. The laundry room, maybe?"

He curbed a grin. "All right, sister dear. Move over." He took her by the shoulders and manhandled her away from the cabinet above the coffeemaker.

"Watch and learn," he said, opening the cupboard door with a flourish. "Ta-da!" He reached in to grab the box of filters. Unfortunately, they weren't there. "Wait a minute…" He moved several mugs and a tin of tea bags. He checked the cupboard beside that one.

"Come on, oh, great one. I'm waiting." She tapped her foot, a smug smile painting her face.

"They were here yesterday. You must have lost them already."

"Oh, no you don't. I already got blamed for using the last of the toilet paper. I'm not taking the rap for the coffee filters, too."

"We'll see about that." Grinning, he hoisted her over his shoulder like a sack of potatoes.

"Put me down!" She pounded his back. "Reed Vincent! I mean it. Put me down this minute!"

"Make me." He carted her into the living room where Mason and Ali were watching a VeggieTales Christmas movie.

The kids were lying on their tummies beside Reed's scrawny Christmas tree, eyes glued to the television screen. At Alissa's squeals, they turned with gaping mouths as Reed dumped their mother unceremoniously into a chair. The minute he straightened, the two were on him like monkeys on a jungle gym.

"My turn!" they squealed in unison over strains of the singing cucumber and talking tomato.

"Throw me in a chair, Uncle Reed!" Mason hopped up and down on one foot.

He picked up the six-year-old and lifted him to his shoulders.

"Me, too! Me, too!" Ali held up pudgy arms.

He scooped her up into the crook of his arm and danced them both around the living room.

Alissa watched from the chair, laughing. "You guys are going to wear Uncle Reed out. Besides, it's bedtime."

"No! Not yet," Mason whined. "Our movie isn't even over."

"I'll just take this bus upstairs." Reed winked at his sister and loped up the stairs, kids in tow. He supervised teeth-brushing, and when they were in their pajamas, he tucked them into the twin beds in the guest room he'd set up just for them.

"Good night, you two," he said, kneeling on the floor between them.

"G'night," Mason whispered.

"Aren't you gonna tell us a thtory?" Ali lisped.

He checked the clock. "It's pretty late, sweetie. I think those

Veggie guys will have to be your story for tonight. But I'll say prayers with you, okay?"

Mason and Ali sat up in bed and swung their legs around, dangling their toes a few inches off the floor.

These had better be short prayers if his knees were to survive. He put a hand on each of them and they bowed their heads and folded their hands in their laps. His throat knotted unexpectedly. His house was going to be unbearably quiet come Friday.

"You start, Uncky Weed," Ali whispered.

He winked at his niece. "Okay. Well, Heavenly Father, thank You for a really good day. Thank You that I got to spend time with two of my favorite munchkins in the whole world. Give Mason and Ali a good night's sleep and bless their mommy and daddy. We especially thank You for giving Mick a safe trip back to Indiana. We love You, Lord, with all our hearts…." He swallowed hard and gave Mason's head a pat. He didn't trust his voice with one more word.

Mason peeped at him through hooded eyes. "My turn?"

Reed nodded.

"Dear Jesus, thank You for Uncle Reed and Mommy and Daddy and VeggieTales and for everything in the whole wide world. Amen."

Ali piped up in a stage whisper. "You forgot to say thank You for all our Cwistmas stuff."

"Did not."

"Yeth, you did."

"Did not. I said 'everything in the whole wide world.' That means *everything,* stupid."

Okay, this prayer time was deteriorating fast.

Ali pouted. "I'm not thtupid!"

"Hey, hey…" Reed gave each head a squeeze.

"Sorry," they muttered.

Ali said her prayers and Reed tucked them in and turned out the lights. "I love you guys."

He went back downstairs to find Alissa stretched out on the sofa.

"Hey, hey… What's this? *I'm* the one who should be lying exhausted on the couch."

She laughed and slung a pillow lazily in his direction. "Give me a break. I do this day in, day out."

"And you do a great job," he said, turning serious. "They're incredible kids, Lissa. I wish Mick could have stayed longer."

"Yeah, me, too, but at least he got to be here for Christmas."

"You guys doing okay?"

A dreamy glaze came to her eyes. "We're doing great. We really are. Life is good."

"I'm glad. He's a good guy."

"Yeah, he is." She stretched her arms over her head and made a pillow of her hands. "What's on the agenda for tomorrow?"

"I need to get a couple of paintings shipped and go do some work on the rental. But I'll be free all afternoon. What do you guys want to do?"

"I'd be happy just hanging out here. A girl can only do so much shopping, you know."

He laughed. "You have done your share of that. You're just lucky Mick left you the car. You never would have fit all your loot on the plane."

He stretched and feigned a yawn. "Well, I think I'm going to turn in."

"Not so fast, baby brother." She patted the couch cushion. "How are you doing? Really?"

He sighed and sat on the arm of the couch at her feet.

He had adored having Alissa and her family here. They'd filled his house with laughter and joy and with noise. Lots of noise.

But he'd been dreading this moment. Alissa was a mother hen. He knew she worried about him, and only asked because she loved him. But he was in no mood to revisit the whole Olivia deal.

"I'm doing fine." He tried to look cheerful.

"Are you really, Reed?"

He shrugged.

"Do you ever hear from her…from Olivia? Has she had the baby?"

He shook his head. "I don't hear from her. A friend told me

she had her baby. A boy." An aching sadness came over him as he spoke the words. He'd hoped so badly to be part of her life— and the life of her child.

Alissa's eyes misted. "There'll be someone else, Reed."

He shook his head. "I'm not so sure. I seem to be batting zilch in that department." Actually, he hadn't even left the bull pen. And had no desire to at this point.

"Reed—"

"Lissa…it's okay. I blew it. It was too soon for Olivia. Even if the whole transplant connection hadn't been a factor…I tried to rush things. I didn't pay attention to what I know God was trying to tell me. What you and Maggie tried to warn me about…"

She sat up on the couch and put a hand on his knee. "Maybe. But I was wrong, too. Please forgive me for judging Olivia before I even had a chance to get to know her."

He bent his head. Now she would never know Olivia.

Oh, for a second chance.

Chapter Thirty-Nine

Strains of Mozart filtered softly through the gallery and a handful of patrons meandered among the display panels in the exhibition hall. Olivia reached into the stroller and unfastened the chin strap on Jon's cap. He stirred and stretched. Olivia held her breath, whispering a prayer that he wouldn't wake up and start squawking again.

She aimed the stroller at the far end of the gallery, where it was quiet and empty. She felt a surge of excitement as she began to walk through the show. She had dug her easel and paints out of storage three weeks ago and had begun to play around with them. It was difficult working around the baby's schedule—if one could call Jon's erratic napping and nursing a schedule. But painting had filled the empty hours and given her a certain sense of accomplishment.

She'd quickly realized that she wouldn't have time to pursue it now that her maternity leave was over, but she'd had fun while it lasted. Maybe she'd pick it up again when Jon went off to college. On a lark, she'd entered one of the first pieces she'd finished in the show. It was a smaller piece, a close-up of Jon. She'd captured him sleeping, his face framed by a soft quilt that had been a hand-me-down from Jayne.

Whether anyone else could see the passion in the piece, she didn't know. But she would never look at it without remembering how she'd fallen in love with her son as she captured his innocence on canvas, working in the quiet of the tiny bedroom, watching him sleep. God had touched something in her heart that night, and she would never doubt His love or His care for her again.

Claire had been right. And Reed. This baby had been part of her healing.

Olivia rolled the stroller gently back and forth as she stopped in front of each piece to study the artist's work and make mental notes of techniques she wished to try. There were some exceptional pieces in the show, but most of them were from the professional entrants. She'd been eligible to enter the amateur category, and felt honored that her piece had been accepted. Looking at the competition now, she let herself feel hopeful.

Working her way around the room, she wondered where her painting was and if there might be a ribbon hanging beside it. She came to the first- and second-place awards for watercolor and mixed media, but she hadn't yet come to the winners of the oil and acrylics category, so there was still a chance.

But that hope was dashed a minute later as she rounded the corner to discover her frame hanging on a Peg-Board display—right next to the winner. The winning piece was a lovely landscape done in gold and orange tones. She couldn't fault the juror's decision, but neither could she help feeling mildly disappointed.

Good grief, Liv, it's your first show in almost a decade. What did you expect? She brushed aside her disappointment, determined not to let it ruin her day.

They made it halfway through the exhibit hall before the baby started fussing. She wheeled the stroller to a quiet corner and got him settled again with his pacifier. At almost ten weeks, he was starting to go longer between feedings. With luck, she'd get through the whole gallery before he needed to nurse again.

She moved through the aisles formed by the movable display panels, enthralled with some of the art. It always amazed her that a few strokes of paint on canvas could stir such fervor. That was what she longed to do with her own work. Make the observer feel something. Evoke a mood or passion. What a gift creativity was! Being amongst all this art made her eager to get home and set up her easel again.

She moved to the opposite side of a bank of displays and took a few steps back for a better view of a large painting that took up most of one panel. She stopped in her tracks. She'd never seen the piece before, but instantly she knew who the artist was. She searched for the telltale signature, then felt a smile tug at the corners of her mouth.

Reed. Her breath caught.

It was a beautiful piece. A stand of dogwoods along a shady country road. He'd captured the mysterious mood of the woods, made her *smell* the musty earth beneath the trees. She thought she knew where the place was. She and Reed had passed it that day on the way to the county park to shoot photos.

She stood there, paralyzed. As much as she'd tried to shut him out of her life, shut his memory out of her mind, Reed had never been far away. Now, standing in front of this canvas, knowing every nook and corner of the studio where it had been produced, she realized she'd never managed to banish one cell of him from her memory. He had been in her thoughts, in her heart, practically from the day they'd met.

Close to tears, she reached to brush her fingertips across his signature. *Oh, Reed.* How was he doing? Obviously he was still painting.

Well, sure he was. Had she really thought her absence from his life would render him incapable of working? *You have a pretty inflated sense of your own worth, Liv Cline.*

"Excuse me? Excuse me… Ma'am?"

She turned to see a stern-faced security guard standing behind her, arms folded across his potbelly. "I'm going to have to ask you not to touch the paintings."

"Oh!" She looked down and realized that her hand still rested lightly on the corner of Reed's painting. She jerked her fingers away as if the canvas were afire. "Oh, I'm sorry. I didn't…"

"No problem, ma'am. We're just responsible to see that the paintings aren't damaged."

What was wrong with her? She knew better. Flustered, she cast about for the nearest exit. She could view the rest of the show when she came to pick up her painting Monday. For now, she just wanted to get out of here.

There was an Exit sign at the far end of the building, but as she started in that direction, she came face-to-face with something that made the surprise of a few moments ago pale in comparison.

Hanging in front of her, gazing at their reflections, as they'd done since she daubed them into life almost a decade ago, were her cows. The painting she'd abandoned at the house. How on earth had it gotten into this show?

She bent to read the label affixed low on the wall to the right of the frame: Cows. Olivia Cline. Chicago. Oil. (Not for sale.) And beside the placard, a yellow ribbon wavered in the draft from the heating vent overhead. Honorable Mention. Her hand went to her throat. Her painting had won an honorable mention and she hadn't even entered it? What was going on? Who had put her painting in the show?

She whirled around, looking for the security guard. He had his back to her, patrolling the main gallery beyond the exhibition hall.

Pushing the stroller ahead of her, she hurried to catch him. "Sir. Sir!"

The guard turned and looked at her, recognition dawned on his face. "Yes?"

"Can you tell me who entered one of the pieces in the show?"

"It doesn't say on the placard?"

"No."

He held up his hands and took a step back. "If it's not on the card, I can't help you, but you could ask that lady over there." He pointed to an elegant, gray-haired woman by the water fountain.

"Thank you." Olivia pushed the stroller over and introduced herself. "I'm wondering if you can tell me who entered one of the pieces in the show."

The woman's name tag said she was the assistant gallery

director. She peered over small reading glasses at Jonathan in the stroller, smiling that smile people reserved for tiny babies. "Which piece are you interested in?"

"Oh. I…I don't want to purchase it. I'm just curious who entered it in the show. It's the large oil over there…with the cows." She pointed toward the corner where her painting hung.

"Oh, yes. That's a lovely piece. There wasn't a placard…a card with it?"

"There was. But I don't know who entered it."

The director looked confused. "I assume it was the artist."

"Um…I don't think so. I'm the artist."

She raised a brow. "And you didn't enter it?"

"No."

"Well, then, I assume whoever owns the piece did so."

"Do you have a record of who that would be?"

"The name is supposed to be on the placard. Let's go check." She led the way to Olivia's painting. Reading the placard, she shook her head. "Hmm." She slipped the placard from the holder and turned it over. "Oh, wait. This is an honorable mention awardee. Let me see who the check was made out to."

Olivia's pulse sputtered. "There's prize money for honorable mention?"

"Oh, yes. Three hundred and fifty dollars. Come on back to my office and we'll see if we can find something."

The director's office was on the basement level of the gallery. She riffled through a stack of identical envelopes searching for the entry number. "Here it is. It's made out to Olivia Cline. Is that your mailing address?"

Olivia read her apartment's address printed beneath her name. She nodded.

"I can't give you the check," the director said. "We have to mail them for security purposes, but they'll go out in Monday's mail."

"And you don't have any other information? Someone will have to pick up the art. It…it doesn't belong to me anymore."

"You don't have a claim check for it?"

"No. I had no idea it was even entered."

The woman shook her head. "I really don't know what to tell you. Everything we have on file is in your name. But the owner evidently retained the claim check." She shrugged. "I guess if you're really curious, you could come and stay from three to five-thirty Monday afternoon and see who shows up to claim it."

Olivia contemplated the idea. Elizabeth wouldn't be crazy about her taking off work early, but she'd have to come pick up her own painting then anyway.

If she didn't get some answers before Monday, she just might take the director's suggestion.

Back at the apartment, Olivia searched for the flier that told about the juried show, but when she finally found it, it gave her no clue as to how her piece could have ended up in the show. Obviously the people who bought her house had sold her painting, but it was odd that someone would have entered it in a competition. Her vanity couldn't help wonder how much the painting had brought.

She thought to call information for her old address in Hanover Falls, but she didn't know the name of the people who lived there. Besides she remembered the Realtor saying it had been purchased as a rental. She didn't remember the owner's name—if she'd ever known it. That time was a blur in her memory. All the paperwork on the sale of the house had come in the mail shortly after the baby was born and she'd put it in her safe-deposit box without even glancing over it. Judy Benton had signed everything in her absence. But the realty office was closed today. She dialed Judy's cell, but it went straight to voice mail.

Olivia hated to call her at home on the weekend. But she wasn't sure her curiosity could wait until Monday.

Chapter Forty

Olivia gathered with the artists clustered at the checkout table, a motley crew that ran the gamut from goateed beatnik to gray-haired octogenarian to sophisticated businessman in a Brooks Brothers suit.

It had been an interminably long weekend with no return phone call from Judy.

Now, with her portrait of Jon tucked under one arm, Olivia rubbed the edge of her claim check until it was frayed, and paced three steps in either direction, holding her place in the queue to check out.

Her cows were still hanging on the display panel at the end of the exhibition gallery. They seemed to be welcoming her, and for the first time, she felt a twinge of regret over leaving them at the house. But it was too late now. And they'd brought her three hundred and fifty dollars! The money was much needed, but she felt funny about having the check come to her when she didn't even know who had entered the piece. Even if they'd intended her to have the check, she ought to at least reimburse them for the entry fee.

She was beginning to suspect Judy Benton herself. The Realtor knew Olivia had left it at the house intentionally and had seemed to admire it. She couldn't imagine why she would have entered it in this show, designating any prize money to go back to Olivia. It didn't make sense.

Judy had known Olivia was in a difficult situation, and she had been very warm and caring, helping Olivia through the complicated transaction long-distance. But entering art shows wasn't exactly the type of perk Realtors were known for—even really exceptional ones.

The queue moved along at an inchworm's pace. Olivia checked her watch. Her babysitter, Mrs. Markham, had agreed to keep Jonathan until six o'clock, but it would take a good half hour to get to the Markhams' house, and she didn't want to come home on the train with a baby after dark.

Her turn came and she signed for her painting. Now to hang out and appear unobtrusive until her mysterious benefactor showed up.

Olivia watched the doors, scrutinizing each new face that came through. Was this the person who would pick up her painting? But she watched with another motive, as well.

Reed Vincent had work in this show. During the months she had worked for him, he usually shipped contest art to the show and paid to have the pieces returned, but what if he showed up here today? It wasn't likely, but even so, the thought terrified her—and sent a little thrill through her at the same time.

Reed's painting was still hanging on the display panel, but it had a purchase award sticker on it, so it most likely would be picked up by the buyer.

At four-fifteen her cows were still hanging and she started to feel foolish lying in wait this way. What did it matter who'd ended up with her painting? Her curiosity would probably only get her in trouble.

She rose to leave. But just then, a new flurry of people entered the building. She studied faces as they came in and kept an eye on the panel where her painting hung.

Moments later, a middle-aged man wearing a black turtleneck and matching stocking cap came through the doors. A graying ponytail protruded from the back of the cap. At first, she thought he was just a last-minute peruser of the show, but it soon became apparent that he was searching for a particular piece. She held her breath as he rounded the aisle where her cows hung.

He stopped in his tracks in front of the painting, then immediately went to work dismounting it from the Peg-Board panel.

Who was he? Judy Benton's husband, maybe? Judy had spoken of a husband, but Olivia had never met him. Well, maybe now was the time. She gathered her things, tucked the smaller painting under her arm and crossed the room to speak with the man.

He had propped the cows against the base of the display and was taking down another frame adjacent to it. Olivia stopped short. Maybe the guy worked for the gallery and was just helping disassemble the show. But then he wouldn't have come in from outdoors that way.

He must be a dealer. The man shucked his jacket and peeled off the stocking cap, wiping his brow with a handkerchief from his pocket. When he turned toward the windows, sans cap, Olivia realized she knew him.

His name escaped her, but he was the owner of one of the galleries that carried Reed's work. Reed had introduced them. Garret or Garth…something like that.

She started toward him, but suddenly realized she didn't have a clue what she would say. She didn't need to worry about that, though, because he spotted her first. Recognition lit his eyes.

"Hi there." He leaned a frame against the panel and started toward her, hand outstretched. "Gavin Chambers. You work for Reed Vincent, right?"

"I used to."

"Forgive me, I'm terrible with names."

"Olivia," she said, smiling and shaking his hand. "Olivia Cline."

He did a double take. "Olivia Cline… Isn't that…?" He turned back to glance at the cows, then scratched his head. "*That* Olivia Cline?"

Smiling, she nodded. "I'm really curious how you got my piece."

He seemed surprised. "I'm picking it up for Reed, actually. He said it was done by a friend, a really promising artist…" He stuck out his hand again. "He was right, by the way. Congratulations on the award."

"Oh…well, thanks." Once again, she took his hand, dipping her head. Her mind swirled with the news that Reed was the one who'd entered her work.

Gavin pointed back to her painting. "Do you want to just take it back with you? Or are you flying?"

"Oh… No. I live here in Chicago now."

"Is that right? I didn't realize…. Well, then I'll just send the piece with you now, if that's okay. Save Reed having to ship it back to you."

Her mind raced. "Um…I think Reed owns the piece. Apparently." This was all getting very confusing. Had Judy sold the painting to Reed?

"Oh, well, that's different," Gavin said. "Then we'll just go with plan A."

"How…how is he? Reed, I mean?"

"He's doing great. Can't paint fast enough to suit me, of course." He brightened. "I'm meeting him for dinner in half an hour. Why don't you come? I'm sure he'd be delighted to see you."

She held back a gasp. "He's in town?"

"Should have landed—" Gavin tapped his watch "—about an hour ago. He'd better have a boatload of art with him, too." He looked down at the painting she still carried. "Are you checked out? Can I wrap that for you?"

"Yes, but, I don't—" She could be face-to-face with Reed just a few minutes from now. Suddenly the idea elated her. "On second thought, I'd love to go." She checked the time. She had less than two hours before she needed to pick up the baby. "I can't stay for dinner, but I'll have coffee."

"Wonderful. And maybe you and Mr. Vincent can discuss who those beautiful bovines actually belong to."

A smile pulled at her mouth. *That* would be interesting.

Chapter Forty-One

The backseat of the cab smelled of gasoline and stale cigarette smoke and Olivia's nerves tangled tighter with every block. Gavin chattered away about the art business, but she had no heart for it now. She was actually minutes from standing in front of Reed. Looking into his eyes again. And she was second-guessing herself every mile of the way.

What had she been thinking? She couldn't just walk up to him as if nothing had happened between them. They'd never even said a proper goodbye. But maybe that's what this was all about for her. That word psychologists the world over seemed so fond of: closure. But as Chicago's skyline towered over them and the jumble of thoughts in her brain started to sort itself out, she realized that it was more than that. Far more.

"Reservation for Chambers?" Gavin leaned over the hostess stand. "There'll be one more in our party. He may already be here."

Olivia panned the restaurant. And suddenly, there he was. Bent over a table by the window, studying the menu, holding it close. Alarm streaked through her. Were his eyes worse? But then he laid the folder on the table and continued to read. She released her breath, but her heart was thumping like a timpani.

Gavin followed her gaze. "Oh, there he is." He started over

to the table, but Olivia grabbed his coat sleeve. "I'll be with you in a minute. I want to…freshen up."

"Sure. Can I order you a drink?"

"No. Thank you. And please…don't tell Reed I'm here. I want to surprise him."

"Women!" He shook his head, laughing. "Always love a surprise, don't you? You go on. I'll save you a place."

Olivia found the restrooms and unbuttoned her coat. She dug in her purse for lipstick and a hairbrush. She stared at her reflection, trying to think what she could possibly say to Reed that would make everything all right, that would give her closure.

Listen to yourself, Liv. Do you really want everything to be all right? What happened to "I can't bear to look at him every day? To look into his eyes…?" She pushed her palms on the counter, steadying herself. Why was she doing this? Why would she subject herself to the very thing that had brought her so much angst? It wasn't too late to just leave. Gavin could tell Reed whatever he wanted. It didn't matter.

Besides, she was due to pick the baby up in a little over an hour. There was no way she could possibly say everything she needed to say to Reed in one hour. Especially not with Gavin Chambers chaperoning them. Better to let sleeping dogs lie. Wasn't it?

She bent over the sink for a minute, collecting herself. Then she straightened and buttoned her coat. With a sigh, she slung her purse over her shoulder, gathered the painting under her arm and walked out the door.

Reed looked up to see Gavin Chambers coming toward him. "Hey, there you are." He pushed back his chair and extended a hand. Gavin's hands were like ice. "Cold enough out there for you?"

"Aw, I'm used to it," Gavin said. "How was your flight?"

"The plane went up and came back down. I'm always pretty happy if that's all there is to tell."

Gavin laughed. "I hear you. Have you ordered yet?"

"No. I had a snack in the airport, so I'm not very hungry. But you go ahead."

"Oh, don't worry. I will." Gavin pored over the menu.

"How was the show?"

"It was a nice show. You won a purchase award, you know. And your friend's oil was an honorable mention."

"Really?" He tried to appear disinterested, but in truth, he wanted to cheer. He'd had a feeling her piece might do well with this particular juror. He wished she'd won the big money, but he'd done it as much for the encouragement as for the prize.

Gavin looked up from the menu. "She does nice work. I might be interested in representing her."

"I'm not sure she's working anymore. But I can give you her contact information if you'd like." He was getting in deep waters here. Olivia didn't even know he had the painting and here he was connecting her with a gallery.

The server came to their table and Gavin waved him off. "Give us a few minutes, could you?"

Reed put up a hand. "Don't wait on me. Order whatever you want. I'd just like a salad. And some coffee, please."

Gavin spent several minutes with the menu. He kept glancing toward the entrance as if he was expecting someone else. Finally he ordered a filet.

When the server left, Gavin gave Reed more details about the show—who his competition had been, some of the new techniques that were being tried. "You haven't done any of those still lifes you were talking about yet, have you?" Midsentence, his eyes strayed over Reed's head.

Reed turned slightly to his left to see what had caught Gavin's attention.

A familiar voice spoke close to his ear. "Coffee on your right."

Olivia? He turned to see a cup of steaming coffee sitting on a large saucer in front of him. Thinking his imagination had gone into overdrive—as it frequently did where Olivia was concerned—he looked up and muttered his thanks to the server.

Olivia stood by his chair, close enough to touch. Smiling.

"Olivia?" He looked to Gavin who was smiling, then back to

Olivia. Locking eyes with her, he scraped his chair back, losing his napkin to the floor. "What…what are you doing here?" he sputtered.

"I should ask you the same." Her laughter was thready. She looked nervous. She looked beautiful. She was slim and elegant in a navy sheath. Her hair was longer, blond tendrils framing her face. He couldn't help it. He opened his arms to hug her.

She walked into his embrace. "Hi, Reed," she whispered against his jacket.

She stepped away and he turned to Gavin. "Gavin, you remember Olivia?"

"Remember her?" He chortled. "I *brought* her."

Reed looked from Olivia to Gavin and back. "What's going on?"

Gavin explained their meeting in the exhibition hall. "Seems you have some 'splainin' to do, Mr. Vincent."

Reed turned to Olivia, his face hot, his tongue tucked into his cheek. "I *can* explain, Olivia."

Gavin apparently realized that the issues between them were a little more serious than he'd treated them. He rose from his chair and dropped his napkin on the table. "Tell you what… Seems like you two have a lot to catch up on. Why don't you split my steak dinner and, Reed, we'll talk tomorrow."

"Oh, no… Please…" Olivia looked chagrined.

Reed joined her protests, but he could have hugged Gavin. They said goodbyes over further protests, but the gallery owner insisted.

When he'd disappeared into the street, Reed turned to Olivia. "You look great. City life must agree with you." He could have bitten his tongue. Why would he encourage her about her move back to Chicago? He hated that she'd left the Falls.

"Thanks. So do you." She toyed with the back of the chair.

"Here… Have a seat." He pulled out a chair for her. "Gavin's dinner will be here any minute."

Her musical laughter broke the ice and she seemed to relax a little.

"I really can't stay but a few minutes, Reed. I have to pick up my son from the babysitter in just a little while."

"You had a son. Claire called me…a couple days after he was born. Congratulations. Let's see… How old is he now?"

"He turned two months last week." She beamed.

"Wow. Two months already. Amazing." Had it been that long? No wonder he'd missed her so much.

She seemed happy. He was glad…or he wanted to be, wanted to be happy for her, even though she'd started a new life that had nothing to do with him.

"Claire said you were back at your old job?"

"That's right."

"You like it?"

She thought for a minute. "I do. It's hard being away from Jon so much."

"Jon?"

"Jonathan…my son."

"Oh…of course." He almost laughed with relief. For one crazy second, he'd thought she was referring to another man. Brother! Nothing had changed. He had it bad for this woman.

The waiter brought Gavin's steak and Reed explained the situation. "And could you bring an extra plate?" Reed asked. "And another coffee, please." He turned to her. "Still decaf?"

"Oh, no." She laughed. "I'll take the fully leaded stuff, please. But I really can't stay long, Reed. I should have left five minutes ago, to be honest."

"Can you call the sitter?"

She shook her head. "I really shouldn't. I…I do that too often as it is."

"Long hours?" Was she just making excuses? He couldn't tell.

"Not more than forty. It's just…it's hard, trying to keep up with work and be a good mom, too. But I'm not complaining. I'm grateful to have the job." She twisted her linen napkin into a rope and gave a halfhearted smile. "So how have *you* been?"

"I'm good," he lied. Except, now that he was with her, maybe he *was* good.

"Gavin said your work is still selling like hotcakes."

He shrugged. "I guess. I have no complaints, either."

She looked at her watch again, then glanced out the window.

"Oh, Reed. It's almost dark. I really do need to go pick up the baby."

He tried to read her. Was she having second thoughts about having come here, or was that true regret he saw in her face. He didn't want to push her. "Do you need a ride? I could take you to get the baby. I…I'd love to see him," he risked.

She seemed to ponder that, then brightened. "You're sure you have time?"

He grinned. "Well, I was supposed to have a dinner appointment with Gavin Chambers, but apparently, he, um…stood me up."

She giggled.

He pushed back his plate. "Let me ask our server to box up this food. You can take it home. I ate a bit at the airport. I'm honestly not hungry."

"While you do that, I'll get my coat and package from the maître d'."

They met at the front door a few minutes later. "Apparently Gavin bought our dinner," Reed said.

"That was nice of him."

He frowned. "I'm parked about two blocks away. Why don't you wait here?"

"That's okay," she said. "I could use the exercise."

They started down the sidewalk, their frosty breaths mingling in the January air. "Here," he said, reaching for her package. "Let me carry that for you… A painting?"

She nodded and her mouth quirked into an odd smile. "It was an entry in the exhibition. The one my cow painting got honorable mention in."

Uh-oh. He'd walked right smack into that one. It was on the tip of his tongue to feign ignorance, but he thought better of it. Instead he tugged on her coat sleeve and stopped her, gently spinning her to face him on the sidewalk. "Olivia, I can explain.…"

"I'm waiting."

He put a hand on the small of her back and steered her out of the way as three loudmouthed, baggy-jeaned teenagers passed them on the sidewalk in front of the parking lot.

"The car's right here," he said. He clicked the remote and the lights on the rental car flashed.

She gave him instructions to the sitter's and they drove in silence, the city traffic matching the cacophony of his thoughts. Finally he blurted, "I bought your painting, Olivia."

"From who?"

He cleared his throat. "From you, actually."

"What?"

"It was in your house."

"I *know* that." She loosened her seat belt and swiveled in her seat to face him. "Do you think you could talk straight for just one minute?"

He sighed and kept his eyes on the road. Might as well get this over with. "I bought your house. The painting came with it."

She sat, mouth gaping. "You did what?"

"I asked your Realtor to do it anonymously if possible. Apparently that was easy since she had power of attorney."

"But why?"

"I didn't want you to have to see my name on the title. To have to deal with that knowledge. That seemed to be something you wanted to avoid."

"Oh, Reed… But why would you buy my house in the first place?"

"I've thought about investing in rental property for a long time. When I was trying to think of some way to…to make things up to you, I realized that one of the things you were praying for was for your house to sell. It was just something I could make happen. And," he admitted, "that house was one of the only things keeping you here. For me to buy it made it easier for you to go. I…I think I needed to do that."

She listened without comment.

"Does that make any sense at all?"

"I think so," she said. "But what about the painting? Why would you enter my—excuse me, *your* painting in the show?"

"Because it's good work, Liv. I know this juror, and I had a feeling you'd win. I figured you could probably use the prize money." He grinned. "But I was hoping for a first-place award."

"You did all that for me?"

"Olivia, I feel terrible about everything that's happened. Some of it wasn't my fault…nobody's fault really. But some of it I brought on because I'm so miserably impatient. I had all kinds of people telling me that you needed time…to grieve, to adjust to a new life, to get through your pregnancy and get to know your baby. But I couldn't help it. I fell in love with you." He stared out the windshield. He'd told her that back in Hanover Falls, and the time hadn't been right. He'd been pushing her. But now it felt proper.

He couldn't read her face in the dim light of the passing streetlamps. But he went on. It was high time they got everything out on the table. "I fell in love with you, Liv, and I was terrified you'd get away. As it was, I drove you away."

She reached to put a hand on his arm. "No, Reed. You didn't do that. I think maybe God did."

Great. She thought it was divine intervention that took her away from him. "You want to explain that one?"

"Turn left at this next street." She pointed ahead. "It's a couple miles." She pushed her hair behind her ears and heaved a sigh. "I've been thinking a lot about this lately. When we discovered that Derek was your donor, I thought it was God's way of telling me that we weren't supposed to be together. And in a way it was. But not for the reasons I thought. I had a lot of healing to do, Reed. When we met, the whole thing with Derek was so fresh. Not just being widowed, but coming to terms with the betrayal in my marriage. Getting used to the prospect of being a mom. Following Derek to a dinky town when I thought I was a big city girl…"

He perked up at her phrasing. Did that mean she no longer felt that way?

"Just so many things I was dealing with, Reed. It was too much to process…and then to have you thrown into the mix…" She smiled softly. "I've done some of the hard work of grieving this past couple of months…coming to terms with what I lost. It's a long process, but I think I know myself better now. I'm starting to realize that it could have been so much worse."

He looked at her with a question, not understanding.

"God gave Derek and me the gift of that last year together. It was a small glimpse of what we could have had if Derek had lived. I don't suppose I'll ever understand why he had to die before we had a chance to make up for lost time, but I've forgiven Derek—and God for taking him."

"I'm glad, Liv. I'm really glad." *But where do I fit into all this?* he wondered. "But what about the whole transplant thing? Isn't that—"

She held up a hand. "I think…I think I put too much stock in that. Maybe I instinctively knew I needed to back away and I was looking for an excuse. But, Reed, I've come to think maybe that, too, was a gift."

"How so?" He worked to keep the rising hope from his voice, but her next words tempered that hope.

"It allowed me to back away from you, to go through the grieving I needed to do. To learn to stand on my own two feet— so I could take care of my son." A slow smile blossomed on her face. "He's so precious, Reed. I never knew it would be like this—" Her voice fractured.

"I can't wait to meet him. I'm happy for you, Liv. I really am."

"Oh, here." She pointed ahead. "Turn at that next light. We're almost there."

Chapter Forty-Two

Reed bent over the infant carrier on the floor in Mrs. Markham's living room. Olivia's heart warmed as he cooed at Jonathan, making a complete fool of himself. And endearing himself to her all over again.

He turned to her with a gentle smile. "You did good, Liv. Really good." He cupped a hand over the baby's head, as though he were dispensing a blessing. "He's awfully small."

"Oh, my. He's gained four pounds since he was born."

"Really?" Reed went back to making faces at Jon while Olivia gathered the baby's things from the sitter and bundled him into his snowsuit.

Reed had insisted on taking them back to the apartment and she was grateful to avoid the train.

The baby fussed most of the way home, so they didn't talk much. "Do you want to come in?" Olivia asked, when they pulled into the apartment complex.

"Are you sure?"

"I'm sure." And she was. She was having trouble remembering what it was that made her think she needed to get away from him so desperately back in the Falls.

But she wasn't the same person she'd been back then, and she knew he wasn't, either.

She fixed coffee and they sat at the kitchen table talking until late into the night, while Jon slept in the bedroom.

"Are you happy, Liv?"

She thought for a moment. "I'm…content. But I'll be honest—life isn't easy. I hate having to take the baby to the sitter every morning. I feel like I've missed so much already. And it terrifies me to think about bringing him up here." She spread her arm to encompass the whole neighborhood. "I have some good neighbors, but the drugs and gangs are here, too. I really wouldn't choose for my son to grow up here."

He gave her a skeptical smile. "But you did. You did choose for him to grow up here…when you left the Falls."

She thought about what he'd said. "I guess you're right. I didn't know what that choice meant at the time. And I didn't know *who* I was choosing it for." She glanced toward the closed bedroom door, love for her son overwhelming her.

"You could come back, you know." Reed's grin was teasing, but his eyes said he meant more, and the spark in them ignited the remembrance of what it had felt like to kiss him.

"Come back to what?" she said, dropping her head. "My job is here now, my—" She'd started to rattle off a list, but there was nothing else to add. Her job was in Chicago. It was what she was talented at, and she liked the people she worked with. But that was all. She didn't know anyone yet in the church she was attending. And she'd grown away from most of her friends now that she had a baby to come home to every night.

When she thought of home now, she thought of Hanover Falls, Missouri, a tiny hick town where the sidewalks rolled up at dusk and everybody got in everybody else's business because they truly cared.

And she thought of the man sitting here at her kitchen table. She felt his eyes on her now and she looked up to meet their blue, blue depths.

And all she saw there was love.

"Come back to what?" she said again, feeling as if she'd just leaped off a cliff.

"To me, Liv. Come back to me."

"Reed, I—"

He held up a hand. "When you're ready. When the time is right." He pointed heavenward. "When *His* time is right." A crooked smile lit his face and he reached across the table and covered her hand with his. "But when it is time, I happen to know of a great job opening. And a house for rent—dirt cheap—with wide sidewalks for tricycles, and a big backyard with room for a kitten or two…"

* * * * *

QUESTIONS FOR DISCUSSION

1. What do you perceive were the problems in Olivia and Derek Cline's marriage? If you were a marriage counselor, what advice would you give them?

2. Olivia did not want to move to Hanover Falls, but she agreed to do so for her husband's sake, in spite of the fact that he'd been unfaithful to her. Do you think she made a wise decision?

3. Olivia felt ambivalent about having a baby. But again, she chose to do so, mostly because it was what her husband wanted. Discuss Olivia's choices in light of Paul's teaching in Ephesians 5:21-33.

4. Reed Vincent was going blind, and had many fears about how that would change his life. Have you ever imagined what it would be like to lose one of your senses? Which sense would you most fear losing—sight, hearing, smell, taste, or touch? How is your choice affected by your career or your gifts? (For example, a musician might fear losing the sense of hearing more than the sense of sight.) How would losing that sense change your life, and how do you think you might compensate for your loss?

5. When Derek died, Olivia was faced with the decision to donate his organs, since he'd signed a donor car. How do you feel about organ donation? Have you discussed such a decision with your family, and have you signed a donor card? Why or why not?

6. If your loved ones have chosen to be organ donors, would you want to know who the recipients were? How would it make you feel to receive a thank-you note from such a recipient? Would you want to meet that person? Do you think

you'd feel resentful toward them or grateful that your loved one's death had provided the gift of life or health for another?

7. Discuss how you might feel if you, like Reed, were an organ recipient, and were given a new lease on life because of an organ donation. How would you feel about knowing someone had to die in order that you might have a new chance at life? Would you want to learn more about the donor whose organs you received, or would you prefer that person to remain anonymous? Why or why not?

8. If you were in Olivia's position, having discovered that you'd fallen in love with someone who had been a recipient of your loved one's organs, what emotions do you think you'd feel? Do you think it would make your feelings for that person stronger, or would it be too "weird" for you to continue in a relationship with them?

9. Do you think you would have chosen to stay in Hanover Falls after your spouse's death the way Olivia did? What motivated her decisions?

10. Olivia fell in love with Reed, her employer. Put yourself in her place and discuss what issues you might deal with under the circumstances and how you would handle them.

11. When she sold her house and got her old job back on the same day, Olivia believed it was too amazing to be mere co-incidence. Does God sometimes move through coincidences? Should we trust such coincidences as God's "method" of guidance? What other confirmation might we seek when we decide a coincidence is a "God-incidence" instead?

12. Talk about Reed's affirmation of Olivia's talents and how that compared to the way Derek had treated Olivia's artistic

endeavors. Do you feel your spouse or other loved ones encourage you in the areas where God has gifted you? Do you find it easy to affirm their talents in return? Why or why not?

13. Talk about the conclusion of the novel. Did you like the way it ended? Would you have made the same decision Reed made? The same decision Olivia made?

Deborah Raney

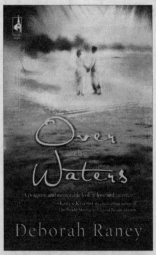

In the Chicago suburbs Dr. Max Jordan has a lucrative business giving Botox injections to wealthy women while fuming over his son Joshua's "wasted" charity work in Haiti with orphans. After Joshua's death, Max flies to Haiti to try to understand why his son chose to work there. While volunteering at the orphanage, Max meets Valerie Austin, whose broken engagement and frustrated longing for children led her to Haiti, too. Sparks fly, and soon Max is reexamining his life's work and his interest in his son's Christian faith.

Available wherever books are sold!

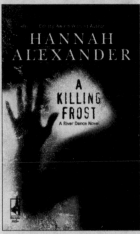

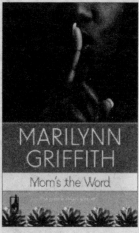

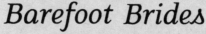